JUST DESERTS

"I always heard you're a real daisy of a businessman. Now I see why folks think it."

Pridemore grinned and tapped his forehead.

"I've got tricks the world has yet to see," he said. He scooted back from the edge, his hand on Bertha's shoulder ushering her along with him. He carried a bow loaded with an arrow on it in his other hand. "We take him alive, you can saw his ears off before we kill him . . . if you've a mind to, that is."

Bertha stared down at the soldiers riding into sight.

"That pig would've had me killed," she said. Turning to Pridemore, she added, "You mean I can do anything I feel like to him before he dies?"

"Have yourself a good time with him, my word on it," Pridemore said with a shrug.

"I could do that," Bertha said under her breath. "I could do that in spades."

Pridemore watched her face flush with vengeance at the possibilities at hand. "Power is a wonderful thing, ain't it, Big Darling?"

"Wonderful and then some."

SCALPERS

—————

Ralph Cotton

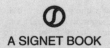

A SIGNET BOOK

SIGNET
Published by the Penguin Group
Penguin Group (USA) LLC, 375 Hudson Street,
New York, New York 10014

USA | Canada | UK | Ireland | Australia | New Zealand | India | South Africa | China
penguin.com
A Penguin Random House Company

First published by Signet, an imprint of New American Library,
a division of Penguin Group (USA) LLC

First Printing, April 2015

 REGISTERED TRADEMARK—MARCA REGISTRADA

ISBN 978-0-451-47157-4

Printed in the United States of America
10 9 8 7 6 5 4 3 2 1

For Mary Lynn, of course . . .

PART 1

Chapter 1

Arizona Territory Ranger Sam Burrack rode his copper-colored black-point dun past a broken hitch rail, over toward a short, wind-whipped campfire fifty feet away. He led a chestnut desert barb beside him. Over the barb's back lay the blanket-wrapped body of the half-breed named Mickey Cousins, who had died in Mesa Grande in a shoot-out with the Ranger and two town deputies at the Old Senate Saloon. Cousins had been a shotgun rider on a desert stage route before falling in with a band of scalp hunters who were under contract with the Mexican government to kill the desert Apache when and wherever they found them.

The leader of the scalpers, Erskine Cord, and his nephew, Ozzie Cord, had been paid to lie in wait and gun down the sheriff of Mesa Grande. While the Ranger was convinced that Erskine had done the actual shooting, Ozzie had been with him, side by side. Erskine, whom Sam had left lying dead on the floor of the Old Senate in the same gun battle that had taken Mickey Cousins' life, had been waging a private war with a particular band of Mes-

calero Apache known as the Wolf Hearts, led by
the seasoned desert chief, Quetos. A bad enough
hombre in his own right, Sam reminded himself.

He had been on the scalpers' trail now for,
what . . . *a week*? he asked himself. Yes, he believed
it had been a week now since he'd loaded Cousins'
body and struck back out on the trail. Time passed
quickly, while you were chasing down scalp hunters
and assassins while a band of Mescalero warriors
was busy killing any white man foolhardy enough
to be out here along the border badlands.

What does that say about you? he asked himself
wryly.

He looked all around the abandoned trading
post when he'd stopped and stepped down from his
saddle. The wooden part of the structure had
burned unobstructed for days. All that remained
standing were two of the original stone walls that
had been here since the days of Spanish rule. The
charred remnants, strewn utensils and bits of
leather shoes and clothing were signs of yet another generation who'd come and gone through
the portal of time. Recent bullet holes dotted the
stone walls; arrows stood slantwise in the sandy
ground.

Twenty feet in front of him past the blackened
adobe walls, a man with dark bloodstained bandaging wrapped around his chest sat in the dirt, staring
at him. Sam saw the shotgun lying across the
wounded man's lap. Two Mexican women busied
themselves preparing an evening meal over a wind-
driven fire.

"Hello the camp," the Ranger called out, stopping at a respectable distance.

The wounded man continued staring at him as he spoke sidelong to the two women.

"Keep . . . cooking," he murmured under his waning breath. A few yards behind the man, a two-wheel mule cart sat with one side propped up on a stack of rocks. A removed wheel leaned against its side. A mule stood tied to a stake by a lead rope, crunching on a small mound of cracked grain.

The Ranger started to step forward and say something more. But he stopped himself as the shotgun came up quickly in the wounded man's hands and pointed at him.

"Easy there, mister," Sam said in a calm but firm tone. "I mean you no harm." He reached a hand up slowly and drew back the lapel of his riding duster. Late-afternoon sunlight glinted on his badge. "I'm Arizona Territory Ranger Sam Burrack."

"What's that mean to me?" the man asked bluntly. His voice sounded weakened and halting. He looked around and off toward the distant hill line. "Is this Arizona . . . ?"

Sam didn't answer right away. He looked at the women, noting for the first time that one was not much more than a child. They only glanced at the Ranger and continued their work.

Finally, "It is, just barely," the Ranger said. He lowered his gloved hand from his lapel and ventured another step forward.

The man eased the shotgun back onto his lap and stared.

"Besides," Sam said, "it wouldn't matter if it's not. I'm in pursuit of a killer. We have an agreement with the Mexican government—"

"*Ha!* The Mexican government," the man said, cutting him off with a sharp tone. "Where was the Mexican government when I was being kilt by Injuns?" He eyed Sam bitterly. "Where were you, for that matter?"

"I expect I was somewhere between here and Mesa Grande," Sam said, keeping his voice civil. He walked closer, leading the two horses until he stopped and looked down at the man. "How bad are you hurt?"

"I've been stabbed deep," the man said. "I fit back a whole band of wild heathens—had 'em leaving too. Dang Injun boy no bigger than a pissant ran out of nowhere, stabbed me twice with a spear bigger than he was." He shook his head in reflection. "And that's how I, Vernon Troxel, died . . . out here, the middle of nowhere, stuck to death . . . by a stinking little nit."

"Take it easy, Vernon Troxel," Sam said, hearing the man's breath and voice getting weaker, shallower as he spoke. He reached out toward the edge of the bandaging, to take a closer look at the wounds. "Maybe you're in better shape than you think."

But the man jerked back away from him.

"Keep your hands to yourself, Ranger," he said. "Only one's going to touch me . . . is my *esposas.*" He wagged his head toward the two women.

Sam looked around at the women, the young one in particular.

"Your wives," he said, still looking at the younger of the two women as they straightened and looked over at Troxel.

"That's right. . . . What of it?" Troxel said, his voice growing a little stronger.

Sam didn't reply; he sat watching Troxel, listening, getting an idea what kind of man was sitting before him.

Troxel coughed up a glob of black blood and spat it away and wiped the back of his hand across his mouth. The young woman, seeing him motion for her with a weak bloody hand, hurried over with an uncapped canteen.

Troxel swiped the canteen from the young girl's hand with a malicious stare. The girl flinched and shied back in a way that told the Ranger she had more than once tasted the back of this man's hand.

"I bought them both down in Guatemala, outside Cobán. They're mother and daughter." He gave a weak, sly grin. "Made them both my *esposas*, legal-like," he said. "Legal as you can get . . . in Guatemala anyway."

A slaver . . .

Sam only stared flatly, but Troxel had seen that same stare in many places across both the American and Mexican frontier.

"You see anything wrong in that, Ranger?" he said, blood bubbling deep in his chest.

"I enforce the law to the best of my calling," Sam said. "I don't judge the laws of another nation." He took the canteen from the man's faltering hand to keep him from spilling it.

"That's . . . no answer," Troxel said, coughing from deep in his chest.

"It's all the answer you'll get from me," Sam said. He didn't like slavers, legal or otherwise. He looked up and all around the pillaged and charred trading post as he capped the canteen. He handed it away to the young girl, who took it hesitantly and then hurried back out of reach. "I'm tracking some mercenaries, white men who rode through here on shod horses," he said, nudging his head toward the wide sets of tracks across the trading post yard. "Looks like the Apache were tracking them too. Were you here?"

"No," Troxel said, "but damn their eyes . . . for getting these Injuns stirred up." He gave a bloody, rattling cough. "I got caught here smack . . . between the two. Damn my luck."

Sam saw his point. The scalp hunters were going to leave bitter feelings between the whites and the desert Apache for a long time to come.

"Can I wheel your cart for you before I leave?" Sam asked.

"I won't be needing a cart come morning," Troxel said with finality.

"You might," Sam said. "Either way, the women-folk will."

"Yeah . . . they will," Troxel said as if in afterthought. His eyes took on a crafty look. "I'd make you a good price . . . for the two of them."

Sam just stared at him for a moment.

"Don't look at . . . me that way," the man said,

struggling with his words. "What good will they do me . . . when I'm dead?"

"As much good as the money I'd be giving you for them," Sam replied.

Troxel closed his eyes and sighed.

"Obliged if you'd . . . wheel my cart," he said. "Obliged if you'd spend the night too. Keep these desert critters . . . from chewing on me before I'm gone."

"I'll fix the cart, and then I've got to go," Sam said. "The womenfolk will see to you. It's only another day's ride to Iron Point."

"Punta de hierro. . . ." The wounded man translated the name Iron Point into Spanish, then spat as if to rid his mouth of bad taste. "What might I find . . . in Iron Point?"

Sam didn't answer. He started to stand.

"Your womenfolk will see you through the night," he said.

In spite of Troxel's waning strength, he grasped the Ranger's forearm.

"No, wait!" he said. "My womenfolk will take pleasure . . . watching critters drag away my bones." He sounded desperate. "Stay the night. Bed down with either of them—bed them both . . . I don't mind. They need a good going-over. But don't leave tonight!"

The Ranger pulled his forearm free.

"Don't say such a thing," Sam said quietly, seeing both the mother and her daughter look over at him from the fire. "I'm on a manhunt."

"Shoot me, then . . . before you leave," the man pleaded. "Shoot them and me. It's best all around." He broke down sobbing. Sam saw the man's mind had taken all it could and was ready to snap. What would he do to the women when that happened, before he turned the double barrels up under his chin and squeezed the trigger?

Sam reached down and picked up the shotgun while he had the chance. The man stopped sobbing long enough to make a futile grab for it.

"Take it easy," Sam said, moving the shotgun out of reach. "I'll wheel your cart. We'll load you on it and ride on to Iron Point tonight."

"Tonight . . . ?" The man sniffled and wiped a ragged sleeve under his nose. "I— I can't go tonight. I'll never make it to Iron Point."

Sam let out a patient breath and propped the shotgun over his shoulder. He looked over at the slaver's mother-and-daughter dual wives and felt something ugly turn in his stomach. The two stared at him; the mother tried to smile, putting herself out in front of whatever bargain Troxel might have struck for them.

"I'll fix the cart," he said to Troxel.

Turning away from the woman's feigned smile and dark hopeless eyes, he led the two horses to where the mule stood crunching its meager handful of grain. The animal looked up and brayed and pulled back its ears, grain clinging to its lips. As Sam walked the horses closer, the mule plunged its bony head down and ate hurriedly.

*   *   *

When the last of the sun's light had sunk below the curve of the earth, the cart and the mule hitched to it stood in black silhouette against the purple sky. With the spare wheel in place and the broken wheel cast aside into the rocky sand, the Ranger and the mother and daughter gathered the remaining cooking utensils and piled them into the cart alongside the wounded, half-conscious slaver. The Ranger noted how the woman tried to keep herself between him and the young girl.

"I speak *inglés*," the woman said quietly. "But my very young daughter does not. So you will speak to me, *sí, por favor*?" she asked hesitantly.

"I understand," Sam said. "Tell your very young daughter to take the seat." There was something about these two he wasn't buying. He gestured up at the front of the two-wheel cart where a rough board lay crosswise front to side as a makeshift driver's seat.

"*Sí . . . ?*" the woman said, looking at him in cautious surprise.

"*Sí,*" the Ranger replied. "She can ride up there. You can ride this one." He nodded at the barb. The woman only stared as he pulled the blanket-wrapped body of Mickey Cousins from across the chestnut barb's back and carried it to the rear of the wagon and secured it down on a narrow board with dangling lengths of tie-down rope.

"My name is Ria Cerero," the woman ventured in a hushed tone of voice. "My young daughter's name is Ana."

"Arizona Territory Ranger Sam Burrack, ma'am,"

Sam said, touching the dusty brim of his pearl-gray sombrero. "If the two of you are ready, we need to mount up and move on out of here." He nodded toward two shadowy wolves who had circled in closer over the past hour, drawn in by the scent of fresh blood. "Get your husband somewhere off the desert floor."

"*Sí*, I understand," Ria said. "But he is not my husband, this one," she added in an ever-more hushed voice. "He purchased me and my daughter from my dead husband's brother."

Sam listened as he ushered her up into the barb's saddle.

"My husband's brother, Felipe, took Ana and me in when my husband died from the fever. But Felipe could not take care of us and his wife and children as well. So he sold us to King Troxel."

"King . . . ?" Sam asked as he settled into her saddle and he swung up atop his dun.

"I meant *Vernon* Troxel," the woman said, correcting herself quickly. She sidled the barb over to the dun and said under her breath, "He has the two of us call him *King* when he is drinking his whiskey and we are . . . all three alone." She lowered her dark eyes in shame. "Please do not tell him I told you this—I only say this to you because you are a man of the law." A fearful look came over her face.

"I won't tell him," Sam said. Letting out a breath, he looked out across the darkening desert flats. "You can talk as we ride, ma'am," he offered, knowing there was more to come.

"*Gracias*," she whispered. "I know I must ask

God to forgive me for what I tell you now, but I wish he would die before this night is through." She immediately crossed herself for saying such a thing. Tears glistened in her eyes.

Sam nodded and leveled the brim of his sombrero. Before he scooped Troxel up into his arms and carried him to the cart, Sam had seen the wispy figures of the two wolves circling farther out in the waning evening light. They were growing bolder, more brazen in their quest for food. He did not want to fire a gun, he told himself. Gazing off into the encroaching darkness, he saw other black forms appear as if out of nowhere and move about, falling onto the wide circling pattern as he and the woman and the mule cart moved forward at a slow pace.

"Careful what you wish for, *señora*," he said quietly. "A night like this, you just might get it."

Chapter 2

In the purple starlit night the small party rode on, the Ranger taking the reins to the mule, leading the fearful animal and its cart at a slow but steady pace. Less than thirty yards out, the wolves had grown bolder. The shadowy animals howled and yipped and continued circling and threatening them. Riding alongside the cart, Sam heard the wounded man groan and mutter to himself inside the cart bed.

"They've come back for me, Pa . . . like I knowed they would," he babbled mindlessly. "They ate Little Charlie's head . . . 'fore I could stop them! Oh my Gawd!" he screamed. "They et *his head*!"

Sam turned his eyes to the woman, who sidled close to him in fear of the looming predators and the man's hallucinations.

"Who knows what thoughts go on inside this man's mind?" she said almost in a whisper. "It is said that all evil in a man's life comes back to him when he is dying." She crossed herself and drew her ragged blanket up around her shoulders. "His evil lies dark and heavy upon us. Can you feel it?"

"There's plenty of evil to go around," Sam said,

not wanting to encourage further discussion on the matter. "What I *can* feel are desert wolves prowling our flanks." He glanced around the purple night. "I hate firing a rifle, but we're going have to do something pretty soon. They're getting too bold." Even as he spoke he saw a large wolf dive forward out of the greater darkness, lunge a few feet toward the mule, then circle back out of sight. "Testing us," he added.

"They smell his warm blood," the woman whispered. She looked up at the young girl and said, "Get down in the cart, Ana."

The girl followed the woman's order quickly. The woman turned back to the Ranger.

"If I slipped a knife into his heart, his blood would stop. We could leave him here for them, *sí*?"

Sam just looked at her for a moment.

Slipped a knife . . . ? Not *stabbed* or *stuck*, but *slipped . . .* , he thought. She made it sound painless, almost merciful. She was right that killing him and leaving him would solve their problem. But he shook his head.

"We're not going to do that, ma'am," he said.

"Then we must roll him out," she urged, "and let the wolves do their own killing."

"Stop it," Sam said.

"No, God forgive me, of course we are not going to do that!" she said, crossing herself quickly. She paused. The two of them watched two wolves move into sight on the darkened trail ahead of them. The wolves stood with their head lowered, as if to bring the mule cart and the riders to a halt.

"Easy, Copper," Sam said to the dun beneath him as the horse grumbled and chuffed under its breath. He drew a taut hand on the reins to the mule cart. Beside him the barb tried to balk, but the woman kept it settled. Sam gathered the dun's reins and the mule's into his leaf hand; he lifted the rifle from across his lap. The mere sight of the rifle coming up sent the wolves back into the darkness.

"All right, it's time we do something," he said.

"I will do it," the woman said without hesitation.

"No, that's not what I mean," Sam said. "Here, hold these animals." He held out both sets of reins.

The woman took the reins with an almost disappointed look in her dark eyes. She watched the Ranger slip down from the dun's back, cocked rifle in hand, and walk to the rear of the cart.

"I don't like doing this," he murmured to himself. He untied the ropes holding Mickey Cousins' body to the board and let it fall to the ground. He took the knife from inside his boot well as he looked at melon-sized stones littering the edges of the trail on either side. "Tough break, Mickey," he said to the blanket-wrapped corpse.

The woman watched the Ranger from her saddle. The young girl peeked over the cart's edge. From in the cart bed, Vernon Troxel awakened slightly and began anew his mindless litany to the wolves.

"I'll kill every . . . damn one of yas! Damn your eyes!" he raged in warning. But his breathing was weak and shallow, and his words fell away into the starlit darkness. The wolves gathered just out of sight and watched the Ranger intently.

As the woman and the young girl watched the Ranger carry out his gruesome handiwork, they turned away from him from time to time and looked at each other with caged eyes. After a moment the Ranger had finished severing Cousins' head from his body and walked back toward them washing his hands in a trickle of water from a canteen. He saw the young girl staring down at him over the edge of the cart.

"Sorry you two had to see that," he said firmly to the woman as he capped the canteen. He took the rifle from under his arm and swung up into his saddle.

"We have seen much worse things than this," the woman replied flatly, handing him the reins to his dun. They heard the rustle of paws out of sight in the sand. "Why did you carry the rocks? Was it to cover the body in respect for the dead?"

"Maybe . . . ," Sam replied, not wanting to talk about it. "Maybe it's to let them know they have to work for it . . . buy us some time to get out of here." He took the reins to the mule cart, turned the dun to the trail and tapped his heels to its side.

The woman rode up close beside him as they heard the sound of wolves running alongside the trail in the opposite direction. Behind them they heard growling, arguing back and forth among the pack.

"You told Vernon Troxel you are hunting the

scalp hunters, the men who are paid by the Mexicans to kill Apache?" she asked.

"Yes, that's right," Sam replied, putting the scene behind him out of his mind. "One of them anyway. He took part in killing a sheriff. Then he escaped jail."

"Not because he kills the Apache and takes their scalps?" she asked.

"In this case, no," Sam said. "It's no longer lawful to take scalps in my country. But these mercenaries stick close to the border. They get the Apache stirred up and get them on their trail. Then they kill them in self-defense, doesn't matter which side of the border they're on." He looked at her. "Sounds rotten, I know, but that's how it's done."

"*Rotten . . . ?*" she asked curiously.

"Rotten means *bad*, *terrible*," Sam said, clarifying the word for her.

"*Bad* I understand, and *terrible* too," she said. She shook her head. "*Rotten* I have not heard, but I will remember. Please excuse my *rotten inglés*?" She managed a weary smile, calmer now that wolves had been pacified, for the time being.

"Your English is not rotten, ma'am. It's a lot better than my Spanish," he said. *In fact. . . .* As he looked at her he wondered how her English could be so good for a peasant Guatemalan, as Troxel claimed her and her daughter to be.

"I learn *inglés* from the mission schools. After the Spanish priests whipped Spanish into our heads, they left, and in my time the mission school taught us *inglés*, only without the whip."

"I understand," Sam said. Although it was not really a satisfactory answer, he let it go. "You must be sleepy." He nodded at the cart. "You and your daughter rest in the cart. I'll wake you when we stop closer to Iron Point."

At the mention of the young girl and the cart, the woman sat upright in the saddle and adjusted herself and batted her eyes to ward off sleep.

"No, I will stay awake and keep you company," she said. "You must excuse my daughter for falling asleep. She is so very young, and she needs a child's rest so she can someday grow to become a woman." She looked at Sam as if to gauge his thoughts on the young girl.

"I understand," Sam said. "Then we'll talk until you get too tired. Then you can get some sleep." Even as he spoke, he knew the woman was up for the night, posting herself as guard between him and young Ana. . . .

Behind them in the night the wolves had scraped away the rocks and gone into a feeding frenzy. The woman looked back once nervously, then turned forward and gave Sam a tired smile. And they rode on.

In the silver-gray hour before dawn, the Ranger brought the mule cart and his dun to a halt alongside a stone-lined water hole that the mule's and horses' noses had brought them to, just off the sand-packed trail. As Sam and the woman stood beside the mule and the horses and let them drink, the girl looked down from the cart's edge and summoned the woman without saying a word. Sam watched as the woman turned away and climbed up the side of the cart. While the two women whispered back and forth, he scanned the other side of the water hole and the cliffs and hill line stretching above it.

"He is dead, Ranger," the woman said quietly over the cart's edge. "*Por favor*, come see for yourself."

But Sam didn't respond right away. He continued scanning the hills and the cliffs that lay shrouded in a silvery looming mist.

"Open the rear gate," he said over his shoulder barely above a whisper.

The woman and the young girl looked at each other, both sensing a wariness in the Ranger's tone.

Sam watched the hills closely as he heard the rear loading gate of the cart creak down to the dirt. When he was certain the cart was open from the rear, he stepped over and turned and looked at the pale lifeless face of the slaver. He glanced up at the bandaging on the dead man's chest, seeing it looked no different from before. He turned his gaze to the young girl, then back at the hills and rock across the water hole.

"Died in his sleep, did he?" he said quietly over his shoulder.

The girl stared to speak, but the woman cut her off.

"*Sí*, yes, he dies in his sleep, this *rotten* man," she said. "You heard him all night, crying out to the dead, as if beckoning them to come for him." Her tone was defensive.

"Yes, I heard him," Sam said, knowing that it

would be pointless to try to suggest that the girl had anything to do with the slaver's death. And if he asked and she admitted it, what good would it do? What purpose would it serve?

The law . . . ? What law? he asked himself, here in the border badlands where men, women and children were slaughtered for the color and shine of their hair.

He still stared off at the hills.

"We did not throw this *rotten* man out on the trail for the wolves to eat while he still lived, *sí*?" the woman said, unsure where the Ranger stood on the slaver's death.

"No, we didn't do that," Sam said, understanding her meaning, giving her and the young girl the relief they appeared to need for some act they might or might not have contributed to.

"If we feed him to the wolves now that he is dead," the woman went on to say, not realizing the Ranger had settled the matter in his mind, "would it be wrong, any more wrong than when you fed the wolves the body—"

"Get the gate up!" Sam said sharply, cutting her off. He gripped his rifle in his hands, ready to raise it to his shoulder.

The woman looked stunned. "I—I did not mean to say you did a bad thing—"

"Get the gate shut *now*, ma'am, pronto!" Sam said, again cutting her short. "We've got company."

He heard the woman gasp; he heard the gate creak up and slam shut as he hurried forward between both horses. Grabbing the watering horses by their bridles, he jerked them back from the water, to the side edge of the cart, making them and himself a smaller target. There was nothing he could do for the mule without turning the whole cart around—no time for that. This would have to do for now, he told himself.

As a last resort before firing the rifle, he scanned the rocky hillside one more time.

"Hello the water hole," he called out, letting whoever was there know he'd seen them, even though what he'd seen was only a slightest movement of a ragged hat along an edge of jagged rock.

"Hello yourself," a gruff voice called out in reply. "I hope you know if we didn't mean to be seen, you wouldn't be seeing us."

"Sounds fair," Sam said. "Now stand and come forward, be seen proper."

"*Proper?* Ha!" said the voice. "If *proper* goes to heaven, I'm plumb bound for hell."

Sam watched as shadowy figures rose among the rocks like ghosts. The man talking was tall and broad-shouldered, dressed in fringed buckskins and a battered Confederate cavalry uniform. The men on either side of him wore slouch hats and ragged coats. But they were smaller, their hair long, beneath drooping hat brims. As they stepped around from behind the rocks, Sam saw knee-high desert moccasins, loincloths. Some carried short-stock rifles; others carried bows with arrows strung and ready.

"That's close enough," Sam said when the seven figures stopped at the water's edge straight across, twenty feet from him. "Who are you? Why are you trailing us?" He had no idea they'd been trailing him, but he tried it to see what he'd get.

"Blame it on these Lipans," the big white man said. "They love tracking folks, 'specially if the folks have horses fit to steal or eat." He touched his hat brim. "I'm the Reverend George Tremble—*former* Reverend, that is. I just got used to saying it." He gave a dark, flat grin. "I'm taking to saving the Lipans here from hell, or at least making them fear it something awful. Unlike some Apache, they druther speak with their hands than their mouths—it makes for better table manners." Again the grin. "But some take it as an insult."

"I don't take it one way or the other," Sam said. "I have nothing to settle with the Lipan. But you'd better break them of that tracking habit," he added, the rifle still level and ready. "I might think you came here to kill and rob us." As he spoke Tremble bent his head a little and looked at the badge on Sam's chest.

"Well, look at you, then, a lawman, no less," he said, trying to sound half-friendly, half-threatening. "I'm not going to lie to you, lawman," he said. "You're about half-right. These fellows want your horses. Myself, being red-blooded, I want the womenfolk." His grin widened. "I told them it would be better to reason with you than just kill you outright, gunfire being as loud as it is."

"You're not getting them," Sam said. He eyed his rifle sights on the center of the man's chest.

"One second. . . ." Tremble held his finger up, signaling a pause, as he turned and signed the warrior beside him. Then he turned back to Sam.

"I'm through talking," Sam warned.

"Now, hold on, lawman," said Tremble. "We're dickering here. He says to tell you we're only taking the two horses and one woman. Is that so bad?" He tried giving a pleasant expression.

"Adios, Tremble," Sam said, squeezing the trigger.

"Wait—!" Tremble shouted, but it was too late. The Ranger's shot split a large silver medallion hanging at his chest, picked him up and hurled him backward onto the rocky hillside. Without wasting a second, Sam levered a fresh round into the Winchester and swung its sights onto the leader standing close by. The Lipan leader had already brought his short rifle up. But before he could get a shot off, the roar of the shotgun from inside the mule cart sent him flying backward. The second roar of the double-barrel sent another Indian to his knees. Bloody, he raked and scraped blindly, taking himself over behind a rock, while the others broke and ran.

Sam got off another shot that caught one of the retreating warriors in the back of his shoulder and spun him like a top. Wild shots resounded toward them as the remaining Lipans found cover and began returning fire. But Sam knew it was too late for them to put up a fight. Their leader was down, and so was Tremble, who was no doubt the *real* leader of the ragged group. Looking up, Sam saw the woman look down at him from the cart's upper edge.

"You are all right, *si*?" she asked. A bullet thumped into the cart's rear gate.

"Stay down," Sam said. "Yes, I'm all right. Are you?" He spoke to the rough plank side of the cart.

"Yes, Ana and I are both all right," the woman said. "What do we do now?"

"Reload and sit still," Sam said. He saw the leader struggling on the ground straight across the water hole. He took aim on the rocky ground just in front of the wounded, bloody man and fired. Dirt kicked up in the wounded man's face. Sam knew the others had seen the shot.

"How do you want him, dead or alive?" he shouted, hoping someone would understand English. When no one answered he called out, "Get up over the hill. When you're gone, I'll leave him here." He waited again, this time watching the hillside, noting that the firing had ceased. As he watched, he eased forward, gathered the frightened mule's reins and turned the cart away from the water hole. The horses turned with the cart, their reins tied to its side. "Keep the shotgun ready," he said to the side of the cart. "We make it to the sand flats we'll be all right. They won't take us on out in the open."

"I am loaded," she said. "Do what you must."

Sam heard the click of the shotgun snap shut.

"Stay inside with your daughter until we reach the flats," he said. "I'll have your horse ready and waiting."

As Sam led the cart farther away from the water, he unhitched the dun and slipped atop it. Once in the saddle, he nudged the dun and led the cart and the other horse at a quicker pace. He heard the woman call out to him from inside the cart.

"Now that this rotten man is dead, Ana and I may choose to go as we please. Is it not so?"

"It's so," Sam said, finding it an odd time to bring up such a thing.

"Then we choose to go with you," the woman said.

"I understand," Sam said, hurrying along, keeping watch over his shoulder. "I'll do my best to get you to Iron Point safe and sound. But from there you two will be on your own."

The woman looked suddenly bewildered, having been long denied the freedom of her own decisions. Sam glanced at her, then back to the trail.

"Don't worry, ma'am," he said. "You and your daughter will be all right. You're nobody's slaves anymore."

Chapter 3

A hard wind had kicked up in the late afternoon as Turner Pridemore and his band of mercenaries swung down from their saddles inside the gates of the old Spanish fortress at Iron Point. Mexican soldiers armed with French rifles ran in from every direction through the swirling dust. They filled the street and watched the rough-looking men closely. The captain of the fort, Luis Penza, stepped out of the Dama Desnuda Bordello buttoning his tunic.

"So, you have bounty receipts for me, eh?" the captain said in good English. A hard gust stood his hair straight up; he pressed it down. Behind him two scantily clad women watched from the bordello's open doorway.

"*Bounty receipts?* Scalps, I say," Pridemore replied, "some long, some short." As he said the word *short*, he cut a sharp stare at the two women's lower bellies. The women stepped back in terror.

"*Buenas noches*, ladies," he said, touching his hat brim toward them. The women stepped back farther.

Pridemore grinned and spat tobacco and wiped

a hand across his dust-streaked lips. He gestured
for his men to bring up the three large burlap grain
sacks they had filled with their wet, bloody tro-
phies. Flies spun and hummed and stayed close to
the bags as the men emptied the grisly contents on
the ground.

"I did not tell you to dump them here in the
street," the captain said.

"You didn't tell me not to either," Pridemore
said.

The captain eyed him closely.

"I have seen you before," he said. "You run the
trading post on the edge of the sand flats. They call
you Bigfoot." He glanced down at Pridemore's
large feet.

"They still do," said Pridemore. He pressed his
hat down on his head and turned his hand toward
the scalps and the swirling flies that regathered
above them between blasts of wind. "I used to run
the trading post. As you can see I've branched out
some." As he spoke above the wind, he pulled a
folded contract from inside his shirt and held it out.

The captain took the folded paper and looked
him up and down, having last seen him wearing a
leather clerk's apron. Now Pridemore wore buckskin and fur clothing he'd taken from a dead scalper
after a recent run-in with the Apache. Breastwork
on his shirt was made up of finger bones entwined
in platted strands of human hair. He wore a stiff
leather hat and battered Mexican boots that reached
halfway up his thighs.

"This contract is not made with you," the captain

said, the paperwork fluttering hard in his hand. "It is made with Señor Erskine Cord. I know this man Cord."

"You don't *know* him anymore, *Capitán*. You *knew* him," said Pridemore. "He got himself kilt in Mesa Grande by a Ranger name of Sam Burrack. I run this bunch now." He gestured at the contract in the captain's hand. "You'll see on the back there that he signed the contract over to me, all legal-like."

The captain turned the contract over and read the back.

"Signed by Cord, witnessed by his *segundo*, Sterling Childs, also recently deceased," said Pridemore. Both Cord's and Childs' signatures were forged by Pridemore, but it wouldn't matter, he'd decided.

It was true that both Cord and Childs were dead. The Mexican government wanted the Apache killed. Turner "Bigfoot" Pridemore and his newly commanded mercenaries were killing them, almost on a daily basis.

"You can see it's all in order, *Capitán*," Pridemore said.

He watched as Captain Penza raised his eyes from the paper and gave him a skeptical look. But then the captain folded the contract and handed it back to him. As the two had spoken, Pridemore's son, Fox Pridemore, and the late Erskine Cord's nephew, Ozzie Cord, had stepped in and begun sorting the scalps into countable rows.

Stepping forward, Captain Penza swatted a hand through the blowflies rising from the scalps.

"No extra charge for the flies, *Capitán*," Turner

Pridemore called out to Penza. He grinned and gave the two women a wink. "You gals sure have some lovely hair," he said with a hungry look. "Shiny as a blacksnake." He started to reach out toward one of the women. They both jumped back away from him, gathering their hair back out of touch and out of the licking wind. "Ah, now, I just wanted to touch it some." He chuckled darkly. His voice dropped to a whisper when the captain turned, facing him. "Maybe another time, then, little darlings." He winked again.

"You, come with me," the captain said to Pridemore in a firm tone. "My men will count the scalps and I will pay you." He gestured to a sergeant and pointed at the scalps in the street. The sergeant instructed his corporal to start counting.

"Where can my men go to drink?" Pridemore asked, looking up and down the wide, dusty street. "Killing Apache is some damn thirsty work."

The captain pointed off toward the far end of the street where a row of plank and adobe hovels stood with ragged tents in the wavering afternoon heat.

"Send your men to *that* cantina," he said. "It is called the Mockingbird."

Pridemore eyed a large tent at the far end of town where a small crowd cheered two men who lay rolling and fighting in the dirt.

The Mockingbird. . . . Pridemore pondered it as he scrutinized the tent.

"What's wrong with *this* cantina?" he asked, pointing at a large adobe cantina straight across the street from them. A bright red-and-green sign read PANCHO MERO'S CANTINA. Mariachi music streamed through the open doors. The dazzling sound of a trumpet rose above guitar, accordion and castanets.

"Nothing is wrong with *that* cantina," Captain Penza said, nodding across the street. "That is why I send you and your men to the Mockingbird." He pointed back in the direction of the large tent where one of the combatants had been handed a long rough board and stood pounding his opponent without mercy. "The owner there is *americano*—a Tejano named Bertha Buttons. She will welcome your men."

"A Texan, huh?" said Pridemore. He grinned. "I like her already." He caught himself in afterthought and said, "Say, does she keep a sporting man around named Diamond Jim Ruby?"

The Mexican captain's expression turned sour at the sound of the name.

"*Sí*, she does have such a man with her," he said. "Do you know this man, Ruby, this woman, Buttons?"

"Know Ruby some, know *of him* a lot more," Pridemore said. "I'll know Bertha when I see her— every Texan I ever knowed has pounded her a time or two." He turned to his men and shouted, "Watch the count, men. We don't want to lose money because one of these Mexicans is missing a finger." He pointed off toward the ragged tent where the man wielding the board slumped and staggered backward, exhausted. "Then go join the fun. I'll be along straightaway with our cash."

The fun . . . ?

"I must warn you, *señor*," the captain said as he and Pridemore turned to walk to his office. "Men with money on them have disappeared from Bertha Buttons' Mockingbird while in the company of Diamond Jim." His voice lowered. "Those unfortunate souls have never been seen again."

"Well, no doubt Jim Ruby robbed and killed them," Pridemore said, taking the news in stride. "He's always been bad about that. That's what sent him and Bertha Buttons packing out of Texas ahead of a rope." Again the grin as the two walked on. "Obliged you told me, though," he said. "I never enjoy consorting with a man I know is sizing me up for a gutting." Now his tone lowered. "If he's a thorn in your side and you'd like to see *him* disappear, *Capitán*, my men's blood is still up from killing Injuns. We'll quarter him out like a steer, if you want us to—Bertha Buttons too, far as that goes."

The captain stopped abruptly and stared at Pridemore, taken aback by the man's casualness on the matter of killing. "You know this man and woman, yet you will kill them so quickly, so callously?"

"At the drop of a hat," said Pridemore. "I said I know Ruby *some*, *Capitán*. I never said we attend the same church. Not everybody we kill has to be a black-haired heathen Injun. Now that I'm back in the business, I'm what you call 'profit driven.' You'd be surprised. Everywhere we go somebody asks—"

"That is another thing I must warn you about," the captain said, cutting him off. He raised a finger for emphasis. "If I find the hair of any of my people among your *receipts*, someone will hang for it this very day."

"*Capitán*," Pridemore said in a firm look of sincerity, "show me a scalp from anyone other than a blackhearted heathen Apache, and I will hang somebody for it myself."

The captain stared at him intently for a moment, as if deciding whether or not he could trust the man. Finally he took a deep breath and let it out slowly.

"Let me say this, Señor Pridemore," he said, lowering his voice again and glancing back and forth along the street. "If this Tejano *puta* and her man were killed while my men and I are away on patrol and above suspicion, it would be a happy day in my life."

Pridemore stared at him. "Happy enough to overcount our receipts by, say . . . twenty-five extra?"

"Ha!" The captain waved the idea aside. "Why would I not have my own men kill them and save that much money for myself?"

Pridemore turned shrewd. "See, I'm thinking you can't do that, because some *federale político* has allowed Buttons to open her cantina here, and you know he'll climb straight up your shirt if something happened to her operation." He pulled his head back with a bemused look. "*Oops.* Did I just hit the target dead-center, *Capitán*, or what?"

"Kill them, then," the captain said. "Kill them and let me wash my hands of them."

"Now, there you are," Pridemore said. "See how easy that was? See how much better you feel already?" The two turned and walked on to the captain's office. "When will you be taking your men out on patrol, and how long are you gone?"

"I will be taking a large patrol out in the morning at daybreak and be gone most of the day," said the captain.

"How many men will you be leaving here?" Pridemore asked.

"I leave only four guards," the captain confided, lowering his voice as if to keep from being overheard. "It would be a good time to take care of the bloody business we speak of."

"Indeed it would," said Pridemore. "Now put Bertha and her sporting man out of your mind. They're dead before we leave Iron Point."

They walked on, the captain not even realizing how fast they had gone from discussing Bertha Buttons and her cantina to having her and her sporting man killed. But Pridemore, seeing the possibilities that having him and his men around brought to mind, smiled and stared straight ahead, aware of the evil aura that surrounded his profession.

"Anywhere we come into a town, it's a good time for folks to get caught up on old grudges and whatnot," he said. He chuckled darkly under his breath.

"So, you are pleased with your bloody craft?" the captain said sidelong.

"Beats the hell out of running a trading post . . . people all the time filling the jakes—keep having to cover them over and dig new ones," said Pridemore, walking on. "You ever fall into one you'll never forget it." He shook his head.

"*Sí*, I believe you," the captain said, walking beside him.

Inside the Mockingbird Tent Cantina, the regular crowds of cutthroats, drifters, rakes, gunmen and thieves had moved aside and made room along the plank bar. A Missourian scalper named Darton Alpine led the rough-looking men across the sawdust-and-mud floor and called out to the bartender as he laid his rifle up across the bar top.

"Whatever you've got to drink, pull it up," he demanded, "and bring on some lively women!" He snatched the first bottle before a Mexican bartender stood it on the bar. He yanked out the cork with his teeth, spat it away and raised the bottle toward the other scalpers. "Here's to hard drinking," he shouted.

Against the side of the tent, a musician stood watching the rowdy men with his accordion hanging on his chest.

"Get to squeezing on that thing," a scalper called out, raising a pistol from his belly holster. "Every time I see one standing still, I want to put a bullet through it!"

The musician struck up a song quickly, seeing the scalper cock and aim the big revolver. As loud, cheerful music began blaring from the accordion,

Alpine laughed and fired a shot straight up through the billowing canvas ceiling. Then he uncocked and lowered the smoking gun. Around the tent men had ducked beneath gaming tables or whatever cover they could find.

"Get used to it, folks," another scalper called out, raising his shot glass. "It's going to be like this all night long!" He raised his revolver and fired a round through the canvas ceiling. "I'm talking about *all* night long."

Another scalper gave out a loud yell. His pistol came up from behind his belt and was cocked on the upswing.

The two youngest of the mercenaries, Ozzie Cord and Fox Pridemore, stood watching at the end of the line of drinkers. Neither of them flinched at the sound of gunfire. As full bottles of whiskey slid down the bar, Fox caught one that managed to get past the other scalpers. He pulled it in close, jerked the cork and kept his hand wrapped around the bottle. Ozzie at the same time grabbed two clean shot glasses from the inside edge of the bar and stood them right side up. Fox filled them.

"Here's to taking hair," Ozzie shouted amid the roar of the drinkers and the loud music. He raised his glass and tossed back the fiery rye in a single gulp.

Without joining his toast, Fox took a shorter sip and let out a whiskey hiss.

"What's the matter, Fox?" said Ozzie. "You've been wound tighter than a Gypsy fiddle all day. You need to loosen up some."

"Maybe you need to *tighten* up some, Ozzie," Fox said. "You've got a lawman after you for jail-break and murder."

Ozzie shrugged it off.

"That ain't nothing," he said. "I plan on having lawmen after me my whole life." He stepped back and gestured a hand up and down at the serious young man. "But look at you! You've got a lot to be pleased about. Your pa, Bigfoot, is our new leader! You've got rid of the clown clothes you was wearing when you joined us." He pictured the polka-dot shirt, striped trousers and black-and-white-checkered galluses Fox had been wearing the first time he saw him. "If I was you, I'd be grinning like an idiot."

"I bet you would, Ozzie," Fox said, staring at him. He wouldn't mention how many of the scalpers called Ozzie an idiot behind his back. But then, for all he knew, the men might be saying the same thing about him. He shrugged a little, sipped the rest of the whiskey and set the empty glass in front of him.

Ozzie refilled his glass quickly.

"You can call me *Oz*," he said, lowering his voice a little. "I only allow my best friends to call me that, to my face leastwise." He raised his shot glass toward Fox with a firm grin.

Fox just stared at him again. Rather than offend the young man, this time he also raised his glass.

"Here's to you, *Oz*," he said.

Ozzie looked elated and threw back his rye.

"So, now we're friends and pards, right?" he said.

"I mean, you know . . . ? After us three fighting the Apache, you and me and your brother, Lucas? God rest his poor bones. I say that makes us pals, huh?"

"Yeah, it does," Fox said, gathering what it took to sound sincere. "We're pals sure enough." He touched his glass to Ozzie's and threw back his drink. All around them the scalpers drank and shouted and now and then fired a bullet up through the canvas ceiling. Scantily dressed women filtered in through the rear fly of the tent, causing the men to whoop and shout all the louder.

"All right, then!" said Ozzie. "Now that we're pals, I suppose you'd like to know all about me killing that sheriff in Mesa Grande?" Fox still stared at him; he knew the young gunman was lying. Everybody knew it was Ozzie's uncle, Erskine Cord, who'd shot the sheriff, who later died from his wound. But he wanted to hear Ozzie's lie. Even at his young age, Fox Pridemore had already learned from his pa that you could garner a lot from hearing how well a man lies . . . and why he does it.

"Nothing would please me more than hearing about it, Oz," Fox said evenly. He managed a tight, friendly smile. "This here's my first time ever being able to get as drunk as I want to. Always before I had to stay sober enough to keep watch over my brother, Lucas." He reached out for the bottle, but Ozzie grabbed it first and poured his drink for him.

"Huh-uh, let me do that, *pal*," Ozzie said. He looked at Fox with admiration.

"All right, then, much obliged," Fox said. He settled back and let Ozzie wait on him. If Ozzie needed somebody to look up to, someone he could tell his lies to and make himself like a big gunman, Fox reckoned he could go along with that . . . for a while anyway.

Chapter 4

The bartender had worked himself into a hard sweat by the time the owner, Bertha Buttons, walked into the wind-whipped tent with a pair of short double-barrel shotguns propped on her hips. A large but shapely woman with broad shoulders and flaming red hair, Bertha stood taller than most men in the ragged tent. Behind her, four young scantily dressed *putas* sauntered in and spread out alongside the drinkers at the bar.

As the scalpers hooted and cheered, the women eyed them like cats eyeing prey and sauntered up to them.

Seeing one of the drinkers raise a smoking gun toward the billowing canvas ceiling, Bertha Buttons cocked both shotguns at once, letting the metal-on-metal sound be heard by all.

"Next man who shoots a hole in my tent, I'll turn him into pig food!" she shouted.

The music stopped; so did the hooting and cheering. Fox and Ozzie watched tensely from their end of the bar. Darton Alpine looked up at the holes in the tent ceiling, then back at Bertha, seeing a determined look on her face.

"We're letting off steam here," he said. "There's no call for breaking ugly on us."

Bertha gestured a nod at the silent accordion player, at the gaming tables, along the bar at the women, at the bottles of rye.

"You've got music, whiskey, gambling and whores," she said bluntly. "If that won't do it for you, get the hell out of my tent."

The men stood silent and tense a moment longer. Then Alpine broke the silence with what started as a deep chuckle and built into a laugh. The other men joined in.

"You fellows heard the lady," he said. "No more shooting the ceiling." As he spoke he looked up at the hard wind whipping across the fluttering canvas overhead. "Although I have to say, I don't see what harm it would do now."

"Don't even think about it," Bertha warned. "I'm collecting a dollar for each and every hole up there." She looked around. "Who's the ramrod of this bunch?"

"That would be Bigfoot Pridemore, ma'am," Alpine said with a flat grin. "He is not a man who tolerates frivolous spending."

The woman looked a little surprised. The shotguns stayed cocked and ready.

"Turner Pridemore?" she said. "The man who ran the trading post out on the desert rim?"

"One and the same," said Alpine.

"I've met Bigfoot," Bertha said. "Where is he?"

"He's collecting bounty money right now," said Alpine. "Soon as he's finished he'll be right here drinking with the rest of us."

"I'll collect for the bullet holes when he gets here," Bertha said, lowering the shotguns a little.

"If I were you I'd walk easy around Bigfoot. He's got his killing bark on," Alpine said. "We all do after all the fine head slicing we done out there." He looked all around and raised his voice. "I could tell you stories that would make your skin crawl, the stuff we saw, the stuff we took part in."

Listening to Alpine, some of the drinkers drew closer to better hear what he might have to tell them about his trade.

Seeing that the drinkers and the women were all interested in hearing the scalp hunter tell them about fighting Apache, Bertha eased her shotguns down some more and stepped back, having made her point about not shooting holes in the ceiling. She had backed almost to the door when Diamond Jim Ruby, a short, thin man with a thick black beard rushed in through the front fly with a shotgun of his own.

"I heard the shooting, and come running," he said, catching his breath.

"Step back, Jim," Bertha said. "I've got them settled down." She looked him up and down, seeing his clothes twisted and hastily attended. "Why's your table closed?" She nodded toward a faro table near the rear of the tent. "We can't make any money if you're going to be off pounding Little Millie every time she raises a leg."

"Don't start accusing me," Jim said in a harsh tone. "I shut down long enough to go eat. I heard from the sergeant that these scalpers were in town." He lowered his voice. "Word has it, they're going to be flush with bounty money most any minute, soon as their leader settles up with Captain Penza."

Bertha gave a grin.

"I know," she said. "Guess who their leader is?"

Diamond Jim just looked at her.

"Turner Pridemore," she said quietly, the two of them watching the drinking and storytelling going on at the bar.

"Bigfoot . . . ," said Diamond Jim. "Then I suspect what I heard was right about him losing his trading post to the Apache."

"I don't care who he lost it to, or how," Bertha said. "Get your table open. I'm rounding up some more whores. We're not letting these birds out of hand until we've got all that bounty money."

"I'm with you, Bertha," said Jim. "Thank the devil for Injun hair." He lowered his shotgun and walked away toward his faro table as Darton Alpine continued his tale at the crowded bar. At the far end of the bar, the two young scalpers, Fox and Ozzie, stood drinking, watching the spectacle going on around them.

"S'pose your pa will get us a big chunk of money?" Ozzie asked, his words taking on a whiskey slur.

"My pa is the best deal-maker this side of hell, Oz," Fox said, his words also sounding tinted with rye. "Ask anybody. My pa's the best at every damn thing."

Ozzie heard the slightest sound of contempt in his friend's words.

"You don't sound very happy about it," he said, pouring the two of them a fresh shot glass of whiskey. "Why's that?"

"Never mind 'why's that?'" said Fox, gripping the shot glass in his fist. "It's my business."

Ozzie gave him a look.

"Sure, it's your business, pal," he said. "But I just told you all about me killing the sheriff in Mesa Grande. Now you don't trust me enough to tell me about why you've got a mad-on at your pa?"

"A *mad-on.* . . ." Fox chuckled and turned to face Ozzie. "Naw, I don't have a mad-on at him." He knew Ozzie was lying about killing the sheriff, but he saw his point. Oz had just told him about killing a lawman. It was only fair that he should reciprocate in kind. "Sometimes it's hard as hell living up to what he expects of me." He raised the glass, drank half of it and held the glass close to his lips.

Beside him, Ozzie drank and nodded and listened.

"All my life I had to work twice as hard, do my chores and my brother Lucas' too . . . him being simpleminded," Fox said. "I had to look out for him, keep him from straying away." He paused, recalling how he, his brother and Ozzie had fought the Apache, and how his brother had died in the battle. "No matter how well I looked out for him, he's still dead anyway."

"That wasn't your fault, Fox," said Ozzie. "I was there. The heathen Apache—Quetos and his Wolf

Hearts killed poor Lucas. I figure that's good enough reason for you to want to kill all them sons a' bitches, far as I'm concerned."

"Yeah, I reckon so," Fox said, staring down at the whiskey near his lips, brooding. "I'll tell you the truth. I'm not glad my brother's dead, but I am glad he's not around anymore." He tossed back the rest of the whiskey in his shot glass and set the glass down hard atop the bar. "There, I said it," he concluded.

"You sure enough did," Ozzie said, giving Fox a drunken grin, knowing his friend had just settled something that had been weighing heavily on his mind. "I say we ought to celebrate . . . get us a couple of gals of our own!" He gestured toward the women playing up to the scalpers along the bar. One scalper had sat a woman atop the bar and buried his bearded face between her breasts.

"Celebrate what?" Fox said. "My brother being killed before my eyes?"

Ozzie stopped grinning.

"No, I didn't mean it like that," Ozzie said. "I mean celebrate you being your own man now— wearing your own skins and bones." He gestured at Fox's shirt with its hair-and-bone breastwork. "With your pa heading this expedition, I can see you being in charge someday yourself."

"I don't want to be in charge of scalping Apache," said Fox. "I don't want nothing I have to take over from my pa."

"I would if I was you," Ozzie said. "Not everybody gets a business like this handed to them."

"My pa will run balls-out wild while there's a contract with the Mexes," said Fox. "But scalp hunting like this ain't going to last long. What do we hunt for bounty when it's over?"

Ozzie thought about it. "I was on my way to being an assassin until that Ranger killed Uncle Erskine. You and me could do that, you know, partner up?"

"Assassins, naw," Fox said. "Maybe when called upon I'd do it. But the big money is robbing. It always has been."

"You mean partner up and rob places, stage-coaches, stores and the like?" Ozzie asked.

Fox thought about it.

"Yeah, Oz, I'd partner with you, outlawing," he said. "We could rob us a couple of places, see how it goes." He gave Ozzie a level gaze.

"Whoo-ee!" said Ozzie. Getting excited. "Hell yes, let's do it! When do you want to start?"

"Soon," said Fox, looking away, staring at the girl with the bearded scalper's face between her breasts. "First, let's get us some gals, like you said. This is my day for doing things I never got to do, breaking loose on my own, so to speak." He held out his glass and Ozzie Cord filled it. They drank their shot glasses empty in one deep swig.

It was well after dark when Turner Pridemore walked into the Mockingbird tent. Outside, a wind-driven rain lashed sideways against the small fortress town of Iron Point as if in vengeance. As Pridemore took off his hat and slung water from it, he walked across the muddy sawdust floor, and the mercenaries along the bar settled their revelry and turned toward him.

"Make room for Bigfoot, men," Darton Alpine said, shoving the drinkers away. The men watched Pridemore expectantly. He stood at the bar and took a hefty leather pouch full of gold coins from inside his coat and held it out at arm's length over the bar.

"There you are, men," Pridemore said. "That's how many heathen Apache we sent to hell with their noggins docked." He dropped the pouch. The gold coins jingled; the men cheered. Diamond Jim Ruby behind the faro table and Bertha Buttons behind the bar both looked relieved, having been running a tab for the whiskey, beer and women until Turner Pridemore arrived.

"Are we going to tally out right now, Bigfoot?" a drunken scalper named Doyle Baines asked.

"No," said Pridemore, "you're all too drunk to be handling money tonight. I won't see my men cheated." He had a second pouch of coins that he'd collected for himself, overpayment from the captain for agreeing to kill Bertha and Diamond Jim.

One of the newer scalpers, Bert Lacy, called out drunkenly, "But I want mine now. This *puta* and me are getting hitched!" A young woman naked from the waist up leaned against him bleary-eyed.

Pridemore looked Lacy up and down.

"Somebody take Bert out back and cut his throat good and deep," he said.

Dead silence fell in, but only for a moment.

Three men reached for Bert Lacy, one already drawing a big knife from his boot. But Pridemore stopped them.

"Jesus, men, I was only joshing!" he shouted.

"So was I," Lacy said in his slurred voice, jerking his buckskin sleeve away from the men. "I ain't getting hitched!" He raised a boot to the *puta*'s rump and shoved her away roughly. "She smells like a wet chicken."

The men stepped back, hooted and cheered; the woman scrambled away. Diamond Jim and Bertha Buttons shared a guarded look from across the large tent. These were dangerous men, their eyes warned each other, as if there had ever been any doubt.

"All right, then, we tally up in the morning," Pridemore said. He snatched up the gold pouch and looked at Bertha Buttons across the bar. "Ma'am, I remember you from Tejas. Is it all right with you and your parrot over there if we settle accounts come morning?"

Parrot over there? This son of a bitch, Diamond Jim fumed in silence.

Bertha tossed the matter aside with the wave of a hand.

"Why, hell yes," she said, knowing it would do her no good to say otherwise. "I remember you too, Bigfoot," she added in a half-flirting voice. "Anytime you pay is fine by me—my parrot too." She grinned and tossed her curly red hair in Jim Ruby's direction. The men laughed.

"Then keep setting us up," said Pridemore, slapping a hand down on the bar top. As he spoke, the young woman Bert Lacy had kicked away sidled up to him and ran her arm around his waist. Looking down at her, he saw the suggestion in her dark eyes. But then he sniffed the air above her head and drew away.

"Not now, little darling. You've made too many friends," he said. "Find yourself some lye soap and scrub everywhere you can reach—come see me later." He gave her a nudge away from him and looked all around the lantern-lit darkness. Outside, rain blew hard sounding like nails thrown against the side of the tent. "Anybody seen my boy, Fox?"

"I seen him," said a veteran scalper, Emilio Siebaugh. "He left here with the idiot, Ozzie. They had whores under their arms."

"And bottles of rye in their hands," a scalper named Early Doss put in. Doss was another scalper who'd been with Erskine Cord when Pridemore took over the bounty contract, after hearing the Ranger had shot Cord dead.

Pridemore nodded and looked around at his drunken scalpers. They were a hardened and dangerous crew, as were all mercenaries he'd ever met. Now that he'd collected the bounty on the Apache scalps, he knew that once these men had their money in hand, they might very well start drifting away, back across the desert floor. He didn't want to let that happen. He needed to keep them busy, keep them banded together. He looked back at Early Doss.

"Give Fox and the idiot time enough to get their

beans baked, then go find them. We've got business in the morning that requires clear heads and steady hands." He grinned slyly.

"Yeah? What's that, Bigfoot?" Siebaugh asked.

Pridemore looked around again, this time noting that there were only three drinkers in the tent who were not members of his group. He drew a long, heavy Walker Colt that he called Ol' Dan Webster from his waist and aimed it at the three. "You plugs beat a path out of here. Nobody likes having you near their whiskey."

Two of the men gave him a stunned look, but offered no argument. They turned away from their half-finished shots and beers and hurried out of the tent into the driving rain. But the third man, an older man with a tangled unruly beard, only stood staring back at Pridemore.

"Are you wanting to die, or just one of them fools who likes getting real close to it before backing away?" Pridemore thumbed back the Walker's hammer and pointed the gun at the man's head.

"Hadn't gave it no thought," the man said quietly, calmly. "I'm looking for work—thought we might palaver about it some."

Pridemore began feeling the weight of the heavy outstretched Colt right away. But he kept it leveled.

"Hear that, men?" said Pridemore. "He wants to palaver with me about a job."

Siebaugh stepped forward, looking the stranger up and down, scrutinizing him closely.

"Bigfoot, I know this old man," he said. "He's

Deacon Sickles, from Alabama. He cut scalps when most of us were still swinging from a teat."

Pridemore let the Walker down, tiring from its weight.

"Are you, now . . . ?" he said to the old man. "I've heard of you too. I heard you not only cut scalp, you're known to take face and all."

"I have done that some," the old man said. "It's mostly a novelty item . . . for foreign dignitaries and the like."

"And you're seeking employment?" said Pridemore. He laid the Walker on the bar, leaving it cocked. Bertha and Diamond Jim watched closely.

"Indeed I am," said Sickles.

Pridemore raised a finger and smiled at the old scalper.

"Give us just a minute here, Deacon Sickles," he said. "I'm sure we've got room for a man like you." He picked the Walker up and let it hang in his hand as he turned away from the bar. He looked back at Sickles over his shoulder as he crossed the muddy floor. "Face and all, huh?"

"That is correct, Mr. Pridemore," Sickles said.

"Just call me Bigfoot," Pridemore said pleasantly. "Everybody does." He stopped at the faro table, grabbed Diamond Jim by his face, raised the Walker and shot him through the heart. Blood splattered around the fresh bullet hole in the side of the tent. Rain blew in immediately.

Behind the bar, Bertha Buttons started to reach down for her shotguns.

"Huh-uh, Bertha," said Pridemore, swinging around and pointing the smoking Walker at her. "Penza wants me to kill you both. But I'd sooner you be in this world than out of it." He gave her a stiff grin.

"So—so would I," she said in a shaky voice. She withdrew her hand slowly from under the bar top. Pridemore looked around at his men, who stood staring curiously. He shrugged.

"A man would be a fool to kill a big strapping redhead like this one," he said. He gestured Bertha from behind the bar. "Come around here, Big Darling. Let's get a better look at you." As Bertha eased around the bar toward him, he said to the others, "Have fun while you can, men. Tomorrow we've got all kinds of work ahead of us."

Chapter 5

In the early-morning light the Ranger had caught sight of trail dust drifting across the flatlands on the far horizon, where sandy bottom slopes reached upward into rocky hill lines. When he drew his dun and the cart beside him to a halt, Ria Cerero reined the barb down on his other side and searched the distant flatlands with him. The young woman sat on her board perch on the front edge of the cart and watched them both quietly.

"What is it?" Ria asked Sam.

"Trail dust," Sam said without turning to her, "less than an hour out."

"How do you know it is trail dust?" the woman asked.

"It's just something you know after a while," Sam said, still scouring the distance as he drew a battered telescope from inside his bedroll behind his saddle. He extended the field lens, raised it to his right eye and searched for the drift of dust again, not finding it. He went on to explain as he searched, "There's not enough wind to pull dust. . . . If it was the wind causing it, it would be a lot wider."

He paused, then added, "Anyway, dust doesn't stir up and drift without a reason."

Ria watched as the Ranger lowered the telescope, collapsed it between his palms and stuck it back behind his saddle.

"But could it be wild horses, even elk?" she asked, not wanting to consider that it might be Indians.

"Could be, but I doubt it," Sam replied, not wanting to spend any time discussing probabilities. He reined his dun to the right, leading the mule cart toward the slope of the hill line alongside them, less than a mile away. "Let's ride up into the rocks and keep moving."

"It is Apache!" Ria said with a slight gasp of fear in her voice. She reined the barb horse quickly and sidled it closer to the Ranger.

"No," Sam said, "Apache don't make dust on their trail if they can keep from it—especially when the Mexican government has scalp hunters killing them for bounty. Apache ride wide of anything soft enough to leave a track, or loose enough to stir dust." He nudged the dun forward.

"You know a lot about the Apache?" Ria asked as they rode along, the girl sitting watching them from her perch.

"No, ma'am," Sam said sidelong to her. "Just enough to keep me alive, so far." He glanced back out and once again saw a thin curtain of dust rise and drift. "I have learned to do the two main things they do out here—keep quiet and stay out of sight."

They crossed the short stretch of flatland separating them from the hill line and put their horses and mule cart upward onto a path that meandered and weaved its way among chimney rock and large boulder. For the better part of an hour they climbed the path until it widened into a trail running along the hillside three hundred feet above the flatlands. The lank mule pulled the cart along steadily, confidently; yet Sam knew the steepness of the hillside would not allow the cart to move any farther up its rigid spine. This was terrain for the sure of hoof, the nimble of foot. The land held no forbearance for man's wheeled endeavor.

"We need to walk," he said to Ria and Ana, the three of them having stopped in the shadowed cover of a cliff overhang. "There's likely an easier trail father up, but we'll never make it with the cart."

"Then—then you think we must leave the cart behind?" Ria asked.

"No, ma'am," Sam said, swinging down from his saddle. "We'll keep moving right along on this lower trail. Whoever's riding toward us, at least we know they're there. We'll listen and watch for them. If we need to, we'll lie low and let them pass without seeing us."

Ria swung down from the barb; Ana stood up off from her board and started to climb over the side of the cart. Seeing the Ranger step over toward the mule cart, Ria rushed past him and reached up and helped Ana down before he got the chance. Realizing the woman's distrust of him toward her daughter was still there, Sam stepped wide of the two and took hold of the mule's harness and steadied the cart.

As Ana collected herself and brushed her black hair back from her face, Ria gave the Ranger an apologetic look.

"Forgive me, Ranger," she said. "I am still fearful for my very young daughter, as you can see. Even though you have done so much for us, it is hard for me to let go—"

"Ma'am, you needn't apologize," Sam said, cutting her off. He turned loose of the mule and rubbed its coarse, bony muzzle. The mule twitched its scarred ears and stared straight ahead.

"*Gracias*, Ranger," Ria said, her arm around Ana's thin shoulders, "for understanding so much."

"You're both welcome," Sam said, a little embarrassed. He nodded and looked back and forth between the two of them. "Let's keep moving," he added, taking the reins to his dun and the mule cart. "Keep as quiet as we can." He drew horse and mule cart along with one hand, his Winchester in the other.

They had moved along in silence for another half hour when he heard the faint clack of hoof against stone on the trail ahead of them. Motioning the women and the two horses off the edge onto the rocky hillside, Sam pulled the mule cart behind a boulder and stood watching from cover as a Mexican guidon banner fluttered into sight above rocks six feet tall.

Good enough. . . .

Sam breathed deep, relieved. He reached his

sombrero out and waved it up and down as a *federale* front scout rode into sight around a mound of large rocks piled up behind a huge boulder.

"Hello the trail," he called out.

The scout, startled, jerked his horse's reins hard, causing the animal to rear slightly before he settled it.

"Come out, show yourself!" he demanded toward the Ranger's sweat-stained sombrero. "Raise your hands *high* and keep them high!" he added as if in afterthought.

Sam leaned his Winchester against the rock and loosened his Colt in its holster out of habit. He placed his sombrero back atop his head.

"Coming out," he said, sidestepping slowly into sight, his hands raised above his hat brim. "I'm Arizona Ranger Sam Burrack. I'm here tracking a wanted man."

The uniformed scout jumped down from his saddle and started walking forward, his big French revolver already drawn and cocked toward the Ranger. Behind him, Sam saw the red, white and green guidon come around the rocks, a Mexican captain and his sergeant riding abreast of the man carrying it. Seeing Sam in the trail, the captain and sergeant halted; the captain raised a gloved hand. Beside him the sergeant called out to the two columns of following horsemen.

"Surround this man," the captain told his sergeant, still surprised at the Ranger appearing as if out of nowhere.

As Sam watched with his hands high, the sergeant led the two columns forward and formed a half circle around him. The scout stood with his revolver still aimed at Sam's head. Sam looked all around at the circling soldiers.

"Arizona Ranger Sam Burrack," he repeated, seeing the captain ride forward slowly and stop his horse in front of the surrounding soldiers.

"I find this one hiding behind the rock, Capitán Penza," the scout pointed out quickly.

"I called out to you," Sam said. "I identified myself."

The scout started to say more, but the captain silenced him with a wave of his hand.

"I saw him call out to you, Corporal," he said to the lying scout. He gave the soldier an angry glance. The soldier stepped back and shut up. Captain Penza turned and looked at the badge on Sam's chest. "What are you doing here, Ranger? Have you run out of outlaws to hunt down in your Arizona Territory?"

A ripple of laughter rose from the men. The captain gave a smug grin.

"No, Captain," Sam said. "I'm on the trail of an assassin who's traveling with scalp hunters your country has a contract with. He had a hand in killing the sheriff in Mesa Grande."

"Oh . . . ?" The captain's interest piqued right away at the mention of the scalp hunters. Sam took note of it as Penza continued. "These mercenaries— *scalpers* as you call them—are wild and dangerous, very hard to control," he said, shaking his head. "They brought in Apache receipts to me yesterday at Iron Point. Is the assassin you seek among them?"

"I believe he is, Captain," Sam said. "But I also want to show you what I brought along to prove that your mercenaries are not only killing Apache but scalping anybody they can whose hair is black enough."

"What do you bring me?" the captain said. He straightened in his saddle and looked all around as if searching the rocks.

"It's in a mule cart back there," Sam said, lowering his hands a little, gesturing behind the rock. "I've got a rifle leaning there too." He gestured a hand toward the rocks on the hillside. "There are two women I sent to hide in the rocks, until I saw who it was coming."

The captain looked at his sergeant seated on his horse beside him, then back at the Ranger.

"Very well, Ranger," he said. "Bring out the two women . . . then show us what proof you bring to me. If my nation's laws are being broken, I will see to it these scoundrels pay."

In moments the mule cart and the horses stood on the trail. The two women shied back from the soldiers and tried to keep out of sight around the rear corner of the cart. Sam told the mounted captain about the two assassins, how one of them was Erskine Cord, the one who had held the contract with the Mexican government. He told him how Cord's nephew had broken out of jail and gotten away.

Yet, assassination and jailbreak aside, the captain's main concern seemed to be that the scalpers had scalped innocent Mexicans and harmless Indians along both sides of the border.

"And this is the best proof I can give you, Captain Penza," Sam said. He upended a burlap sack and let Mickey Cousins' half-scalped head fall to the ground. He righted the face upward with the toe of his boot for the captain to take a better look.

"*Santa Madre . . . ,*" the captain said. He crossed himself and looked at his sergeant for verification.

The sergeant stepped down from his saddle and stood over the severed head.

"Yes, *mi Capitán*," he replied grimly, staring down at the blood-streaked head in the dirt. "I have known Mickey Cousins for a long time. . . . This is him." He looked at the Ranger. "The white streak is missing from his hair. But I saw one of the scalps—I mean *receipts*—with a white streak in it." He shook his head. "It looked familiar, but I never imagined it to belong to this man. Mickey Cousins was a good scout."

"Yes, I too recall a receipt that had a white streak in it," the captain remarked, pondering the half-scalped head. Mickey Cousins' eyes were barely parted and seemed to stare up at him. "Who cut off his head off?" he asked Sam.

"I did that," Sam said. "I had no choice. At the time we had a badly wounded man with us. Wolves were getting bolder at the smell of his blood. I had to leave either Mickey Cousins' body or the wounded man behind. I knew if I started shooting at the wolves with a rifle, Apache would ride in from every direction."

"It is a wise thing you do, Ranger," the captain said. "Where is this wounded man?"

"He's dead and buried back alongside the trail," Sam said, jerking his head in that direction. "There's a couple of Lipans dead back at the water hole too," he added. "I expect the desert wolves have eaten well this whole trip." He looked at the captain, sensing that something was bothering him. But he had no idea what it could be.

"And now you are continuing on to Iron Point," the captain asked him, "even though the mercenaries will no doubt be gone by the time you arrive?"

"I'm on their trail until I get the man I'm looking for," Sam said. "I'm also taking these women there where it's safe, so they can rest up and be on their way. Are you headed back to Iron Point now?"

"Yes, right away," said Captain Penza. "I must stop these scalpers and see to it they pay for their crimes." He gestured down at Mickey Cousins' head. "This in itself is enough reason to hang them. There is no way of knowing how many other innocent people have died at their hands."

Sam watched him. Yes, something had the man troubled, he was certain of it.

"I'm obliged if we can ride back with you," he said. "It would make the women feel better having more guns around."

For a moment the captain appeared to have a

hard time considering the Ranger's request. Finally he said, "No, I am sorry, Ranger, that is out of the question."

Out of the question?

Sam noted that even the sergeant looked a little taken aback by his captain's words.

"It would slow us down too much," Penza offered, seeing the look in both his sergeant's and the Ranger's eyes. "We must hurry to catch these men." He looked at the sergeant, then back at the Ranger.

Sam stepped in close, keeping his words just between himself and the captain.

"These women are going to be in great danger if we should happen to run into Apache between here and Iron Point," he said. "The scalpers have the Wolf Hearts and every other band worked into a frenzy."

"I realize this is true," the captain said. "And I will leave some soldiers to escort you and the women, of course. But I must keep moving and ride quickly in order to catch these murderers. The soldiers will see to it you and the women take your time and get there safely, even though it will take longer."

It dawned on the Ranger that the captain didn't want him getting to the scalpers first. *Why?* he asked himself, looking into the captain's troubled eyes.

"On second thought, that won't be necessary, Captain," he said. "I believe if we stay off the main trails and keep in the hills as much as we can, we'll be all right." As he spoke he slid a look at the sergeant, who still looked surprised at the captain's actions.

"Very well, suit yourself, Ranger," Captain Penza said, taking on a rigid tone. He turned to the sergeant and said, "Turn this patrol around. We ride back to Iron Point immediately."

"*Sí, Capitán,*" the sergeant said, snapping to attention. He turned to his horse and stepped up into his saddle.

"Wait," Sam said as the sergeant settled into his saddle. He stepped forward, rolled the severed head back into the burlap feed sack, picked it up and walked to the sergeant's horse. "Don't forget Cousins," he said.

The sergeant looked to the captain for permission to take the feed sack. When the captain nodded, the sergeant took the sack and passed it along to the soldier nearest him. Then he nodded at the Ranger and straightened in his saddle. Sam stepped back to the horses and the mule cart and stood beside the women as the patrol turned around on the trail and rode away.

"So, we continue on our own alone," Ria said warily as the patrol rode out of sight around the rocks, the guidon leading the way.

"We'll be all right, ma'am," he said. "The way they're announcing around every turn, we might be better off without them." He reached around before Ria could stop him and lifted Ana up onto the side of the cart. Fear flashed across Ria's face. But then she settled and looked relieved when the Ranger turned the young woman loose. Ana scrambled the rest of the way up over the side of the cart and climbed up onto her makeshift seat.

"*Sí*, Ranger," Ria said. "You have brought us this far. I know you will take us to safety."

Chapter 6

Before daylight Turner Pridemore and his men had assembled and readied their horses behind the town livery barn. They stood hidden in the purple, shadowy darkness still watching Captain Penza and his sergeant lead the twenty-four-man patrol ride out of Iron Point. Beside Pridemore stood his son, Fox, and Ozzie Cord, the two still weaving from all the whiskey they'd poured down their gullets less than two hours earlier.

When the soldiers had ridden out of sight, Pridemore looked the two drunken young men up and down. He shook his head in disgust and turned to Darton Alpine.

"Keep these two here, Dart," he whispered. "They're no good on the trail."

Alpine also looked the two up and down, seeing Ozzie stagger in place and almost fall.

"I've got four guards we have to kill here," he said in a lowered voice. "Are these two up to it?"

"They best be," said Pridemore, "else I'll bullwhip all the hide off Fox's back and feed this one's eyes to a buzzard." He studied Alpine closer with a questioning gaze. "Maybe I'm putting more on you and Chase than the two of yas can handle?"

"Don't worry about nothing. Malcolm and I have this place covered. Right, Malcolm?" Alpine replied quickly, looking around at the burly buckskin-clad scalper standing nearby.

"We got it under control, Bigfoot," said the veteran mercenary, Malcolm Chase. He carried a long saber wound down the length of his right jaw. He held a two-pound ironmonger's hammer in his thick fist, fastened to his wrist with a leather strap. "Once I crack a man's nut, it'll still be cracked when he crosses Jordan."

"Good," said Pridemore. "There's four of them and six of you, not counting Fox and Ozzie. I better not come back and hear any excuses." He looked at the older scalper, Deacon Sickles. "Did you take care of things, Deacon?"

Sickles stood rolling down his wet buckskin shirtsleeves, his big knife in hand.

"I did," he replied.

Pridemore nodded, then gestured toward Fox and Ozzie. "It they don't sober up and get into the spirit of things, tie them up and throw them in the barn. I'll deal with them when I get back." He looked toward the other men gathered in the shadows, waiting beside their horses, holding their reins.

"Let's get to it," he said, taking his horse's reins from an outheld hand.

Alpine looked around at the men he'd be working with as Pridemore and fifteen of the mercenaries mounted quietly and rode away. He gave Deacon Sickles a grin in the shadowy darkness.

"How does it feel, Sickles, going from riding alone to riding with a whole damn army?" he said.

"Comforting," the older scalper said. "Even more so when I'm rubbing money agin my leg." He patted his empty trouser pocket.

"It'll come soon enough," said Alpine. "Bigfoot is a leader with vision."

"I sensed it right off," said Sickles.

Alpine looked around at the other faces watching him, waiting for his orders. Aside from Sickles and Malcolm Chase, there stood a newer scalper named Ed Adams and his half-breed Cherokee sidekick, Philbert Ohiola—Ohio Phil to the men. Phil wore a tall, bent and battered silk top hat atop a head that he kept shaved for safety's sake. He carried an old iron-head trade hatchet shoved down behind his belt. Next to Adams and Ohio Phil stood a scalper named Ian Pusser, who had ridden off and on with Erskine Cord's mercenaries from the group's origin.

Alpine gestured a hand to the east, ushering the men's attention to the sliver of silver light mantling the horizon.

"Any minute now the sun is going to lift its lid," he said quietly yet firmly. "When it does I want a man behind every one of the four guards." He looked from face to face. "When you hear me give off a crow call, kill them quick and quietlike and leave them where they lay. Once the sun's up and they're all dead, we'll gather in the street and let this town know who's in charge."

"Any fool who thinks four Mexican guards can handle the likes of us is asking for a bloodletting," said Chase, swinging his ironmonger's hammer back and forth calmly on his wrist.

"Hey! *Malcolm!*" said Alpine in a stiff tone. "Don't talk while I'm talking. This is business here."

"Excuse the *hell* out of me," Chase said without ceasing to swing the thick hammer. "Next time I'll raise my hand."

Alpine just stared at him, knowing if anything went wrong here, he himself would be the first person Pridemore blamed. He started to say something more, but before he could, Fox Pridemore stepped forward, hearing what was going on and trying to sober up and take part in it.

"Want me and Oz to ready some horses, just in case things don't go right?" he asked, working to control the thickness in his tongue.

"No," said Alpine, "you two stay out of the way till you're sober. Besides, there's to be no riding away from this. Either this thing works or we all die right here." He looked all around at the faces. "Any questions?" he asked.

The men stood silent until finally Chase raised a hand like a courteous schoolboy, the hammer still swinging calmly at his side.

Alpine just stared at him coldly.

"Can we get on with this?" Chase said in a bored tone. "I ain't et yet."

Damn it to hell!

Alpine seethed, but he kept his anger to himself and motioned the men away. As they moved away silently, like lingering apparitions in the grainy purple darkness, he took a position out of sight behind the livery barn. For the next few minutes he watched as the sliver of light on the eastern sky widened slowly above the earth. When the sun domed the jagged edge of the earth like a bald man peeping over a picket fence, he cupped both hands over his mouth and cawed out three times along the empty street.

Standing in the dead silence, Alpine heard not a single sound come from the two-man guard post at the wide gates to Iron Point. Neither did he hear any sound of a struggle come from the single guard post at the far end of town. Nor did any sound come from the Apache lookout post above a large boulder facing toward the hill line a mile behind the old fortress. The only sound he did hear was a sour and abrupt belch that Ozzie Cord let out, followed by Ozzie laughing and apologizing drunkenly.

"This son of a bitch," Alpine growled, stomping off in the direction of the gurgling belch.

When he got to where Ozzie and Fox lay on the ground against the rear side of the livery barn, he saw Ozzie raise a bottle to his lips. Without hesitation he reached down and slapped the bottle away. It crashed and broke on the rocky ground.

"For two cents I'd blow your damn head off," he

growled, keeping his voice low. His cocked Colt jammed against Ozzie's forehead.

"Don't shoot, Dart!" Fox said to Alpine. "I'll sober him up; I swear I will. I'm not drinking, see?" He spread his hands to show they were empty.

Alpine knew this was not the time to be firing a gun—not just yet. He eased his gun from against Ozzie's head and uncocked it.

"See that you do, Fox," Alpine said. He glared at Ozzie. "It's a good thing Fox here had enough sense to sober up. He's in charge of you until I say otherwise. Have you both got that?"

"I've got it," Ozzie whined.

"I got it," Fox said responsibly. "He'll do no more drinking, I promise you."

The two stared as Alpine walked away. Looking sidelong at Ozzie, Fox grinned and pulled a bottle of rye up from behind his back. He took a long swig and passed the bottle to him. The two muffled their laughter, hands over their mouths like naughty children.

Alpine walked on a few yards toward the sound of a hammer tacking nails into a board. When he got closer, the tacking stopped and Deacon Sickles looked over his shoulder at him.

"Am I starting too early?" Sickles asked in a hushed tone.

"No, you're good," said Alpine. "It's time the town wakes up and sees what we're doing here." He looked around and saw two of his men walking in from different guard posts. "How long before you're done and ready?" he asked Sickles.

"Another nail or two, I'm finished," Sickles said,

turning back to the board. "This ought to put the fear of God in them."

"Damn right it will," said Alpine. He raised his Colt again and wagged it back and forth. "All right, here we go."

Pridemore and half of his men lay strewn along a rock ledge overlooking the trail where they had spotted the patrol riding back toward Iron Point. The other half of the scalpers lay in wait along the trail below, every third one with a bow and a quiver of arrows beside him. Overhead the scalding noon sun beat down, casting a harsh wavering whiteness over the rock desert badlands. Beside Pridemore, Early Doss looked up at the burning sky, then looked down and batted his eyes against the sun's glare.

"By now, I expect Alpine and his lot has Iron Point under their thumbs," Doss said to Pridemore.

"They better have," Pridemore said. "We get back there, I best see every gold coin and peso stuffed into a bag, ready to carry off." He allowed himself a tight grin, staring down at the rocky hill trail. He looked on his other side at Bertha Buttons, who lay shielded from the sun beneath a ragged serape. Under the serape her dress hung torn and soiled. Her left shoe was missing, her hair tangled and dusty from the trail.

"How you holding up, Big Darling?" Pridemore asked. He reached a hand over and brushed her hair from her eyes. Her rouge had been smeared from her cheek to her chin.

"Better . . . than I expected, Bigfoot," she said, careful not to say anything that might upset the mercenary leader. "I—I worry about my saloon, my girls. I really should be there—"

"Now, now. . . ." Pridemore cut her off with a finger up against her parched lips. "You don't need to be there. You just think you do. I left orders for my men to take care of things."

"I know you did, and I'm grateful," said Bertha. "The truth is, this desert is roasting me alive. It's been a long while since I've trekked outside Iron Point." She looked all along the row of men for a canteen. "Could I get some water?"

Pridemore reached his hand over and patted her rouge-smeared cheek.

"Soon you can, but not just now," he said. "I believe we've got to toughen you up some. If you're going to be my gal—my partner so to speak—you'll need to get by for long stretches like this without water, food and whatnot." He drew his hand away. "My last gal never got the hang of it, bless her heart. She fried like bacon before the desert finally et her innards." He rubbed the back on her hand as if stroking the head of a pet cat. "That poor sweet darling . . . ," he murmured. An Apache bow lay on the rock beside him.

Fried like bacon . . . ? The desert ate her innards . . . ?

Bertha just stared at him for a moment. She looked off along the row of filthy buckskins, of a grisly assortment of human hair and bone ornamentation. Then back at Pridemore. They were insane, every single bloody last one of them. She'd never met a scalp hunter who wasn't.

Turner Pridemore had never been known as a madman before. Was this madness something that joining these mercenaries had brought out in him? Was this what scalp hunting did to a man? She didn't know; she didn't care, she concluded to herself. All she knew was that she had to find a way to stay alive until she could either get away or scratch out a safer place herself.

"You're right about food and water," she said, forcing a thin smile in spite of her parched lips. "I've always said, it takes more than food and water to sustain a gal."

"So true," Pridemore said. "And whatever sustenance a gal like you needs, I will bring it and lay it at your feet. You'll never flee another hanging posse, Texas or otherwise, so long as you're with me."

"Here they come now, Bigfoot," Early Doss said on Pridemore's other side.

Pridemore affectionately tapped the tip of his finger on Bertha's nose and grinned at her.

"I want you to keep quiet here for a minute, Big Darling," he said. "We're fixing to kill us a bunch of Mexican soldiers."

"Captain Penza's patrol?" Bertha asked, seeing the soldiers follow their guidon into sight. The scout had fallen back closer to the men, riding about ten yards ahead of them.

"Right you are," said Pridemore, "the very son of a bitch who paid me to kill you and Jim Ruby. He believed with you two out of the way he could slip somebody of his own in to run the saloon."

Bertha thought about it.

"So, now, with Jim Ruby out of the way, you figure killing Penza will make you and me partners?" She leveled her gaze. "You realize I have a Mexican official I pay every month."

"I understand," said Pridemore. "He won't even have to know. Who knows? Someday he might even die himself."

Bertha stared at him in feigned admiration. "I always heard you're a real daisy of a businessman. Now I see why folks think it."

Pridemore grinned and tapped his forehead.

"I've got tricks the world has yet to see," he said. He scooted back from the edge, his hand on Bertha's shoulder ushering her along with him. He carried a bow loaded with an arrow in it in his other hand. "We take him alive, you can saw his ears off before we kill him . . . if you've a mind to, that is."

Bertha stared down at the soldiers riding into sight.

"That pig would've had me killed," she said. Turning to Pridemore, she added, "You mean I can do anything I feel like to him before he dies?"

"Have yourself a good time with him, my word on it," Pridemore said with a shrug.

"I could do that," Bertha said under her breath. "I could do that in spades."

Pridemore watched her face flush with vengeance at the possibilities at hand. "Power is a wonderful thing, ain't it, Big Darling?"

"Wonderful and then some," Bertha said, staring at the captain from high above him. "Bigfoot," she offered, feeling less afraid, more protected than she'd felt in a long time. "I can see where you and I might make a nice place for ourselves."

Chapter 7

———

Captain Penza's patrol straightened out around the turn in the trail and rode between two high-reaching hills towering on either side of them. From behind the cover of rock and from atop cliff overhangs, Pridemore's men took all the time they needed. As the scout dropped farther back, searching the upper hill lines halfheartedly, the scalpers homed their rifle sights on the unsuspecting soldiers.

The well-coordinated ambush erupted so fast and furious that the soldiers hardly knew what hit them. As the first hard-pounding volley of fire exploded on either side, the mercenaries squalled and shouted among the rocks like wild Indians.

"*Apache!* Take cover!" the sergeant bellowed, yanking his horse around as bullets sliced through the air around him. Soldiers fell from their horses, many never getting their guns raised. Their rearing horses fell too. The captain's horse reared and twisted wildly midair and came down, turning back onto the trail alongside the sergeant. But before their animals could get the move completed, a bullet from Pridemore's rifle knocked the captain's horse off its hooves. Two bullets hit the sergeant at once and slung him from his saddle in a wide spray of blood. As the captain hurried to the cover of rock, Pridemore took close aim and sent a bullet slicing through the back of his leg. The captain fell forward and crawled away quickly.

In seconds the soldiers were bunched up in the trail, a third of them already down, dead or dying. The fighting wounded threw themselves from their horses and ran to what cover they could take among rocks at the low edge of the trail. A few lay in the trail in the shelter of downed horses. Rifle fire butchered the animals where they lay. Arrows flew in from the hillsides; Pridemore's men yelped like coyotes. They shouted war cries they had learned from their many Indian battles.

Seeing the fight was rapidly drawing to a close, Pridemore fired three arrows down into the dead horses below, then tossed the bow out onto the rocks. Return fire from the ambushed soldiers was sporadic and waning. Looking down, Pridemore saw soldiers on foot bounding away over rock and brush along the high hillside.

"Another terrible attack by the heathen savages," he said, rising into a crouch, pulling the woman up beside him. "Keep your head down, Big Darling. One of these bullets is apt to find you whether they're seeking you or not."

"Careful, Bigfoot," said Early Doss, still firing at the soldiers in retreat among the rocks. "They might yet get collected and fight back."

"Naw, little chance," said Pridemore. "These

boys are so scared of Apache they see them when they look down the jake." He gave a dark little laugh, then added, "Get finished up here; then search the hillside. You see any soldier's hair long enough to look Apache, take it. Bullets cost money—we got to make *something* out of all this."

He gave a tug on Bertha's hand, pulling her along, the two of them moving crouched among the cover of rock. Looking down at the soldiers and horses lying dead with arrows in them, Bertha gave a faint smile.

"My, my, Bigfoot," she said, "you manage to play every angle, don't you?"

"I do indeed," Pridemore said. "If I felt like doing it, I could convince the *capitán* that my mercenaries showed up just in time to chase away the Apache and save him and what few men he's got left." He chuckled as they moved down toward the trail.

Bertha giggled and ran her hand back over her tangled hair, straightening it as best she could.

"What they don't know," Pridemore said, "is that the Wolf Hearts and the rest of the Mescaleros have moved on out of here. We whupped them bad. They've rode south to lie up and lick their wounds. No telling when they'll be back."

They stopped for a moment while three scalpers ran in behind a stand of rock and finished off three soldiers.

"Will you go after them?" Bertha asked.

"Naw, we'll wait, get them when they come back this way. When the Mescaleros move out, the Lipans get a little bolder, start thieving horses and goats here and there." He shrugged. "They're Apache too—hair pays the same."

Bertha shook her head.

"I'm impressed," she said as they walked out on the trail, the firing all but over. Farther along the rock hillside, halfway up, a voice cried out in terror. Bertha winced.

Pridemore grinned.

"There's a man I'm betting should have seen a barber before riding out here," he said.

On the trail, scalpers gathered on either side of Pridemore and walked forward slowly with him, keeping quiet as they approached a place where the soldier's heavy gunfire had resounded earlier. Half circling the spot, Pridemore raised a hand, holding the men back as he grinned listening toward the rocks. Then he turned the grin to Bertha.

"Capitán Penza? Are you in there?" he called out. They all listened for a silent moment. After a tense pause the wounded captain replied.

"Yes—yes, I am here," he said, sounding stunned at hearing the words of a white man. "Who . . . is out there?"

"Hell, it's me, Bigfoot, and my mercenaries, Captain," Pridemore called out. "Lucky we came by. We just run off two dozen heathen Apache before they made dinner out of yas."

"Pridemore, thank God it's you!" the captain called out, almost sobbing with gratitude. He stood up from behind a waist-high rock, his bloody hands clasped together as if in prayer.

Pridemore turned to Bertha and grinned.

"See? What'd I tell you?" he said just above a whisper. "This world is mine."

Around Pridemore his mercenaries laughed at the easily duped captain.

Captain Penza looked confused.

"What is funny, Bigfoot?" he said. "Many of my men are dead. Why do your men laugh?"

"Hell, they're all crazy, *Capitán*," said Pridemore. "I should have told you."

"*Sí*, loco," Penza said indignantly. He looked at Bertha Buttons, her clothes ripped and hanging, one large breast almost completely bare. "What is she doing here?"

Pridemore reached around and pulled Bertha forward, prisoner-style, and held her forward roughly for the captain to see.

"I lured her out here, *Capitán*," Pridemore said causally. "I figured you might want to see me cut her throat — no extra charge for watching, of course."

Bertha gave Pridemore a look of terror as he raised a big knife from his boot well. She tried to jerk away from him, but he held fast.

"I did not *want* to," said Penza, recovering quickly from the ruse Indian attack. "But since you brought her . . ." He looked back and forth, the scalpers having settled down from laughing, serious now. "What about Jim Ruby?"

"Next place you'll see Diamond Jim is in hell, *Capitán*," Pridemore said. "Watch close now." As Bertha tried to pull away, he tightened his grip on her and laid the edge of the big knife blade across her throat. Penza clenched his teeth; a dark gleam of satisfaction came to his eyes, a faint smile.

"Ziiii-iip," Pridemore hissed through his teeth, running the dull edge of the knife across her flesh so quickly that Bertha gasped out loud and threw her hands up around her throat.

For an instant Penza's faint smile widened, his eyes gleamed sharper. Then his eyes turned confused as he saw no blood either ooze or spew from between Bertha's clutching fingers.

Even the mercenaries looked a little bewildered by Pridemore's actions.

Bertha swooned a little in relief; she started to sink to her knees, but Pridemore caught her, steadied her.

"Easy, now, Big Darling," he said. "I thought you'd know it was all in jest." He let her rest against him. "I wouldn't hurt you. We've still got to consummate and whatnot." He grinned at her, then looked back at the captain, who'd begun to see this as a madman's ugly game.

"See, Capitán Penza," Pridemore said. "I told her you paid me to kill her, but I didn't want her to take my word for it." He looked at Bertha and handed her the knife by its handle.

"You double-crossed me. . . ." Penza slumped, knowing that only death awaited him.

"Well, yeah, sort of," said Pridemore. "Look at her and then look at yourself. I couldn't kill this big strapping beauty." He squeezed Bertha. "And I do maintain a rigid rule against giving refunds."

Bertha straightened and looked at the knife in her hand. She gave the captain a cold, bitter stare.

"Thanks, Bigfoot," she said, gripping the knife tightly. Three of the scalpers moved in fast and held the captain by his outstretched arms.

"Capitán Penza, Bertha's going to cut a few odds and ends off you. I told her she could, if she had a mind to"—he watched the seething woman stalk forward—"and now it appears she certainly *does* have a mind to."

Behind the livery barn, Ozzie and Fox plunged their heads down into the cool water of a horse trough and held them there for a moment. When they rose and slung their wet hair, Fox wiped his face with his hand and looked around and batted his red-rimmed eyes. "No more whiskey for me, Oz," he said. "I don't remember much of last night or this morning, but what little I do ain't good."

Beside him Ozzie took a drink from their last bottle of whiskey and handed the bottle toward him.

"What'd I just tell you?" Fox said with hangover testiness to his voice. "I'm not getting drunk all over again."

Ozzie shrugged and stood the half-full bottle on a short hitch post.

"Neither am I," he said. "But I'm not going to go around hurting all day when a stiff drink will put me back on my feet."

Fox thought about it. With each beat of his pulse, his head pounded like a hammer on a tin tub.

"Hell, give it here," he said, reaching a hand over toward the hitch post.

Ozzie chuckled, picked up the bottle, swished its contents, then handed it to him.

"You remember us robbing the mercantile?" he asked as Fox took the bottle. "Remember us tying up the owner and me bashing him over the head with my gun barrel?"

"Yeah, sort of," said Fox. He took a quick drink of whiskey and made a sour face. When he lowered the bottle, he felt the lumpy coins and dollar bills he'd stuffed down in his trouser pockets. The whiskey spread like warm coals throughout his chest and shoulders. He felt his head already begin to settle.

"I went back and killed him while you was chasing that whore with the shoeing tongs," Ozzie said matter-of-factly. "Figured it beat taking a chance him telling anybody."

"You didn't have to kill him," Fox said. "He wouldn't dare say nothing, not after everybody here seeing Diamond Jim's face nailed to a board. Nobody even wants to come out on the street."

"Still and all, it's never good to leave a witness behind," said Ozzie. "My uncle taught me that." He chuckled aloud, picturing Diamond Jim Ruby's entire face, beard, scalp and all, stretched out and tacked to a pine board. "How'd old man Sickles ever learn to do something like that, you reckon?"

"*Practice* is all I can think of. He's had lots and *lots* of practice," Fox said.

"If you ask me, old Deacon Sickles is a little peculiar," Ozzie offered, lowering his voice a little as if Deacon Sickles might hear him.

Fox stifled a laugh, looking over at Diamond Jim's raw faceless head, the wide, dead grin. Lidless eyes stared up at the boiling Mexican sun.

"You think so, huh?" he said.

The two laughed and slung their wet hair. Finger bones and ornaments clacked and clattered on their breastwork. Fox was feeling better. He wiped his face again and looked off along the corral fence where Diamond Jim's body lay in the dirt. Corral horses gave the grisly body a wide berth. They stood back and sniffed toward it, then blew out a breath and walked away.

"Did we eat any breakfast this morning?" Ozzie asked.

"I don't think so," said Fox. "Are you hungry?"

"I could eat," Ozzie said.

"Let's go eat, then," said Fox, picking up his hat and rifle from the hitch post.

"Yep, let's look at Diamomd Jim's face again on the way," said Ozzie, almost childlike.

They walked from the livery barn to the street and on to Iron Point's public well in the center of a dusty plaza. The board with Diamond Jim's face tacked to it leaned against the front of the well, facing the gates toward anyone entering town.

"Who are they waiting for?" Ozzie asked Fox, the two of them stopping at the well and looking toward the iron gates of the old fortress.

Fox just looked at him for a moment.

"For any of the soldiers . . . ?" said Fox, trying to

jog Ozzie's memory. "Oz, you *really don't* remember much," he added.

"Like I said, not a lot, just killing the store owner," Ozzie replied.

The two chuckled, turning to the board with Diamond Jim's face stretched on it. Flies walked on the nose cartilage that lay atop a flattened cheek. Fox fanned the flies away. From a few yards away a couple of townsmen watched warily. The streets of Iron Point lay empty, save for occasional townsfolk who ventured forth one and two at a time to see the face of Jim Ruby tacked on rough pine.

Looking at the face, Ozzie chuffed and shook his head.

"I can't make no sense of it," he said, cocking his head this way and that, studying Ruby. "He was an ugly sumbitch anyways."

Skinned from the back of the head forward, Ruby's face looked small inside the large circle of skin scalp and beard. His eyelids were gone, as were his lips. His ears had been kept intact on the grisly souvenir.

"After my pa and the others hit the army patrol," Fox said, dismissing Ruby's face, "Pa figures any soldiers that manages to get away alive might come running back here."

Ozzie shook his head and turned away from Ruby.

"Stupid soldiers," he said.

"Yeah . . . ," Fox said. He gazed in contemplation at the iron gates, and beyond them, out across the distant flatlands below. At the gates Darton Alpine looked back at the two and motioned them toward the rear trail out of town.

"Right away, Dart," Fox called out to him. To Ozzie he said, "He wants us to cover the other end of town. Let's go."

"What about something to eat?" Ozzie said.

"We'll get something on our way," said Fox.

"Hell," said Ozzie, "no soldier's going to go all the way around town and come the back way—not while they think Apache is on their trail."

"I know it," said Fox, "but let's do like we're told. Maybe he'll forget about us getting drunk on him." They started walking, rifles in hand. "Anyways, I've been thinking," Fox added. "I figure when Pa gets back, he's going to have us pillage this town and burn it on our way out."

"So?" Ozzie grinned, looking all around. "That's sounds like fun to me."

Fun?

Fox just looked at him as they walked.

"It might be *fun* for the two of us if we got the jump on everybody and took whatever money we can find ahead of time. Don't you think?"

"Oh yes, indeed I do," Ozzie said, grinning. He looked all around. "How we going to do it without being seen by Alpine?"

Fox looked him up and down.

"We just go to all the back doors," he said, "shake a gun in the owner's face. Tell him if he don't keep his mouth shut, he'll be leaning on the well beside Diamond Jim."

Ozzie laughed and clapped his hands together in excitement.

"Damn! I like it!" he said. "You must think just like your pa when it comes to business."

"I ought to," Fox said solemnly. "That's who I learnt it from. Now that I'm no longer saddled with my brother, I want to put my learning to work. Maybe strike out on my own before long."

"I hear you, *El Zorro*," said Ozzie. "You need a pal covering your back, I'm your huckleberry."

"'El Zorro'?" said Fox.

Ozzie grinned.

"Yeah, you know, 'The Fox'?" He made a strong fist. "The way the Mexes say it, *Astuto como el zorro* . . . ?"

"Crafty as *the fox*," the serious young man translated. He spat and said, "I don't know about that, Oz. I just know the only way out for me is to shoot my way out, fight my way out and never look back."

Ozzie looked all around, puzzled. He shrugged and spread his hands.

"Your way out of *what*?" he asked as they walked.

"Any damn thing . . . every damn thing," Fox said grimly without looking around. They walked on in a tight silence until finally Fox's dark brooding seemed to lift a little. He let out a breath and glanced sidelong at Ozzie.

"El Zorro, huh?"

"Yeah." Ozzie grinned. "What do you think of it?"

"It'll do," Fox said. He managed a slight smile,

realizing there were a lot of things about Ozzie that reminded him of his dead brother, Lucas. Ozzie still had a lot of kid in him, Fox realized. But he was smart enough to know how to stay alive. That was worth a lot.

"El Zorro," Fox murmured to himself, getting a feel for it. He was not a young man given to frivolity, but he liked it.

And they walked on.

PART 2

Chapter 8

The Ranger and the women had heard the gunfire from a long ways off. With little other choice they had continued moving steadily in that direction throughout the day. In the late afternoon, they stopped at a turn on the hill trail when three soldiers stood up on the hillside and waved down at them. One soldier wore a bloodstained handkerchief wrapped around his upper arm; another soldier rode slumped in his saddle with a hand pressed to his side.

"Ranger, up here," one soldier called out in English, recognizing Sam from when they'd met earlier on the trail. As he spoke the soldier bounded through the rocks down toward the trail. The two wounded soldiers stood watching, their French rifles in hand.

Sam stopped his dun and the mule cart and sat watching. The woman, Ria, stopped the barb beside him. The young girl sat at the front of the cart.

"We heard shooting earlier. What happened?" he asked.

"Apache! Quetos and his Wolf Hearts ambushed

us," the soldier said, reaching the trail and stopping. On the hillside the other two walked down slowly, cradling their rifles. "Thank God we saw you before you go any farther. They will kill you." He waved a hand at the trail leading to Iron Point. "They are everywhere."

Apache . . . ?

Sam was skeptical. Looking out across the sand flats below and back along the hill trail in the direction of Iron Point, he saw no trail dust, no signs of life on the rugged Mexican badlands. He'd yet to see anyone ride away from fighting Apache without warriors in hot pursuit. From the condition of these three, the Wolf Hearts would have ridden them down long before now and killed them on the spot.

"Where's your captain?" Sam asked.

"Dead, I think," the soldier said. Then he stopped and said, "Or maybe he got away, I don't know. We saw a chance to retreat and we did so. Were we wrong?"

Sam just looked at him, getting an idea these men were in the midst of deserting when he and his little party happened along.

"I don't know," Sam replied. "Sometimes a retreat is the only move to make. Where are you headed now? Where're your horses?"

The other two soldiers had stopped a few feet away and stood watching.

"Where are we headed? Where are our horses?" the soldier repeated, as if needing time to come up with some answers. "Our horses are over there." He gestured a hand toward the hillside. "We are headed back to Iron Point, of course — to defend the fort against the heathen Apache."

"I see," Sam said. He picked up his canteen by the strap around his saddle horn and swung down from his saddle. The women watched him step around and hold the canteen out to the soldier.

"Ah, *gracias*, Ranger," the man said. He took the canteen, started to uncap it.

"You're headed the wrong way," Sam said, leaning in close to the soldier as if sharing a secret. He eyed him closely.

The soldier looked surprised, nervous, feeling pressed by the Ranger.

"We are?" he said. He glanced over at the two men as he raised the canteen to his lips. But he stopped suddenly when he felt the tip of the Ranger's gun barrel stuck up under his chin.

"You try signaling them to fire, I'll lift the top off your head," Sam said quietly.

"No, no, *señor*! You have us wrong!" the man said, hearing the Colt cock in the Ranger's hand. "*Por favor*. Let me explain to you —"

But Sam was having none of it.

"Tell your pards to drop the rifles," he demanded, cutting the man off.

The soldier's eyes flashed toward the men. Sweat beaded thick on his forehead.

"Okay, lay down your rifles, both of you!" he shouted. "I told you this would not work. That this man is too smart to fall for any trick —"

"Shut up," Sam said, gripping the man by his

shirt with his free hand, the barrel of the Colt still in place under his chin. "Tell them to drop every weapon they've got. If they hold out, I'll kill you first. Don't forget, *yo hablo español*."

"This one speaks Spanish," the soldier said to the men in their own language. Then he quickly ordered them to disarm, and looked back at the Ranger. "There, you see, no tricks." He gave a shrug, his head cocked high on the tip of the gun barrel.

"Ria, you and Ana search those two," Sam called out to the women. "See to it they're unarmed."

"I will search them," Ria replied. She motioned for Ana to remain in the cart.

Sam watched her climb down from her saddle and hurry over to the wounded soldiers. He looked at Ana, who had sat back down and folded her hands on her lap.

"Ana, find some bandages for these men," he called out to the young woman.

"Please do not blame us for what we do, Ranger," the soldier said. "We are in desperation here. We know the Apache will kill us if they catch us."

"You've got no horses, do you?" Sam said. "You were going to take ours, right?"

"It is true, God forgive us," the soldier said. "We have no horses . . . no food, no water." He lowered his eyes to the canteen in his hand. "Yes, we are going as far from this place as we can get. The patrol is dead. What else can we do?"

Sam lowered the Colt from under the man's chin when he looked around and saw Ria give him a nod. The soldier drank from the canteen and gestured toward the other two men.

"Ana, come take the water to the men," he said, seeing the young woman step down from the cart with bandaging in her hands.

"No, Ana, stay where you are!" Ria called out, hurrying toward the canteen in the soldier's outstretched hand. "I will do it."

Sam stepped back from the soldier; he lowered the Colt to his side but kept it cocked. He watched Ria take the canteen from the soldier and hurried to Ana to get the bandaging.

"We're going to give you a canteen," he said to the sweating soldier. "You know there's a water hole back there."

"*Sí*, yes, we know," the soldier said.

"We'll give you the bandaging and part of what food we have."

"*Gracias,*" the soldier said humbly, his head lowered in shame for what he and his companions had planned to do.

"Here're your choices," Sam said. "We're going to Iron Point—"

"But, Ranger, the Apache!" the soldier blurted out.

Sam silenced him with a firm stare.

"You three can follow along with us on foot." He motioned the other two soldiers over closer as he spoke. "Or you can take your chances and head for your next nearest outpost."

"The next nearest outpost is the old mission fortress near Rio Santo," the soldier said. "It is a two-day ride—walking, I don't know." He shook his head a little at the prospect and looked at the other two as they walked closer, stopped and listened.

Sam noted the bloodstained bandages on the two men.

"We had a wounded man back there and the wolves got awfully bold on us," he warned.

"Better we face the wolves than the Wolf Hearts," the sweaty soldier said. He paused, then said, "Perhaps you should go with us, Ranger. When we reach the outpost we will have over a hundred armed soldiers around us."

"We're headed on to Iron Point," Sam said in a voice that invited no more discussion on the matter. "Unless the womenfolk want to go to Rio Santo with you." He looked at Ria and Ana as the two walked in closer. But Sam already knew that Ria wasn't about to allow these soldiers around Ana, not for a minute, certainly not for a long trek across the Mexican badlands.

"No," Ria said flatly, "we are going to Iron Point with the Ranger." She stared at the soldiers and looked them up and down with wary distrust in her dark eyes.

"There you have it," Sam said to the soldiers. "We'll get you outfitted best we can. I'll unload your guns and pitch your bullets up on the hillside. We'll be cleared out of here by the time you find them."

"But, señor—" one of the wounded soldiers started to protest.

"Keep quiet," the sweaty soldier snapped at him. "It is only fair that he does so."

Sam continued. "It's up to you whether you go to Rio Santo and report what happened out here, or skin out somewhere else and be deserters." He stared at the soldiers.

"*Sí*, Ranger, it is up to us," the sweating soldier said, calmer now, seeing they might stand a chance. "We will go to Rio Santo and report to the commander. You have our word."

When the Ranger and the women had ridden on a full two miles, too far for the three soldiers to catch up with them after having to scour the hillside for their bullets, Sam slowed his dun and looked back along the trail.

"Do you think they will go to the fortress at Rio Santo, Ranger?" Ria asked. "Can you count on them, after what they were going to do to us?"

"I don't know," Sam replied. "They were in desperate straits. Fear and desperation make a man do a lot of things—things he wouldn't do otherwise." He turned back to the trail and put the dun forward. "Soldiers are trained to obey orders," he said, riding on, leading the cart, the women right beside him. "Take away the orders they're used to getting, some of them don't know what to do."

"That does not excuse them for what they had planned for us," the woman said. "Had you not put your gun under his chin, they would have killed us without batting an eye. They would have ridden away on these horses and left our bones to the desert floor."

"Maybe," Sam said. "Luckily we'll never know."

They rode on in the darkening hills until the sun was gone and stars began dotting the purple sky. They did not stop again until they found themselves on a narrow trail skirting around a moonlit valley where bodies of man and horse alike lay strewn about, being pulled and picked upon by a pack of frenzied wolves.

"Stay back here," the Ranger said. "Hold the cart."

"Santa madre de Dios!" the woman whispered. She crossed herself and sidled her horse closer to the cart where Ana sat on the board, a blanket wrapped around her. The mule had grown fearful and balked at the cart reins as Sam held them over to Ria. Both horses shied back from the sound and the scent of the wolves. Even at thirty yards the sound of snarling and eating filled the night.

"They're too busy to care about us right now," Sam said. He swung down from his saddle in the purple moonlight and handed Ria his dun's reins. "Ana, throw out something I can use for a torch."

"I will get it," Ria said quickly.

"No," Sam said firmly, "you hold the animals."

Ria stayed in her saddle; Ana hurriedly gathered an old shirt and a slim pick handle and pitched them over the side of the cart.

No sooner had Sam fashioned the wadded shirt and the pick handle into a torch and lit it than he heard a faint voice coming from a stand of rocks to his left. Instead of venturing closer to the wolves to count the dead, he walked sidelong to the rocks, his rifle in his right hand, his left hand holding the torch burning above his head. As he neared the rocks he heard the voice again. This time he saw a soldier's chewed-up boot reach from among the rocks and scrape at the ground. He hurried over to it.

"*Por favor*, help me, *señor* . . . ," a weak voice moaned as the torchlight spread down over the rocks brokenly.

Hearing the man speak English, Sam said, "Keep quiet. Wolves are everywhere." As he whispered, he stooped and dragged the man from under the rocks where he'd burrowed himself a den from which to fight off the scavengers. As Sam dragged him into sight, he saw the bloodstained bandages around his waist; he saw the chewed-upon forestock of the French rifle that the man had used to jab at the wolves' muzzles when they tried to dig him from his lair.

"Thank God, thank God, thank God . . . ," the soldier chanted in a rasping whisper until his voice trailed away.

Sam laid the torch down long enough to lift the man over his shoulder. At the cart, Ria and Ana watched him rise and carry the wounded man, torch, rifle and all, beneath the flickering dome of firelight.

"Ranger, they see us!" Ria said, struggling with the nervous horses and the balking mule.

"They're not bothering with us just now," Sam said. "They've taken an easier meal."

Ana had hurried to the tailgate of the cart and pushed it open. Sam laid the wounded man into the cart, lifted the gate and held it while Ana slipped the iron gate pin back into place.

Sam stepped back and held the torch close to the ground, examining the many hoofprints scattered in the dirt. He saw no unshod prints, only the iron shoes of the soldiers' horses.

"Ranger, we must leave!" Ria said.

Sam turned and took his dun's reins from her and swung up in the saddle, the torch above his head. The dun was steady enough, but tense, agitated by the wolves, the fire flickering so close above its back.

"Get moving, ma'am," Sam said to Ria. "I'm right behind you."

As Ria turned the barb and pulled the mule by the cart reins, Sam rose in his saddle, drew the torch back and heaved it in the wolves' direction. The torch fell well short of the thirty yards, but it hit the ground and caused the feeding animals to hunker back. In the shadowy firelight Sam caught glimpses of arrows sticking up from the dirt, from the bodies of the dead, both men and horses alike. Then he turned the dun and rode away behind the cart.

"Thank our Holy Mother they will not follow us," Ria said as he rode up beside her and took the cart reins.

"So far they haven't," Sam said, keeping the mule moving along at a quick but safe pace.

Farther along the trail, they stopped where the moonlight shone full and unobstructed. Sam and

Ria met Ana at the back of the cart and stepped inside when she opened the rear gate.

Ana kneeled beside the soldier and poured a trickle of canteen water onto his lips. Sam stooped down beside him.

"Did Apache attack your patrol?" he asked, already having begun to form an opinion of his own.

The man shook his head weakly.

"No Indians . . . scalpers," he managed to say. "They capture . . . my captain. The woman from the . . . Mockingbird Cantina. She stab . . . him in the heart. . . ." His voice trailed; his eyes closed. Sam gave Ana a nod and she poured another trickle on his lips and wet a cloth and laid it on his blood-crusted forehead.

"He hides there in the rocks ever since the battle?" Ria asked as if in disbelief.

"I would say he did," Sam replied, "first from the ambushers, then from the wolves." He shook his head slowly at the enormity of it. "He must've seen everything that happened back there."

"I did . . . ," the wounded man whispered.

Seeing his eyes open a little, Sam leaned in closer.

"Take it easy, we're going to get you to Iron Point," he said. He adjusted the wet cloth on the soldier's forehead.

"She stabbed . . . my *capitán*," he whispered. "The leader . . . hit her in the face . . . for stabbing him. . . ."

"The mercenary leader hit her for stabbing the captain?" Sam asked, trying to make sense of it.

"He hit her . . . ," the soldier said. Again he closed

his eyes. This time there was a sense of finality to his action. He tried to grip the Ranger's forearm, but his strength failed him; his hand fell to his side. A long breath escaped his lips.

Ria and Ana both crossed themselves.

"You risked your life to save a dead man," Ria commented quietly.

Sam just looked at her.

"He wasn't dead at the time," he said. He stood up in the cart and dragged the dead soldier out of the cart to the side of the trail. As he picked up rocks and laid them over the body, he reminded himself that he was here in pursuit of one man, Ozzie Cord. The rest of these men, scalpers . . . mercenaries, whatever they wanted to call themselves . . . were the Mexican government's concern. After all, it was the government who employed them.

He stopped covering the body and looked off across the purple sky above the rugged badlands. This was a bloody land. He knew it coming in. A man with no solemn reckoning of death had no business here, he reminded himself.

"Amen," he said silently to the pile of stones. With that, he turned and walked to the dun and stepped up into his saddle. In moments the small party of travelers was gone. Above the desert a moon lay golden and silent in the purple velvet night.

Chapter 9

In Iron Point four dead soldiers lay in the trail at the main gates to the fortress. Alpine and his men had lifted the soldiers' scalps the afternoon before. But he'd left the bodies sprawled in the dust overnight. The dead served as a message to the townsfolk to do as they were told, and as a reminder to Turner Pridemore what a good day's work he and his men had done in their leader's absence.

Inside the battered, crumbling wall of Iron Point, most residents were still afraid to go about their daily business. A factor that Pridemore liked to see.

"You could never pull these shenanigans in, say . . . Texas, California . . . or anywhere else, I don't expect." He chuckled, looking all around the streets, all of them empty save for his men and a few hardcase border outlaws. "Ornery Americans wouldn't stand for it."

"That's a fact, Bigfoot," Darton Alpine said, feeling proud of himself.

Standing by the front gates grinning, Pridemore rolled a dead soldier's scalped head back and forth a little with the toe of his tall Mexican boots.

"You know what's wrong with this country, Dart?" he said, tilting his chin to take in the aroma of a young pig cooking slowly on a spit out in front of the Mockingbird Tent Cantina.

"A lot of things I can think of," Alpine said.

"Not enough guns," Pridemore said. "These folks barely have enough armament to hunt dinner, let alone fight Apache." He shook his head and looked down at the soldiers. "Course, they're stupid to boot," he added, again rolling the scalped head back and forth. "Look at these poor sumbitches. They ran here fleeing the Wolf Hearts." He chuckled. "The Wolf Hearts have cleared out. We whupped them so bad they'll not be seen for weeks—months even."

Pridemore walked back through the open gates and stood before the public well staring down at Diamond Jim's sun-curing face. "Now, see, this right here is why it's always good to have an old hand like Deacon Sickles around. This strikes the fear of God in everybody in town."

"No question about it," said Alpine, looking at the face, the flies walking on it.

Pridemore cocked his head, looking down at the face. "I'm told the English pay high for these kinds of American keepsakes. Ol' Deacon might be onto something here."

Alpine couldn't see the potential. But he kept quiet about it.

Pridemore looked all around, stretched his back and looked over where Bertha Buttons supervised an elderly Mexican turning the pig on its spit.

"What other news you got for me, Dart?" he asked. "All of it good, I hope?"

"It's not all good, Bigfoot," Alpine said cautiously. "While we were getting this town braced and broken, that idiot Ozzie Cord lit out of here. Nobody is saying, but I get the feeling these townsfolk would like to gut-shoot him."

"Tell them to fire away. I've heard worse news than that in my life," Pridemore said, again the grin. "Good riddance, *idiot*," he called out to the surrounding hillsides.

"The thing is, your son, Fox, lit out with him."

That stopped Pridemore.

"*Fox* . . . rode out with Ozzie Cord? You don't mean it, Dart," he said, surprised. "Now, that's a different thing altogether. Are these folks down on him too?"

"I get that feeling, Bigfoot," said Alpine. "I saw grumbling and whispering going on when the two walked down the street. Of course everybody shut up when I asked about it."

"Maybe you didn't ask hard enough, Dart," Pridemore said pointedly. "Sometimes you need to ask with a whip in your hand, acting like you already know the answer."

"I'll start at one end of town and whip my way to the other, if you want me to," Alpine said.

Pridemore seemed to consider it for a moment.

"This town is ours to do with as we see fit," he said. "They might hate us for some things, but they damn sure worship us for keeping the Wolf Hearts out of their rectums."

"They'll stay out of our way and leave us alone—that's for sure," said Alpine. "Want me to ask around easylike what that idiot Ozzie and Fox might have done?"

"Not just now," Pridemore said. "Fox is good at looking out for himself. If he lets an idiot like Ozzie lead him astray, I reckon he'll have to account for it. He's been itching to get away on his own for a while now."

"I can send some men out to look for him," said Alpine. "Leave Ozzie nailed to a tree if you want me to."

"Keep that 'nailed to a tree' thought," said Pridemore. "Let's see if they come back. I know my son. If Ozzie ain't careful, Fox'll get enough of his foolishness and stick a bullet in his brain—"

Pridemore stopped talking when Philbert Ohiola trotted past the guard at the main gaits and came toward them.

"Top of the morning, Ohio Phil," Pridemore said, his hand resting on the butt of the big Walker Colt sticking up from his waist. "The way you come running up, I was thinking Ol' Dan Webster here might have to greet you." He tapped his fingers on his Colt and eyed the rifle Ohio Phil carried across his chest at port arms.

"Sorry, Bigfoot," Ohio Phil said, letting his rifle slump to his side. "There's two riders on horseback and a mule cart just cleared up onto the trail. One's a white man wearing a badge. Pusser saw it through his spyglass."

"White man wearing a badge, you say . . . ?" said Pridemore. He looked at Alpine with a grin, then back at Phil Ohiola. "Think somebody ought to tell this fool he's not in Texas?"

"Seems like we should," Alpine said, going along with his boss's wry humor.

"All right, I just come to tell you," said Phil Ohiola. "Pusser's still out there keeping an eye on them."

"Good work, Phil," Pridemore said. "You and Pusser pull back and let them past you."

"It could be that Ranger," said Alpine.

"I hope it is," said Pridemore. "I ought to thank him. Hadn't been for him killing Erskine Cord, I might be back at the trading post, swatting flies off rattlesnake meat, serving it for chicken soup."

"I'm just saying . . . ," Alpine replied.

"Don't worry about it," said Pridemore. "He's not after any of us. If Ozzie was here I'd hand him over to the Ranger just to watch him wiggle."

"Anything else . . . ?" Phil Ohiola asked in his deep, solemn voice.

Pridemore looked the hatless half-breed up and down, noting his shaved head.

"Tell me, Phil," he asked amicably. "When are you going to let your hair grow out?"

"No time soon, Bigfoot," said the serious half-breed. He rubbed his shaved and weathered cranium.

Pridemore nodded back toward the gates.

"That's all, Phil," he said. "You and Pusser stay sharp out there."

"If it is the Ranger, I can drop back out of sight and stick a bullet in him," Alpine said as Ohio Phil trotted away, his rifle dangling at his side.

Pridemore had taken a thin black cigar from inside his buckskins and stuck it in his mouth. He eyed Alpine up and down.

"You're doing good work here, Dart," he said. "Stop trying too hard to please me." He pulled out a long match, hiked a knee and struck it down his trouser leg. "I had a whore in Abilene acted like that. Turned out she tried to nut me in my sleep." He held the flaming match to the cigar but stopped first. "You would not want me showing you the scar."

"No, I wouldn't, Bigfoot," Alpine said.

"Good," said Pridemore. He puffed the cigar to life and flipped the match into the dirt. "Go gather a few men around us. Tell Chase to goad whoever this is wearing a badge. We'll see what he's made of."

"Got it," said Alpine.

But before he could turn and leave, Pridemore stopped him. "If this *is* the Ranger, I want to first off try to make him feel welcome." He gave a skeptical grin. "Maybe he'll even tell us about gutting Wilson Orez with his own knife."

Alpine gave him a curious look, then nodded and moved away.

It was midmorning when the Ranger and the women made it up the last few yards of the trail with the creaking, slow-rolling mule cart. As the animals climbed to the old fortress on the craggy hill, Sam was a little surprised to find no guards standing at the open gates. He entered the town ahead of the woman and the cart, and came to a halt, rifle in hand, seeing the throng of buckskinned mercenaries lounging against the town well facing him.

At the center of the rugged-looking group, Turner "Bigfoot" Pridemore sat in a large, high thronelike Spanish chair as if awaiting him. The Ranger looked around warily as the women and the cart stopped beside him. Ria sidled the barb over closer to him. She and Ana sat staring in silence.

"Top of the morning, lawman!" Pridemore called out, hoisting a tall Spanish goblet that sloshed liquid over its rim as he raised it out toward Sam. He wore a wide scowl of a grin on his face. "I'm betting every dollar in the bank that you be Arizona Ranger Samuel Burrack." As he spoke he waved a hand, inviting Sam to step down and come forward.

"You bet right," said the Ranger. "I am Sam Burrack." He handed Ria his dun's reins and swung down from his saddle with his thumb across the hammer of his rifle. He nodded at Pridemore walking toward him. "You're the man they call Bigfoot— owned the trading post over on the edge of the sand flats." He stopped a few feet away.

"*Owned* is right," Pridemore said. "It was mine until the heathen Apache ran it over and killed my elder son." He eyed the Ranger closer. "Have you ever lost kin to the savages, Ranger? 'Cause let me tell you, it hurts something awful." He looked at Sam for an answer. When none came, he nodded all around at his men, who returned his nod in agreement. Then he swigged from the goblet and wiped his buckskin sleeve across his lips.

Sam cut to the point. "I'm tracking one of your men for killing the sheriff in Mesa Grande."

Pridemore wagged a big finger.

"Say . . . I heard about that," he said. "You'd be talking about the idiot, Ozzie Cord, nephew of the late Erskine Cord." Again the scowling grin. "Of course you know all about that, you being the one made him the *late* Erskine Cord."

"I killed him; that's a fact," Sam said. He glanced around for Ozzie but didn't see him. "I had him jailed, but your men broke him and his nephew out."

"Huh-uh, not my men," Pridemore pointed out quickly. "That was Cord's men. They're all dead now," he lied. Waving the matter aside, he added, "Anyway, I harbor no ill feeling toward you. Fact is, you killing Erskine is what got me the contract to kill Apache for the Mexican government. I ought to thank you."

Having seen no soldiers along the streets, Sam wondered if the *federale* patrol he'd met on the trail and later found lying dead had been the entire military presence. He caught the waft of roasting pork from the spit out in front of the tent saloon and saw Bertha Buttons and a Mexican woman attending it.

"As for the idiot, Ozzie," Pridemore continued, "he's not here. I wish he was, 'cause watching you kill him would be better than watching a wrestling match. Oh, and by the way, I'd be rooting for you."

"I'd be rooting for Ozzie," said a huge scalper standing beside Pridemore's chair. The scalper stood a head taller than Sam and stared down hard and cold at him.

"I forgot to mention, Ranger," said Pridemore. "I've no ill feelings, but my friend Malcolm Chase here was broken up over Erskine's demise."

"That's right, I was," said the huge man. He stepped forward just enough to the side to reveal the face tacked to the board, leaning behind him. "I still am," he said. He handed his rifle off to the man beside him.

Seeing what was happening, Sam continued staring at the face on the board as if engrossed.

"Hey, Ranger!" Chase demanded. "Look at me when I'm talking to you—" He'd reached two fingers out as if to gouge Sam on his shoulder and get his attention. But he never completed the move.

The butt of the Ranger's Winchester came up full stroke under the big man's chin and lifted his face high. As Chase staggered back a step and his face bounced back into place, Sam stabbed the Winchester butt full strength. The blow crushed the big man's nose and both lips and splattered blood in every direction. Chase flipped backward and hung over the stone edge of the well, his big booted toes pointing to the sky.

Some of the men winced at the sight and sound of the Ranger's action. No sooner had Sam made the hard stab with the rifle butt than he swung the rifle around and cocked it in his hands, ready to fire in any direction.

"Jesus, Ranger!" said Pridemore, holding a hand out sidelong to keep his men back. "You didn't have to break *violent* on the man. You call that a fair fight?"

"I don't call it a *fight* at all," Sam said firmly, rifle poised, ready.

Pridemore chuckled.

"You got me there," Pridemore said. He looked at his men and nodded toward the downed scalper. "Get Malcolm out of there before he ruins the water," he said. He looked back at Sam and said, "You can lower the rifle. Nobody else is going to try you. Hear that, men? Leave the Ranger alone," he called out.

Sam lowered his rifle a little and nodded at the face on the board.

"Who's this?" he asked.

"That's Diamond Jim Ruby," Pridemore said. "I have a man who is developing this sort of curio item. I think it's a peach of an idea. What say you?"

Sam didn't reply. Instead he looked toward the open door of the command office of the *federales*.

"If you're looking for the soldiers, they ain't here," Pridemore said, anticipating him. "They rode out on patrol, ain't come back yet. We're getting concerned. You didn't happen to come upon them, did you?"

"Yes, I did," Sam said, going along with the man's ruse. "The ones I saw were dead."

"Them damn Apache!" said Pridemore. "Feared just this very thing. Full of arrows, I'll wager."

"Yes, full of arrows," Sam said, flatly, letting his eyes tell Pridemore that he didn't believe a word of it.

Pridemore shrugged.

"Well, there we have it," he said. "Something just *told me* I was going to have to take this town over, bad as I hated to." He looked around at his men. Two of them held Malcolm Chase seated on the edge of the well. One held a wadded cloth to his bloody face. Chase slumped sidelong, knocked out. Pridemore cut his eyes back sharply to the Ranger and said, "Have you got any problem with me running things here for a while?"

"Under the Matamoros Act, the Mexican government allows American lawmen to come here in pursuit of wanted men," Sam said. "Anything else that happens here is between you and the *federales*. I have no say in it."

"I'll be dogged," Pridemore said with feigned interest. "You mean if I stood up and pissed right here in the street, you couldn't do nothing about it?" Behind him his men muffled a laugh.

"Not as long you keep it off my boot," Sam said without cracking a smile. The men laughed again.

"You and I are going to get along, Ranger," Pridemore said. He stood up and waved Bertha Buttons over from the roasting pig. "Come get these folks, Big Darling," he called out to her. Then he looked back at Sam. "Bertha here runs the Mock-

ingbird Cantina." He gestured toward the large
ragged tent.

The Mockingbird Tent Cantina. . . . Sam recalled
the dying soldier telling him about the cantina
owner being with the mercenaries—how the leader
of the men had hit her after she'd stabbed Diamond Jim in the heart.

Pridemore pointed at the grim face on the pine
board. "She used to be this one's woman, but she's
more or less mine now." He grinned again. "Enough
of all that . . . I *can* feed you folks, can't I?"

"Obliged," Sam said, looking around and seeing
the hungry look on Ria's and Ana's faces. He
looked over at Bertha Buttons, who came walking
toward them. Even from halfway across the street,
he saw her black swollen eye.

"Which way did Ozzie Cord go?" he asked Pridemore.

Pridemore looked at him for a second, then said,
"North, Ranger. He rode out of here headed north.
He knows you're on his trail. Probably wants to get
somewhere and lie low. How soon are you going
after him?"

"Soon as I get my horses grained and watered,"
Sam said. He nodded at Ria and Ana Cerero. "I
need to get them situated here until they get ready
to head home."

"Hear that, Bertha?" he said as the big woman
walked up. "These women need to get situated for
a while."

Bertha looked the women over.

"I can make room for them," she said.

Before Sam could speak for the women, Ria swung down from her saddle and walked over to them.

"I am Ria Cerero," she said to Bertha, "and this is my very young daughter, Ana. We are not saloon girls, but we will sew and cook and clean your saloon for you and your women . . . if you will allow us to?"

Sam listened. From the sound of Ria, she knew her way around these kinds of women.

"Honey, I can use you and your daughter's help starting today. My girls' clothes are falling apart." She smiled and stepped over and reached out for Ria to take her hand.

Sam started to say something to Ria, but before he could, she stepped over, pulled him aside and said to him, "It is good, Ranger. We have worked in such places. We will work and rest here and prepare for our long journey home."

Sam only nodded, knowing it was Ria's decision to make.

"All right, ma'am," he said. "You and your daughter do what suits you, I'll get on with my manhunt." He gathered the reins to the horses and the mule cart.

"Anything else I can do for you, Ranger?" Pridemore asked, seeing Sam turn and gather the reins to the horses and mule.

"I'm good," Sam said. He touched the brim of his sombrero and led the animals toward the livery barn. As he walked away, Pridemore leaned closer to Alpine.

"Get some men on his trail soon as he leaves," he ordered. "I'll go to the barn in a few minutes, see what he's got to say in private with Ol' Dan Webster here cocked at him." He patted the big Colt in his belt. "Some folks find it easier to talk man-to-man."

Chapter 10

In the livery barn, the first thing the Ranger did was walk to the rear doors and swing them open to the air and sunlight. Returning to the horses and the mule, he watered and grained the animals. When a young boy came from the Mockingbird carrying a wooden plate filled with roasted pig and flatbread, Sam sat down on an empty crate beside the horses and ate his fill. As he finished, Turner Pridemore stepped inside the barn and stood facing him from ten feet away. The scalper leader's right hand rested on the butt of his big Walker Colt. Sam looked up as if he'd been expecting him.

"Have we got more to talk about?" he asked quietly. Even though Pridemore had come in alone, Sam saw scalpers waiting outside the front door.

"Yeah," Pridemore said. "Figured we best talk alone, make sure we both understand each other."

"Talk, then," Sam said. He set the wooden plate aside and stood up, his hand at his side near the butt of his own Colt.

Pridemore said, "We both know it won't be long

before more soldiers show up wanting to know what happened to Captain Penza and his men."

Sam kept a level gaze on the mercenary leader.

"I have no doubt they will," he said. "If you're wondering what I'll tell the *federales*, I plan on telling the truth."

Pridemore gave him a questioning look.

Sam said, "That I found soldiers lying dead in the trail, wolves eating them. It looked like an ambush."

"What else?" Pridemore asked.

"I'll tell them I saw arrows in the bodies of man and horse alike," Sam said. "But I'll also tell them I saw no unshod tracks of Apache horses." He wasn't going to mention what the dying soldier had told him. The situation here was shaky enough without revealing that a dying witness had identified who killed the captain and his men.

Pridemore's palm rubbed back and forth on his gun butt.

"So what?" he said. "Apache steal lots of horses, especially Quetos and his Wolf Hearts. Seeing shod horse tracks don't mean it wasn't Apache who ambushed Penza."

"I didn't say it meant anything one way or the other," Sam relied. "I said I'd tell the *federales* what I saw, and that *is* what I saw." As he spoke he reached over and picked up his Winchester from where it leaned against a stall door. Checking the rifle, getting ready for the trail, he said, "I expect they'll make what they will of it." He casually levered a round into the rifle chamber. "See any problem with that?" he asked, turning back toward Pridemore.

Pridemore noted that the Ranger had left the rifle hammer cocked, his finger inside the trigger guard. Seeing the barrel tip slightly toward his chest, Pridemore realized in a sudden flash that whatever advantage he thought he'd had on the lawman was gone. Without a clue, without a threat, easy and calm, the Ranger had just gotten the drop on him.

This sneaking son of a bitch!

"Move your hand down off your gun," Sam said quietly, sounding almost as if it were a request rather than a command.

Pridemore looked at him almost in disbelief, keeping his hand on the big Colt.

"Huh-uh," he said. He gave his stiff trademark grin. "Do you realize how many men are out there, waiting to do whatever I tell them to?"

Sam said, "Do you realize that *none* of them are standing between you and this rifle barrel?" He took a slow step forward, the rifle tip only inches from the mercenary leader's chest.

Pridemore saw the dark, deadly look in the Ranger's eyes and realized there was no more room for talk here.

"Whoa, now, easy!" he said. His hand dropped from the butt of the big gun. "That was nothing against you, Ranger. I often find that keeping my hand on Ol' Dan Webster here helps me think."

"Then *think* of this." Sam said. "If I wanted you dead, you'd be dead right now. Your men might kill me, but you'd never know about it. Are we clear?"

Pridemore stared at him. He wasn't used to a man making such a bold statement, standing this close, willing to back it up in spite of the odds being against him.

"We're clear," he replied.

Sam took a step back but kept his rifle cocked and ready.

"What is it you really come here to talk about, Bigfoot?" he said.

Pridemore eased down and let out a breath.

"My boy, Fox, is out there riding with that idiot Ozzie Cord," he said. "I want to hear you say you're not going to kill him."

"You're not going to hear me say that," Sam said. "I'm not hunting your son. But if he casts his lot with Ozzie Cord when I catch up to them, he'll have to deal with me."

"I come here to reason with you in private," Pridemore said, starting to bristle a little as he spoke.

"You came here to see if you can buffalo me one-on-one," Sam said. "That won't work. I expect you'll next try to bribe me." He saw that his words stung Pridemore, who had brought along a pouch of gold coins tucked inside his buckskin shirt.

Pridemore kept control of his temper.

"I might not need to buffalo or bribe you, Ranger," he said, cooling down. "I taught my boy how to fight, how to shoot. He knows how to kill if a situation comes to that." He offered his grin. "It just might be that you're the one getting ready to reap the whirlwind."

Sam let the comment pass.

"When you taught him all that, you should also have taught him how to stay out of bad company," he said. He stepped back to his dun and gathered the reins to both horses. "Outside . . . ," he said, gesturing the rifle barrel toward the door.

Pridemore didn't move.

"Tell me something, Ranger—you know so much," he said. "What makes you think I won't have my men kill you right here, right now? Save us all the trouble."

"Are you asking *me* or *yourself* that question?" Sam said. He stepped forward, a menacing look in his eyes.

This time Pridemore turned and swung the large door open.

"He's coming out, men," he said through the doorway. "Let him through." He looked at Sam. "This will be the only talk you and I ever have," he warned. "Nothing better happen to my boy."

"I hope it doesn't," Sam said. "Now step out." He still held his rifle tipped in Pridemore's direction.

"Easy, men," Pridemore said, walking out through the doors, expecting the Ranger right behind him. But instead of the Ranger following him, Pridemore turned at the sound of pounding hooves and saw the Ranger and the two horses ride out the open back door at a quick pace.

"He's cut out the back," Pridemore said, he and his men hurrying to the edge of the barn in time to see the Ranger atop his dun, the barb right beside him. Both horses leaped up over the low corral rail and rode off along the rear trail out of town.

"Get after him, men," said Alpine.

"No, wait," said Pridemore, stopping them. "Nobody in Iron Point witnessed anything we've done, except tacking Diamond Jim's face to a board. We don't want to be seen riding off to kill a lawman, no matter which side of the border he's from." He stared off at the dust riding behind the Ranger's horses as if in dark contemplation.

Alpine sidled up to him.

"What about sending out some men to trail Fox?" he asked.

"Get them sent," Pridemore said. "I don't want Fox anywhere between the Ranger and Ozzie Cord when the lead starts flying."

Fox and Ozzie had ridden all day on the strength of Ozzie telling of a place in the desert hills that his Uncle Erskine had once mentioned. The small hill town, Poco Aldea, or Little Village, was rumored to be ruled by a gang of Mexican gunmen and banditos known as the Perros Locos—the Crazy Dogs. Fox had also heard his father mention the place when he talked about his days of adventure and exploits on the wild Mexican frontier.

"Why are you so interested in this pissant of a town?" Ozzie had asked him earlier in the day.

"I'm not," was all Fox had replied as they rode on across the desert floor.

It was later in the evening when the two rode up to a hitch rail out in front of a small adobe cantina in Poco Aldea. The Little Village stood on a steep hillside overlooking a short land spur of sandy flat-

lands between the hills line and wide desert floor.
Fox realized before they had put their horses up
the hillside that they were being watched. He found
it strange that Ozzie, in spite of knowing the town's
reputation for harboring bad men, appeared surprised when they stepped down from their saddles
and were met by six Mexican gunmen walking out
of a darkened alleyway.

"Buenas noches, americanos," said a half Mexican, half Texan wearing a black dusty Mexican
business suit and a tall sombrero. "I saw you *los
necios* on the sand flats before dark." The gunmen
gave a quiet chuckle. "Do you know it is not wise to
travel *unaware* in these dangerous badlands?" He
eyed the two young *americanos* up and down, Fox
wearing a long duster over his buckskins, the tails
spread down his horse's sides.

Jackasses, huh . . . ?

Fox ignored the insult and swung down easily
from his horse and stepped around it. Ozzie stepped
down awkwardly, seeming unsure what to do about
the guns pointed at them.

As Fox stepped into sight, the gunmen saw a
short-barreled ten-gauge shotgun appear in his hands
as if from out of thin air. They had neither seen the
short gun lying inside his saddle cantle under his
duster tails, nor heard the hammers cock.

"Who's *unaware*?" Fox said flatly. He deliberately kept his face stoic, refusing to copy his father's stiff grin.

"Ah, *señors*," said the Tex-Mexican, him and the
other gunmen stepping back at the sight of the

large sawed-off's barrels aimed at them. "Sometimes we joke with all the pilgrims who pass through
Poco Aldea." He shrugged and gave a slight nervous grin. "It is not always a good idea, I admit."

Fox cut a glance at Ozzie, who had now gotten
himself collected and held his hand on his holstered
Colt. Then he looked back at the Tex-Mexican.

"I see where it could become a hazardous practice," Fox said quietly, wearing the same flat stare.
He wagged the sawed-off at the man. "Want to tell
your pals to trim down, keep me from blowing your
brains all over their shirts?"

"*Sí*, I can do that," the Tex-Mexican said. He
reached an arm out slowly to his side and motioned
for the men to lower their guns.

"I'm Silvar Stampeto. Maybe you have heard of
me and my *compañeros*, the Perros Locos? We are
known as bad hombres."

"The Crazy Dogs? No, I've never heard of you
or Perros Locos," he lied. He eyed the men, then
looked back at Silvar Stampeto. "Maybe you're not
trying hard enough."

Stampeto gave a short chuckle and looked at his
gunmen.

"We are 'not trying hard enough,' he tells me,"
he repeated to his men. He said to Fox, "I must
consider that myself when I make plans for us." He
tipped the barrel of the gun up and uncocked it.
Fox kept the shotgun leveled and ready.

"Just so you know from now on," Ozzie cut in,
"my pard and I are men you want to steer clear of

unless you're looking for trouble." He tapped his fingers on his holstered gun. "Next time you might not get a chance to crawfish."

The gunmen's eyes flared at Ozzie.

"The Perros Locos crawfish from no one," a big powerfully built Mexican said.

"Easy, Paco," said Stampeto. He looked at Fox. "Is your pard always so quick to bad-mouth a man?"

"Call it *even* for your jackasses' remark," Fox said.

"Ah, so your Spanish is good, eh?" said Stampeto. He gestured at the human finger bones and other grisly human ornaments on the bib of Fox's buckskin shirt. "No kin of yours, I hope," he said.

"Barely acquaintances," said Fox. "We're mercenaries. We've been cutting scalps for the Mexican government. My friend here speaks his mind. Rein your pals in or we'll stop talking altogether."

"Scalpers, mercenaries . . . ," said Stampeto, overlooking the threat. "Then it is true, you are some bad hombres."

"I wouldn't lie to you," Fox said.

"I would like to hear all about the scalp business," said Stampeto, slipping his gun back into his holster, even as Fox kept the shotgun leveled and ready.

Fox cocked his head slightly and said, "You pay for the whiskey, make up for your rudeness, maybe we'll tell you how to kill Apache and lift their hair—government won't have to pay us to do it for you."

The big Mexican, Paco, bristled at Fox's words. Yet, staring closely at him, hearing him talk about scalp hunters jogged his memory.

"I know this gringo," he said, gesturing a thick hand toward Fox.

"Best watch your language, big boy," Ozzie warned the huge Mexican.

The Mexican ignored Ozzie.

"His father is the one they call Bigfoot," he continued. "He ran the desert trading post. The Apache wiped him out."

"Ask me how many of those heathen Apache are still alive," Fox said coolly.

Stampeto looked closer himself.

"I've been to that trading post," he said to Fox. "Are you the one they called Fox—the one who wore the strange-looking clothes?"

Fox kept himself in check.

"Maybe . . . for a while," he said.

Seeing Fox's embarrassment, Ozzie walked forward and stood beside his friend.

"His name is Fox. I call him El Zorro," he said. "We just robbed every store and business in Iron Point. We've got more robbing to do all across Mexico. Right, *Zorro?*"

Fox just stared at him.

"Hell, so what if I talked about it?" Ozzie said with a shrug. "We've got nothing to hide from these boys. We might even rob this place before we're through."

"You don't rob this place," said Paco. "This whole hillside is *our* place. Tell him, Silvar."

"Yeah, this whole hillside is ours," Stampeto said, dismissing the matter. He looked back at Fox and said, "So, El *Zorro*, what about that whiskey I'm buying—?"

"Nobody calls my pard El Zorro but me," Ozzie said.

"Take it easy, Oz," Fox said. "I'll decide what I get called and what I don't."

"Oz and El Zorro . . . ," Stampeto said. He gave a thin smile. "And here I was thinking my name was peculiar." He paused, then said, "If you two are interested in stealing some good old cash and gold coins, we likely could use a couple more good gunmen."

Fox looked at him.

"I was just thinking the same thing myself," he said. "When you say *we*, who are you talking about?"

"You know . . ." Stampeto shrugged. "We mean these men and myself, and our jefe, Carlos Montoya."

"So you're not the boss, you're the *segundo*—the number-two man in charge?"

"Are you too good to talk to the number-two man?" Stampeto asked on their way into the weathered adobe building.

"No, I'm not too good," said Fox, looking all around the shadowy candlelit cantina. "I'm just figuring who I have to kill to take over this lousy band of banditos."

"'Take over these banditos,' he says." Stampeto laughed, as if certain that Fox was joking. He slapped him on his back and ushered him on to the bar.

"You are pretty funny, *Zorro*, *mi amigo*," he said, still laughing. "You make me laugh." He kept his hand resting on Fox's shoulder. "I hope we ride together real soon."

"It's almost a sure bet we will," Fox said, slipping from under his hand as the gunmen lined up along the dusty tile-topped bar.

In a moment bottle corks were pulled; shot glasses were filled and slid along the bar. The bartender lifted a hefty leather pouch of Mexican brown cocaine and plopped it onto the bar and jerked its drawstring top open.

"*Cocaína*, on the house! *Saludos, señors!*" he said. He lifted a generous pinch of the substance and sprinkled a mound of it onto Stampeto's outstretched palm.

Stampeto threw back the cocaine, licked his palm and tossed back a shot of rye.

Fox only watched, listened and waited patiently.

Chapter 11

———

For the next two hours Fox sipped his whiskey sparingly, just enough to keep up with the others. Ozzie, on the other hand, drank fast and steadily, setting a quickened pace for Paco and the rest of the Perros Locos gunmen to keep up with, Fox noted.

"Your friend drinks like he has a hole in his gullet," Silvar Stampeto commented. He and Fox had drunk slower, discussing the craft of scalp hunting, and of robbing Mexican banks and French mining companies.

"My friend does as he pleases," Fox replied, not even realizing why he took a prickly attitude toward Stampeto's comment. "Anybody don't like it, guess what they can do?" he said pointedly.

"*Fácil, fácil,*" said Stampeto, filling their shot glasses with amber rye.

"*Easy* yourself," said Fox, translating the Tex-Mexican, committing the conversation back to English. He kept his hand away from the glass and stared at Stampeto.

"I mean no offense." Stampeto shrugged. "I too

am a fast drinker, except today you and I are talking about business, so I show restraint." He offered a thin smile, raised his shot glass and glanced at Fox's glass with question. "*Saludo*, eh?"

Restraint?

Fox cooled. Not knowing why he'd taken such offense to begin with, he picked up his glass and raised it and tipped it against Stampeto's.

"*Saludo,*" he said.

"Good," said Stampeto. He nodded at the sawed-off still hanging in Fox's hand. "Again, I mean no offense. But do you always carry this shotgun against your leg?"

"Not always, but tonight," Fox said, staring evenly at him as he sipped and set his glass down. "When am I going to meet this Carlos Montoya?"

"Soon," said Stampeto. He wiped the back of his hand across his mouth. "But I can tell you it is up to me to decide who rides with us and who does not." He wagged a finger to make his point. "So, don't worry. I like you and your friend."

"That's a relief," Fox said flatly. "You like being the Perros Locos' *segundo*?"

"*Sí*, I like it," said Stampeto, the cocaine having kicked in, loosening his voice. "Although I must say there are times when I know I am put upon."

Fox gave him a questioning look.

"Like tonight?" Stampeto continued, speaking a little quicker. "It should be Montoya, the leader himself, not the *segundo* who meets you and your friend when you ride into our town—"

"You want to be my *segundo*?" Fox asked, cutting Stampeto off.

Stampeto started to laugh, but then his grin faded as he saw the seriousness in Fox's face.

"Do I have a choice?" he said, glancing at the shotgun against Fox's thigh.

"Everybody has a choice," Fox said grimly, his thumb close to the sawed-off's hammers.

Stampeto looked around quickly as if making sure no one was listening to them.

"If Carlos Montoya is dead, I work for the man who has killed him," he said. "It is the way things are done here." He leveled his dark eyes at Fox. "My first loyalty is to Perros Locos."

His first loyalty . . .

"When do I meet this man?" Fox asked again; this time his words were more demanding.

"I told you, *soon*," Stampeto repeated.

"You said he should have met us coming into town," Fox reminded him. "Is he in town somewhere?"

"*Sí*. He is with a woman," Stampeto said. He took a large pinch of cocaine from the pouch, threw it back in his mouth, washed it down with rye and let out a whiskey hiss. "We saw you coming on the sand flats, don't forget. Carlos knows you are here."

"With a woman," Fox said flatly.

"*Sí*, she thinks she is his wife, so he will be finished with her soon," Stampeto said.

"Where is he?" Fox asked.

"I told you he is with a—" Stampeto stopped

when he realized what Fox was asking. "Oh. He is in the woman's *armario* behind this place. Hers is the first *armario* on the right," he added, giving Fox clear directions.

First cubicle *on the right.* . . .

Fox turned from the bar and walked to the rear door. As he walked past Ozzie, who stood sloshing a bottle of rye in one hand and waving a shot glass in his other, Ozzie turned and looked at him drunkenly. A brown shadow of cocaine showed on his lips.

"Where you headed, Zorro?" he asked.

"Nowhere," Fox said over his shoulder. "Stand at the end of the bar in case I need you there."

Listening, Paco started to step in behind Fox and follow him. But when he heard Stampeto call out to him he stopped, looked around and saw the *segundo* shake his head, stopping him. Paco gave a half-drunken shrug. He looked at the other drunken gunmen and turned back to his shot glass on the bar.

Only a few seconds after the back door closed behind Fox, the sound of a shotgun blast brought a tense silence over the drinkers. They stood staring as if frozen in place. A second later when a second blast resounded, they all turned to Stampeto for some kind of direction.

"Everybody stand fast," he said. "See who walks through the door." He looked away from his gunmen to Ozzie, who stood at the far end of the bar with his Colt in hand, out and cocked.

The men turned toward the rear door as it swung

open and Fox came in leading a naked, blood-splattered woman by her arm. The shotgun smoked in his hand. As he walked past Ozzie he pitched him the empty shotgun and drew his Colt and cocked it toward the Mexican gunmen, who had bristled and looked to be on the verge of reaching for their own guns.

"Too late, fellows, the party's all over," Fox said, dragging the woman forward.

"Let him pass," Stampeto called out. "That is an order. Zorro is our leader now. He has killed Carlos." As he spoke he reached for the pouch of cocaine.

The gunmen looked at the woman in Fox's grip. Montoya's blood ran down her face, her belly, thighs, calves. Tissue and bone matter clung to her long black hair. Fox shook her a little to get her to speak.

"It—it is true. Carlos is dead," she said shakily.

A silence lingered behind her words. Behind the bar a small swarthy bartender stood ready, his hands spread along the clay-tiled edge.

"All right, *mi compañeros*," said Fox, "the next bottles are on Oz and me. Now drink up—think about how you're going to spend all the money we'll make together."

Ozzie and the Mexican gunmen cheered and turned to the bartender, the gunmen having first looked to Stampeto for his approval.

"You work fast, *mi amigo*," Stampeto said to Fox.

"I hate a dawdler," Fox said. He shoved the

woman to the bar beside him and waved the bartender over. "Do you have a woman here?" he asked.

"*Sí, mi esposa,*" the small man said, looking worried.

"Good," said Fox. "Then you have your wife get this woman cleaned up and dressed—made to look fitting." He flipped a strand of the woman's hair as if disgusted. "I won't tolerate a woman looking unfitting."

"Her name is Terese Montoya," said Stampeto, who stood waiting to carry out any orders Fox might give him.

"Not anymore," said Fox. He pushed a strand of blood-streaked hair back from her cheek as she stood staring down at the floor, a forearm covering her bare breasts. "Now she's Terese Pridemore, till I say otherwise."

"But . . . he is *mi esposo,*" the woman said, gesturing at the blood down her front.

"He's nothing but a glob of dead meat, little darling," Fox said. "You're my *esposa* now." He put the tip of a finger on her chin. "See . . . that's how we do it where I come from," he explained patiently. "You kill a man, you get to take everything he's got, his wife, his guns, horses and whatnot." His words reminded him of what he'd heard his father say over the years. He smiled a little. "You understand that, don't you?"

"*Sí,* I understand," the woman said, again lowering her dark eyes. "You kill him, so now I am yours?"

"There it is," said Fox. "I couldn'ta said it any better." He looked at Stampeto. "You're still the *segundo* here, Stampeto," he said. "But let me warn you. If you don't do what I say, when I say it, I will kill you graveyard dead and give Ozzie your job." He looked back and forth along the bar, then back to Stampeto. "Let everybody get liquored up tonight. Come morning we ride. We're going to start robbing everything Mexico has to offer." He turned to walk away.

"But where do we ride to?" Stampeto asked.

"You tell me, *segundo*," Fox said over his shoulder. "You're the one who's been thinking about all this."

In the gray hour of morning, Ozzie managed to sober himself on hot, thick coffee at the cantina bar and walk half staggering back to the cubicle where Fox and the woman had spent the night. Seeing Ozzie looming in the doorway, the woman stood up naked from where she sat on the edge of the bed and ran out a rear door, grabbing a serape on her way. Ozzie stood staring at the door she slammed behind herself.

On the bed, Fox sprang awake and grabbed his Colt from its holster hanging from a short bedpost. Upon seeing Ozzie, he relaxed back onto the bed and stared at him, the Colt cocked in hand.

"Does that girl not own any clothes?" Ozzie asked, struggling not only against the rye, but also against the effects of the powerful brown Mexican cocaine still boiling in his brain.

"She does," Fox said in a tired voice. "She just has a hard time keeping them on." He uncocked the big Colt and slid it back into the holster. "How's everybody feel about me killing Carlos Montoya?"

"Everybody's good with it," Ozzie said. "If they're not they've been keeping it from me. He stooped and picked up Fox's boots and pitched them over beside the bed. "Montoya had played out his string with everybody. They were ready for somebody to kill him. They just didn't know it." He watched Fox swing up onto the side of the bed and push his hair back from his face. "I palavered with the cantina owner," he continued. "He's been paying Montoya almost half of every dollar he makes here, the whiskey, the *putas*."

"That tells me why the Crazy Dogs haven't been doing much robbing," said Fox. "The leader was squeezing money from this place. He wasn't taking care of his men."

"If you say so, Zorro." Ozzie shrugged. "I've got no mind for that sort of figuring. Anyway, I think he's nervous, wondering how it's going to be dealing with us."

Dealing with us. . . .

"What did you tell him?" Fox asked.

"I told him I'd talk to you, see what you had to say, you know, about how much he's going to pay us, the way he paid Montoya."

Fox didn't answer. He just looked at his friend as he stood up, stepped into his trousers and pulled them up around his waist. He had a lot to consider today, he reminded himself, getting his gang into shape. He stepped into his tall Mexican boots one at a time, pulled them up just below his knees and pushed his trousers down over the wells.

"Ease up some calling me Zorro," he said, buttoning his fly, looping his suspenders up over his shoulders.

"But I thought it was all right, me calling you Zorro," Ozzie said, a little childlike hurt showing in his voice. "Else I never would have—"

"It *is* all right," said Fox, cutting him short. "I'm just saying don't overdo it." He picked up his buckskin shirt from a stool, put it on and smoothed it down, the bone work clattering slightly on his chest. "What happened to all the cocaine?"

"*Whew*," said Ozzie, "that was powerful stuff." He put a hand to his head in recollection.

Fox just looked at him solemnly, waiting for an answer. Ozzie finally got it.

"Oh, it's still on the bar back there," he said, thumbing over his shoulder. "There's plenty left. Want me to get you a taste or snort of it?"

"Get rid of it—all of it," Fox said. "Any man I catch using it while we're on the prowl gets a bullet in his head." He picked up his gun belt and swung it around his waist. "Make it known, loud and clear."

Ozzie looked stunned.

"Zorr—I mean *Fox*," he said, correcting himself. "These are Mexican banditos. They need their cocaine like a preacher needs verse."

"They can find cocaine anywhere we stop on the trail," Fox said, adjusting his gun belt on his hip.

"I'm not having it traveling with us . . . whiskey neither. It takes a man's mind off his business."

Ozzie considered it for a moment, watching Fox pick up a large knife in its fringed sheath from beside the bed. Lifting the back of his shirt, Fox shoved the big knife down into the back of his trousers.

"All right, then, I guess I agree with you," Ozzie said. He gave a grin. "It sure had my mind off business last night."

"I'm glad to hear you *agree* with me, Oz," Fox said a little stiffly. He turned facing him, adjusting his Colt in its holster.

"So . . . what should I tell the cantina owner?" he asked.

"Tell him nothing," Fox said. "Get the Crazy Dogs sobered and ready to ride. Soon as we're mounted, we're burning the cantina to the ground."

Ozzie chuckled. "Yeah, right," he said.

"Stop laughing. I'm not joking, Oz," Fox said, with a trace of warning in his voice.

Ozzie collected himself quickly.

"We're burning the cantina, the *putas' armarios*, anything else Montoya and the Crazy Dogs had going here."

"But this is their graze, their stomping ground!" said Ozzie. "This is where they always come back to."

"Not anymore. That's why we're burning it," Fox said. "We're not coming back here. It's gotten too easy for them here. Montoya had them lying around here not robbing anything, getting drunk, feeding money into a cantina he owns part of."

"What if they don't go for it?" Ozzie asked.

"They'll go for it," said Fox. "If they're real banditos, they'll see how bad things have gotten here. If any of them are not real banditos, it won't matter. We'll shoot them on our way out of town."

"And the woman?" Ozzie asked. "What about her? Is she going with us?"

"Yes, for now," Fox said. "The men see her with me, they know my takeover is complete. When I get through with her I'll drop her off somewhere . . . give her some gold coins. She's a looker. She'll be all right."

"When can I break the news to Stampeto that he's not *segundo*, and I am?" Ozzie asked. He grinned. "I can't wait to see his face, then shoot him down."

"Not now, and not for a while," Fox said. "Let him think he's my second-in-charge. We both know he's not. Everything he does I'll make him answer to you."

"You mean I'll be in charge and he won't even know it?" Ozzie chuckled, liking the idea.

"Something like that," Fox said, eyeing him closely. "Now go find him and let him know what we're fixing to do here. Just don't let him know why." He picked up his battered hat and set it atop his head. "Stupid bastard should've have known to do all this for himself."

Chapter 12

When the first thin mantle of sunlight stood just above the eastern rim of the earth, Fox, Ozzie and Silvar Stampeto sat atop their horses. Sidled close to Fox, Montoya's widow, Terese, sat on a paint horse that Fox had taken from the town livery operator at gunpoint. The four watched high-licking flames roil upward in a cloud of thick black smoke from the felled and burning roof timbers. Behind the four sat the other four Mexican gunmen. Paco Frulio sat slumped in his saddle, his red-rimmed eyes barely open.

"I will miss this place," Paco muttered under his breath. He stared blurry-eyed at the dead cantina owner lying in the street where Ozzie's bullet had killed him. His shirt had been scorched brown from the intense heat. A shotgun lay close to his out-stretched hand.

"Juan Peddersal did not have to die this way," a gunman named Sergio said under his breath to those around him. "For a gringo he was not so bad." He slid a taunting look at a half-Missourian, half-

Mexican outlaw named Otis Seedy. Otis only gave him a sour look and spat in the dirt.

"Suppose El Zorro takes Juan's *esposa* and marries her as well?" he said.

The men chuckled among themselves, knowing Juan Peddersal's wife to be a monstrous woman whose odor alone both animals and children alike avoided.

"By Fox's own words she belongs to Ozzie Cord, the one who killed Juan," said Sergio.

"Ha, this is loco," said Paco. "I never hear such a thing as man's *esposa* belonging to the man who killed him, and I have rode with banditos my whole life." He brushed the idea aside with a wave of his thick hand. "This was all gringo talk."

"I never hear of it," said Sergio, "but Zorro is the leader. He can say as he wishes, and make it become so."

"Zorro . . . ," said Paco, barely hiding his disgust. But he didn't elaborate. He spat down at the ground and looked back at the burning cantina. Like the others, he was still a little addled from last night's whiskey and cocaine. Fox, having heard the gunmen talking guardedly twenty feet behind him, glanced over his shoulder in time to see all five of them look away.

"Want me to go shoot one of them in the foot?" Ozzie offered in a quiet tone, his hand going to his gun belt as he spoke.

Fox gave him a look, knowing he was serious.

"They'll feel better when they've got money jingling in their *bolsillos*."

Ozzie just looked at him dumbly.

"In their *pockets*, Oz," Fox translated.

"Why didn't you say 'pockets,' then?" Ozzie replied. Fox saw an instant of dark anger stir in Ozzie's eyes. But then it was gone.

"Next time I will," he said, realizing how his words had belittled his thick-witted friend. He'd seen his brother, Lucas, have those same flashes of anger, and he knew they never lasted long. But now it was time to make quick repair. "You and I could use some cash in our *bolsillos* too, eh?" he said, reaching over and pushing his fist against Ozzie's shoulder.

Ozzie stared straight ahead, but he gave a slight grin.

"Yeah," he said, "my *bolsillos* always need money in them."

"Sí, dinero en nuestros bolsillos," said Silvar Spampeto, trying to include himself in their camaraderie. But Fox only turned in his saddle and stared at him.

"Did you decide upon a good place for us to rob, my *segundo*?" he asked the nervous Stampeto.

Stampeto straightened in his saddle, seeing the no-nonsense look on Fox's face.

"Yes, I think of several," he said.

"One at a time," Fox said.

"Yes." Stampeto nodded. "There is a nice fat French mining company three days' ride from here — the Mexico-France Consorta Tierra Mineral. They pay their employees every month around this time. They open a large safe and set up a pay line the first of every month. Afterward I hear there is much fi-esta, dancing and drinking and—"

"I don't care about their payday party," Fox said, abruptly cutting him off. He considered the date. "That's only five days from now. Do they keep their payroll money on hand or have it sent in every month?"

"Unlike the Germans who have their payroll brought by the *federales* every month, these French like to keep large amounts of money on hand."

"Why haven't the Perros Locos robbed this place before now?" Fox asked him.

"Because Carlos Montoya said it is too far to ride," Stampeto replied.

Hearing him, Ozzie turned in his saddle to face Fox as if in amazement.

"Three days, *too far to ride* . . . ?" He stifled a laugh and shook his head. "No wonder his men didn't care that you killed him," he said to Fox. "Lazy beaners. . . ."

Stampeto's dark eyes moved back and forth between the two of them. Terese Montoya sat staring blankly at the raging fire and the body of Juan Ped-dersal. The heat had burned away the back of his shirt; the skin beneath had peeled, blackened and curled.

"Any towns between here and there worth raising?" Fox asked.

"There are two," said Stampeto with a slight shrug. "There are women and whiskey in Big Sand, and some nice horses at Ranchero Casa Robos just before you get there."

Fox let out a breath.

"All right, *segundo*," he said. "That's where we're headed. You get with the men, let them know what a sweet payroll this French mining company's going to be. Get them lathered up over it."

"*Sí*, I will do this, Zorro," Stampeto said, feeling as he'd been taken off the hook.

"On our way there, be thinking of where we're heading next," Fox put in. "Soon as you figure it out, tell Oz all about it. He'll tell it to me." He turned his horse. "Let's ride," he added, nudging his horse forward, leading the woman beside him.

"Yeah, you just bring any ideas to me. I'll tell Zorro," Ozzie said to Stampeto with a sharp chiding little grin. "Get the men and follow us. Hurry up about it." He jerked his horse around and rode off behind Fox, liking the way this was all working out for him.

Silvar Stampeto grumbled to himself as he turned his horse and rode to the men who still sat slumped in their saddles.

"Tell me, amigo," said Paco, his dark eyes red-rimmed and bloodshot, "why does this man burn down such a fine place as Peddersal's cantina?" He gestured a hand toward the *putas*' plank cubicles flaming up behind the blazing cantina. Women ran back and forth grabbing what meager belongings they could salvage. "What did Peddersal and these *putas* ever do to him?" In the dirt near the roiling fire, the dead owner's back sizzled like a pig on a spit. Burned hair smoked on the back of his head; his ears appeared to be melted away.

"El Zorro does not want us riding back here," said Stampeto. "Unlike Montoya, he wants us to stay in the saddle and make money." He rubbed his finger and thumb together in the universal sign of greed. "I say he is right. I do not choose the life of a desperado gunman so I can lie around and do nothing." He looked around. "What about the rest of you?"

"I feel like I have swallowed a rattlesnake," said a hungover young Mexican gunman named Ricardo Mirano. "We did not have to ride today. We could do this *mañana* when we are—"

"Shut up, Ricardo," shouted Stampeto. He gigged his horse over to the young man, yanked his sombrero from his head and slapped him back and forth across his face with it. The young gunman bowed down and covered his face with his forearms. Before Ricardo could go for his gun, Stampeto snatched it from his holster and held it up for everyone to see.

"Look, he cannot move quick enough to defend himself? And he calls himself a bad hombre, a bandito, a Perros Locos?" He threw the gunman's sombrero to the ground in disgust, but held on to his pistol.

The men sat staring. Stampeto backed his horse and addressed them angrily.

"This grocery clerk, Fox—El Zorro—comes into our town and takes us over so quickly none of us even realize it is happening until it is done. He kills Carlos Montoya as easily as snapping his fingers. That is how sorry we have become in conducting our business!"

He looked at each pair of bloodshot eyes as Ricardo stepped from his saddle and retrieved his sombrero. The Perros Locos men stared back at him.

"Listen to me, all of you," Stampeto said. "El Zorro means business. He is leading us to rob the mining company we have wanted to rob for so long. Montoya has turned us into drunken fools. But once we get the taste of our business back into our mouths, we will be bad hombres again, and men will fear us." He looked back and forth and shrugged. "As it is, no one fears us anymore. But I promise you, when we get back to work, no one will ever walk in and take us over again."

The men looked at each other, their eyes lowered in shame.

"We agree with you, Stampeto," said Paco. "We should have robbed these French miners months ago. We will go wherever this Zorro takes us. Only . . . can we first have some whiskey to settle our senses?"

"If I catch you drinking I will kill you," Stampeto warned somberly, "because if I do not kill you, this man will kill me, for not doing my job." He paused, then said, "If you cannot stay sober, ride away now and save yourself. If you want to ride with the new Perros Locos, come with me, and El Zorro will make us rich."

The men looked at each other again.

"I have long dreamed of robbing these French *bastardos*," Otis Seedy said. He spat in contempt. "It's worth being sober just to see the fear in their eyes while I drop the hammer on them." He nudged his horse forward to stand beside Stampeto. Behind him the others followed, including Ricardo, whose face was red-streaked from the bite of his sombrero across his cheeks.

For the last three miles along the lower hills trail, the Ranger had followed the high rise of black smoke adrift on the desert air. At length he stopped the dun on a rocky cliff overlooking the charred remnants of the small village below. From there he could see a few men and women walking in a straggling line toward the hill line off to their west. They carried their earthly possessions on their shoulders, and on the backs of donkeys and horses too old to properly support a saddle and rider.

The day before, he'd sensed someone on his tail. But that was to be expected, he'd told himself, knowing that Turner Pridemore's son was riding with the man he was tracking. *So be it.* The main thing for now was not to let them know that he was onto them being there. He'd deal with them when the time came. They would either come forward and confront him when they thought they had the advantage, or manage to get ahead of him and set up an ambush—something he wouldn't let happen if he could keep from it. For now he'd simply tolerate them. Swat them when the time was right, he told himself.

He nudged the dun forward onto a downhill path, the speckled barb beside him.

"There he goes," said Malcolm Chase, one of the

three scalpers Pridemore had sent to follow the Ranger. "I could drop him from right here and be done with him." Chase spoke with a terrible nasal twang and a thick lisp owing to the crushed nose and mouth Sam had given him with his rifle butt. Chase lifted his rifle from across his lap.

"Hold it, Malcolm," said Bernard Stevens, a scalper who'd joined Pridemore right after he took over the mercenary band. "Your face is swollen the size of a mule's ass. You're lucky you can even see your rifle, let alone aim it."

Chase gave him a hard stare.

"I want to kill the son of a bitch," he said, "for doing all this to me." He gestured at his swollen face. "You got any objections, Stevens?"

Stevens looked at Ian Pusser, the third horseman, then back at Chase.

"Yeah, I suppose I do," Stevens said. "Dart said Bigfoot wants us to follow this lawman, make sure if he kills Ozzie he don't kill Fox Pridemore at the same time."

"Listen to you," Chase said with contempt. "You act like this law dog has already got everybody killed and in the ground." He spat unevenly through his swollen purple lips. "I say I go on and kill him and be done with it. We can tell it however suits us when we get back. Who'll give a damn?"

"Huh-uh, I don't work that way, Malcolm," said Stevens, shaking his head.

"Nor do I," said Pusser, who sat listening with his wrists crossed on his saddle horn. "Nobody loves killing a lawman more than me. Having been one myself, I know what rotten sons a' bitches they are. But Dart said follow and keep watch. That's what I intend to do."

Chase stare at the two, his nose and lips swollen, purple and blood-crusted. His eyes were puffed out and black as a raccoon's. Anger flared inside his chest. But he took a deep breath and calmed himself.

"Okay, first off," he said in a controlled tone, "Darton Alpine can kiss where I scratch. I was with this bunch before he'd learned to shake himself after pissing. If you two don't want to help me kill this Ranger, I'll kill him myself." Keeping his rage under control grew harder the more he spoke. His voice trembled. "If I can't see to shoot him, I'll ride up and stove his head in with a rock!"

"Huh-uh," Stevens repeated. "'Follow and keep watch,' is what Dart said."

Chase raised a finger and wagged it at Stevens.

"Do not 'huh-uh' me again, Stevens," he warned. "I will yank every limb from your body."

Pusser and Stevens straightened in their saddles, neither of them prepared to give an inch.

"Follow and keep watch . . . ?" Chase said with sarcasm. "What the hell does that even mean?"

"Well," said Stevens, "it means—"

"Shut the hell up, Stevens!" said Chase, cutting him off. "You're both warned here and now. First chance I get to kill that Ranger, he's a dead man." He jerked his horse around in the direction of the rising black smoke. "So's anybody who tries to stop me." He kicked the horse out at a trot and rode away.

Pusser and Stevens watched him for a moment, then looked at each other.

"I ain't letting him get in a stew with Bigfoot just because the Ranger broke his nose," said Stevens.

"Me neither," said Pusser. "But he's right about one thing. Alpine didn't make it real clear what him or Bigfoot wanted us to do to this Ranger." He shook his head and yanked his horse around. "I hate it when folks ain't clear what they want."

"Me too," said Stevens. "Once you kill an hombre, there's no way to bring him back. Maybe Malcolm is right . . . just kill the Ranger, and say he ambushed us. Who's going to care?" They booted their horses in the same direction as Chase.

Chapter 13

———

A few remaining Mexican elders sat in a row on a short adobe wall and watched as the Ranger rode the last few hundred yards into their smoldering village. An empty water bucket lay on its side at one old man's feet. His feet and sandals were blackened from the soot of the windswept fire. Behind the elderly villagers, all that remained were a few roofless adobes. A loose corner of the livery barn roof—the only tin roof in town—flapped and rattled on a gust of wind like the tongue of a lunatic.

When the Ranger stopped his horses, an old man stood up, a relic of a Spanish muzzleloader rifle in hand, and picked at the seat on his blackened peasant trousers. He rolled the bucket away with his bare foot and stepped forward.

"Buenos dias, señor," the old man said, keeping the barrel of the ancient muzzleloader lowered. He swept a hand toward the smoldering village. *"Bienvenido."*

A woman's voice behind the old man said in Spanish, "Tell him it was gringos like himself who set fire to our homes."

The old man looked troubled at the woman's request and scratched his head.

"Yo hablo español," Sam said, letting the man off the hook.

"Ah, he speaks our language," the man said to the others in border English. He looked relieved at not having to translate.

"These men who burned your town," Sam said, "were they young men dressed in buckskins—lots of breastwork on their shirts?"

"Ah yes," the old man said. "They rode in and took up with the bad element of our village, the Perros Locos. They eat much cocaine and drink much whiskey. Then they burn our town and leave." He shrugged as if struggling with the random insanity of it. "What did we do to them?"

"You did nothing," Sam said. He swung down from his saddle, his rifle in hand, and walked forward carrying a canteen of water he'd taken from its loop around his saddle horn.

The old man took the canteen as Sam held it out.

"Gracias, señor," the old man said, eyeing the badge on Sam's chest behind his open duster lapels. "I am Ramon Decarias."

"I'm Arizona Ranger Sam Burrack," the Ranger said. He knew the village still had water—he saw a waterwheel and a donkey twenty yards away. Yet his was a gesture of kindness, and the villagers knew it. They stood up slowly and drew closer to the canteen as the old man drank and passed it around.

"You can fill your canteens at the well," the old

man said, pointing off to the low stone wall where the donkey stood at the wheel. The animal had gone back into harness the moment the fire and smoke died down.

"*Gracias,*" Sam said. "These Perros Locos," he asked, "how many are there?"

"Six . . . no, wait, five," Ramon said. "It is said that one of the gringos—I mean the *americanos*—killed the leader of the Crazy Dogs and left his body to burn in the flames." He pointed off to where a spiral of thin smoke still swirled above a pile of rubble that had been the women's cubicles. "Do you want to see him?"

"No, not particularly," Sam said. But seeing the slight disappointment in the old man's eyes, he said, "*Gracias*, in a minute. First I want to water my horses and find them some shade to rest in. The man I'm after is a scalp hunter—thinks he's an assassin. The man riding with him is a scalper too. So nothing they've done is going to surprise me."

"Ah, these scalp hunters are very bad hombres," the old man said. "Now I understand why they burn our village. They know no other way to live except the violent way—" He stopped talking, seeing Sam's attention drawn to the sound of a long war cry coming from the sand flats he'd ridden in on.

"*Señor*, look!" said one of the elderly women, pointing out a roiling rise of trail dust.

"I see him," Sam said calmly. To the old man he said, "Get your people back, Ramon—take cover."

"Do these scalp hunters return?" the old man

asked, already shooing the people back toward the remnants of their homes.

"This is *another* one," Sam said, recognizing the big, burly Chase as he rode screaming forward. "This one most likely wants to kill me." He kneeled and raised the rifle to his shoulder and methodically adjusted the long-distance sights. He'd been expecting these men to come calling any time. But why only one of them? Because of the broken nose . . . ? he asked himself, taking close aim on Chase's wide chest as the rider rose and fell with the horse's long, bounding stride.

Chase's war cry sounded part Apache, part rebel yell. Sam saw the man's rifle poised out to the side like the balancing outrigger on a boat. He knew that nothing short of killing the man was going to stop him. He could think of no reason why Chase would come charging at him out in the open this way. But that would make little difference once the scalper got close enough to draw his horse down and start shooting. This was the best place to put a stop to it.

Here goes. . . .

Sam took close aim on Chase's chest and held it level as the horse's pace raised it up and down, in and out of his gun sights. He drew a breath, let a puff of it out and held it. When the horse came into its down stride and Chase fell into sight, he squeezed the trigger.

But in the split second before the rifle responded to his command, he saw Chase, horse and all, pitch forward into a hard roll as rifle fire exploded farther back in the trail dust behind him.

What was that?

Sam let off the trigger without firing a shot. He lowered his rifle a few inches and stared out above the sights. For a moment the fallen horse and its rider disappeared in the roiling dust. Through the dust, Sam heard two more rifle shots, saw them blossom orange in the thick sandy veil. Somebody out there on Chase's back trail had just shot his horse out from under him.

Who?

Sam watched and waited, the rifle fire falling silent after the second two shots. As the dust started settling he saw no sign of the other two men who'd been following him through the hill country. Whatever this was about, he still had to water his horses and get them rested, he reminded himself. He stood up, uncocking his rifle and dusting his knees. A few feet away his dun and the speckled barb looked haggard, dusty, sweat-streaked and thirsty.

The copper dun chuffed, scraped a hoof and grumbled under its breath.

"All right, I'm coming," Sam said quietly to the tired animals. He kept an eye on the settling dust as he picked up the reins to both the dun's and the barb's lead rope. Then he started walking toward the well, where the waterwheel donkey had stopped once again and stood staring toward him and his thirsty horses.

After resting and graining the horses, the Ranger ate a meal of jerked elk from his saddlebags and corn tortillas cooked on a charred outdoor kitchen.

The burned-out kitchen stood behind the spot where the cantina and the women's cubicles used to stand. Under the insistence of the old townsman, Sam walked a few yards and looked at the burnt lump of char that had been Carlos Montoya.

"The young scalper took this bandito's widow with him when he left," Ramon said, gesturing toward the unrecognizable body with heat still wavering above it, "because this is what outlaws do in your country, *sí*? They take whatever belongs to the man they killed?"

Sam looked at him curiously.

"I've never heard of it," he said. "But these mercenaries are good at making up the rules to their game as they go along."

"*Mercenarios* . . . outlaws. Which are these two men?" the old man asked.

"Probably both," Sam said. "Scalp hunting draws the worst sort of men from both sides of the border, from every occupation."

The old man paused. Sam saw something on his mind.

"What is it, Ramon?" he asked.

"We know that you are in a hurry to catch up with the man you are hunting. But the others bid me to ask you this," the old man said hesitantly. "Will you accompany us to the dead horse so we can butcher it and bring the meat back? The fire has left us without much food." He nodded out onto the sand flats where the settled dust now revealed the fresh carcass of Malcolm Chase's horse lying sprawled in the sand.

Sam thought about how hospitable the old folks had been in sharing their tortillas with him in spite of being short on food for themselves.

"Yes, of course I'll help you and your people carry the food back here," Sam said. Even as he spoke he gathered the reins to both horses. "I was going there anyway, to see if I can figure out why two of them killed one of their own."

"We have four donkeys to carry the horse meat," the old man said. "We'd like you and your gun with us in case more of these *mercenarios* are out there." He held up his muzzleloader with an ironic little grin. "The only way I know this will fire is to fire it. Then the only way to know it will fire again is to reload it and fire it again." He shrugged. "I will never get caught up with it."

Sam nodded. He had no reason to think the scalpers would be out there in the heat, the sun and the dust waiting for him in such an exposed position. But he treated the elder's fears seriously.

"I understand," he said.

He and Ramon walked over to where the others stood waiting.

"The Ranger has agreed to escort us," Ramon said. "So let us go quickly and gather the meat before the vultures beat us to it."

The people looked relieved and grateful, and they hurriedly took stock of themselves and whatever butchering tools they carried.

As they fell into a line and filed off toward the downed horse, Sam lifted an elderly woman who held a naked infant in her arms swaddled in her serape. He sat the woman and child both atop the dun.

"*Mi gran hijo,*" the old woman said, smiling across empty gums as she patted the baby's head.

"Yes, and a beautiful grandson he is," Sam replied in his border Spanish.

The dun blew out a breath in discontent, wanting none of it. Yet he settled and acted with civility as Sam led him and the speckled barb forward.

"We all do our part, Copper," he said quietly to the dun, rubbing its muzzle as they walked on, Sam with his rifle in hand. The barb walked alongside carrying the Ranger's trail supplies.

When the Ranger and the elderly villagers reached the spot where the horse lay stretched out dead in the sand, Sam dropped the reins to his horse and lifted the old grandmother and her naked grandson down from the dun's saddle. He unhitched the dead horse's saddle and with the help of two elderly men pulled it free from the downed horse's side and pitched it away.

Sam then stepped back as the elderly villagers fell upon the fresh horse carcass with skill and utility. Overhead a pair of vultures appeared high up and began circling long and lazily in the white-hot sky.

"We beat you today!" Ramon called to the dark circling birds in Spanish. He waved a bloody knife overhead and grinned and nodded at the Ranger. Sam touched his sombrero brim in acknowledgment and looked off and all around the area. It concerned him that Malcolm Chase's body was not lying dead on the ground. He walked out slowly away from the dead horse, looking all around on the sand.

Seeing the look of the Ranger's face, Ramon handed his knife off to one of the other butchers, picked up his muzzleloader and hurried over to Sam, who now stood about where he figured a man would fall if thrown from a downed horse.

"You feel something is not right?" he asked Sam quietly.

"Yes," Sam said. He nodded at the ground by his feet. Large dark splotches of blood lay randomly among a line of meandering boot prints leading off to a low rise. "Stay here, keep an eye on your folks while I look around."

"*Sí*, and you be careful, Ranger," Ramon said in a whisper, watching closely as Sam ascended the low rise and walked down out of sight.

Sam followed the boot prints until a few yards ahead of him he saw where they disappeared, as if their owner had been plucked up from the face of the desert and flown away. As he looked off far to the left, he realized what had happened here. He jerked back around toward the end of the boot prints. But he hadn't moved quick enough. He saw Malcolm Chase standing facing him with sand pouring from his shoulders, his hat, his rifle.

"Huh-uh, Ranger, I've got you!" Chase said, seeing Sam had fallen a second short of leveling his rifle. "A man learns a lot killing Apache. Pitch it away."

Sam needed a second. He stalled.

"I don't throw away rifles," he said calmly. But he lowered the Winchester, took his right hand off it and let his hand drift down onto the butt of his Colt as he spoke.

"Get your hand off the Colt too!" Chase said. "I've heard how you do, you sneaking bastard."

Sam took his hand off the Colt, running out of moves now. He looked at the dark blood down Chase's thigh, a large black circle on his left shoulder.

"You're hit bad," Sam said. "You'll need help getting out of here—"

"Shut up, Ranger," Chase shouted, his voice weakening a little from his hours in the sand, and under it. "The only reason you're alive this minute is that I need some help. Here's the deal. Tell your beaner amigos to patch me up after I kill you, and I promise I'll let them live. Otherwise no dice. I'll kill them all after I blow your head off."

"Your deal sounds shaky," Sam said, needing an edge, looking for it, hoping for it. Drawing against a cocked rifle hammer was never good—he knew, having been on the other side of this play too many times to count. "Why should I believe you'd keep your word after I'm—"

"To hell with it," said Chase, cutting him off, feeling himself growing weaker. "I'll make them help me at gunpoint." He steadied the rifle at his shoulder. Sam saw him tense himself for the shot. Here it came. Sam had to make the move—no choice—slim though his odds were.

He snatched for the Colt, already knowing it was taking too long, even as his Colt was up and aimed, his finger ready to press back on the trigger. All he needed was a split second—

But he didn't get it. Instead he heard the powerful explosion of a huge-caliber rifle shot. Confusing, though, since he saw no smoke or fire fly from Chase's rifle barrel. Instead he saw the scalper's head explode like a busted bucket of red paint and raw eggs from the nose up.

"This time it worked! This time it worked!" shouted Ramon behind him.

Sam spun instinctively toward the rifle shot, his Colt cocked and ready. He let his gun and his hand fall to his side, seeing Ramon hold the big muzzle-loader up over his head in a large cloud of silvery black powder smoke. He breathed in a deep breath and let it out, realizing how fortunate he'd been in escorting the elderly villagers out to collect their horse meat. Had he ridden out alone . . .

But you didn't, did you? he reminded himself, already wanting to put the close call behind him.

"Now I must reload and wait and see if it works the next time," Ramon called out, trotting down the rise to him. "I know you said to wait up there." He stopped ten feet away, the big ancient rifle leaving a trail of smoke behind him and a stream still curling from its barrel. "But I am old and do not always do as I am told. Forgive me, Ranger."

Sam only gave a faint smile and nodded.

"Good shooting," he said, lowering his Colt back into its holster.

"*Gracias*, Ranger," said Ramon, fanning the smoke away from his rifle. "Now to reload, and wait and see if it works the next time I try to fire it." He crossed himself quickly. "By the saints, I hope it does."

"So do I, Ramon," Sam said. He looked toward the dead man, then off into the distance. *One down, two to go,* he told himself. Then he and Ramon turned and walked back up the rise toward the elderly villagers. The elders had looked up at the sound of the gunshot, yet upon seeing no harm done went back to gathering their food.

Chapter 14

———

Twice the two scalpers had started to ride out onto the sand flats to make sure their rifle fire had killed Malcolm Chase, but each time something had stopped them. The first time, when the dust had settled enough for them to get a clear view of their handiwork, they spotted the Ranger and the elderly villagers trekking out to butcher the dead horse. Their second attempt, the loud blast of the big rifle had resounded at the same time they stepped into their saddles.

They stopped and looked at each other warily. Instead of riding out to investigate, they straightened high in their saddles and stared out, only to have their view blocked by the low rise on the other side of which the Ranger and Ramon stood over Chase's body.

This was their third attempt at making sure Chase was dead, although by now they were both certain he was. They'd watched the villagers butcher his horse, pack it onto the donkeys and haul it back to the blackened rubble that had been their homes. The Ranger had ridden with them, lagging behind, keeping watch on the sand flats as they left.

When they rode their horses at a walk past the hooves, hide and innards of Chase's butchered horse, three greasy black vultures looked toward them and stretched out their wings and scowled them away from their gory feast.

"It all yours, boys," Stevens called out to the bold scavengers, glancing back over his shoulder at them. "We've et."

"Speak for yourself," said Pusser. "Those horse steaks looked pretty good while they was parting out Chase's cayouse."

"If you're that hungry, I'll wait for you," Stevens said, giving a taunting grin, nodding back at the bloody mess of horse entrails.

"You know what I meant," Pusser said crossly.

They rode quietly on, following the Ranger's and Ramon's footprints to the top of the low rise. When they stopped they looked down at a lone young vulture picking through the former contents of Chase's cranium. A few feet from the vulture a mound of fresh-turned sand supported a stack of rocks.

"Think they buried ol' Malcolm?" Pusser asked.

"Yeah, that's what I figure," Stevens said quietly, his hand on his holstered gun as he looked all around.

"Meaning he wasn't dead after we shot him," Pusser offered.

"One would only think so," said Stevens, still looking all around the small sandy basin. "It's doubtful anybody would waste a bullet on a dead man, don't you think?"

"Yeah," Pusser agreed. He paused, then said, "So . . . you figure the Ranger finished him off?" trying to work it out in his mind.

"I would not find that *hard* to believe," said Stevens, getting a little testy from all the questions. "If I ever see him I'm going to ask him, first thing."

"Are you crowding me?" Pusser asked, getting a little testy himself from Stevens' snide answers.

Without answering, Stevens turned his horse and nudged it toward the charred remnants of the village in the flat, shapeless distance.

Pusser clenched his jaws and rode alongside him.

When they got closer to the burned-out village, they saw the people stretching a large canvas from the top of a blackened stone and adobe wall slant-wise to the ground. Rocks were laid to hold the canvas in place both atop the wall and along the ground, forming a lean-to-shaped shelter. Seeing the two scalpers riding in, Ramon and another man stepped out of sight, Ramon with his muzzleloader reloaded, the other villager with Malcolm Chase's rifle. In addition to carrying his muzzleloader, Ramon wore Chase's gun belt around his thin waist.

"*Hola* the village," Stevens said as the two reined up a few feet from the ongoing work.

A large elderly widow named Natilizar stepped back from the work on the shelter and gave the two scalpers a nod.

"*Hola,*" she said. "You can see that our village has burned, and we are preparing a place of refuge from the wind and the sand."

"Yeah, yeah, we see all that," Stevens said impatiently, looking around for any sign of the Ranger. "We just need to get our horses watered . . . ourselves too. We'll be on our way."

"We never hang around where work's going on," said Pusser with a slight grin.

"Over there is our well," the widow said. She gestured toward the donkey at the waterwheel. "You are welcome to fill your canteens before you leave."

Stevens stared at her coldly.

"Are you rushing us off?" he said. "What if we're hungry?"

"Yeah," said Pusser, "what if we wanted ourselves a good fresh horse steak?"

"We have no horse meat," said the widow. But upon seeing by the look in their eyes that they knew better, she said, "None to spare, that is."

"Fix us a steak," Pusser said, getting demanding. "You best not spit on it either."

Stevens gave him a surprised and annoyed look and said to the woman before she could respond, "Where's the Ranger? We know he's here."

The widow looked back and forth between the two, getting nervous.

"Are you going to fix us a gawl-damn steak, or am I going to have to thrash the living hell out of you?" He started to rise and swing down from his saddle.

"Forget your gawl-damn steak for a minute!" said Stevens. He looked back at the woman. "We just want to know if we're going to get waylaid unsuspecting." He looked all around again.

The widow looked panic-stricken.

"She told you the truth." said Ramon. "The Ranger is not here. He left." He stepped around the corner of the charred wall, the flintlock in hand, cocked and ready. Chase's black-handled Colt stood in the holster at his waist.

"Oh, did he, then?" said Stevens, his hand still clamped around his gun butt. "I know who that black Colt belonged to." He nodded at Ramon's waist.

"*Sí*, I know you do," Ramon said solemnly. "But now it belongs to me . . . me and all of us."

On the other end of the fifteen-foot-long wall, the other Mexican villager stepped into sight with Chase's rifle against his shoulder, cocked, aimed, ready to fire.

"Well, well . . . ," Pusser said in a low, even tone. "Look what we've got here." He sat ready to draw his pistol and start firing.

"You must ride on," Ramon said in a steady voice, "or we will kill you both." He stared at them. "The Ranger is gone, your *compañeros* are dead and buried. There is nothing here for the two of you—nothing but trouble," he warned.

"The only thing worse than a Mexican getting a bath is a Mexican getting a gun," Pusser said. He glared again at the widow and added, "But I'm having me a gawl-damm steak before I leave this burned-out hull—"

"Shut the hell up about your damn steak!" Stevens shouted at him. "The Ranger's gone, Malcolm is dead." As he spoke he lifted his hand slowly from his gun butt and stepped his horse back. "This is loco."

"*Sí*," said Ramon, nodding, "it is loco." He looked at the widow. "Wrap some meat and give it to them."

"By God, that's more like it," Pusser said. He eased the grip on his gun butt and gave Stevens a look.

"*Gracias . . . ,*" Stevens said, looking around at the workers who had stopped and stood watching. The widow walked away behind the wall and returned right away with meat wrapped in a bloody canvas cloth.

As she handed the meat up to Pusser, Ramon said to Stevens, "If you follow the Ranger, you will run into a band of six young Apache. We saw them only moments after he left."

"Good try," said Stevens. "Knowing the Apache is our game." He rattled the finger bones and bits of scalp and memorabilia on the bib of his shirt. "We know they've all cut out to the deep hill country."

Ramon started to say more, but he stopped himself.

"Go with God," he said, raising a hand as Stevens turned his horse and nudged it back toward the trail.

"Watch your language, old beaner," Pusser said. "God wants to go with us, he better bring his own skinning knife." He followed Stevens with a smug look, hefting the wrapped horse meat in the palm on his hand.

*   *   *

Knowing the scalpers were playing cat and mouse with him, the Ranger didn't stop until well after dark when the many shod hoofprints he'd followed from the village became lost in the darkness. He'd traveled all day in silence, keeping the horses quiet and out of sight, avoiding any open stretches or turns on the hill trail. When the sun dropped he'd continued on, adjusting his eyes to the grainy dark until he knew he could safely go no farther. Then he eased off the trail onto the rocky hillside and made a dark camp, keeping the horses a few yards away from his bedroll against the back side of a large boulder. The prints he followed would be there in the morning. One of the horses wore shoes that had an extra-thick ridge at its center. Another horse wore shoes with two missing nails. Easy tracking, Sam told himself.

In the moments before sleep overtook him, he recounted the events of the day. With Malcolm Chase dead, he told himself, one down, two to go. . . . If he could avoid killing the other two, he would. If not, he wasn't going to let them stop him from getting the man he was after.

He had made the right move escorting the village elders out to butcher the horse. Had he gone alone, he realized, there was a good chance Malcolm Chase would have killed him. It was not something he wanted to dwell on, but he had to acknowledge it was a close call. These mercenaries had spent enough time hunting down Apache that they had learned a lot of their ways. Hiding under the sand was a trick he knew himself, yet Chase had managed to pull it on him—almost gotten away with it. He had to watch his step, he told himself, turning onto his side, closing his eyes for the night.

In spite of the bone-tiring day he'd spent in the desert heat, he slept a light and shallow sleep, the way he'd trained himself to do. The sleep of a tracker, he called it, or the sleep of an owl. Even so, in the middle of the night, his light veil of sleep was pierced by the quiet sound of horses walking past his camp on the trail beneath the boulder. Having also trained himself not to awaken with a start but rather open his eyes slowly and search out whatever sound had awakened him, he did so without moving an inch.

And there it was, the slightest rustle of horses' hooves, of men speaking under their breath in the darkness. But it wasn't English, he realized after a moment of listening, nor was it Spanish. As the riders drifted past him like ghosts in the night, he recognized the short, low, choppy words of Apache. The fact that he heard them and their horses at all made him doubt his findings. Apache traveled as silent as a wisp of desert breeze.

Yet there it was again. He listened closely. Lipan, he decided. Even as he reaffirmed his conclusion, he realized by the thickness and the slur of their voices that the warriors were drunk. That explained a lot, he thought, rolling silently up from his blanket into a crouch. Colt in one hand, Winchester in the other, he eased over to the back side of the boulder, leaned his rifle against it and stood between the horses, keeping their attention away from the passing horses.

"Good boys," he whispered near their pricked ears as the last faint click of hoof moved away on the trail to his left. He slipped his Colt back into its holster. "What say we take a different path? It's getting a little crowded up here."

The horses stood silent as he rubbed each of them on its muzzle. After a moment he unhitched them both, saddled the dun and tied his supply pack atop the barb. In the pale moonlight he led the animals around from behind the boulder, to a thinner trail leading farther up on the steep hillside. By the time he'd found a stop to his liking, the sun had drawn a fine silver thread along the distant horizon. "A long day followed by a long night," he told himself, slumping down against a boulder and closing his eyes, the horses' reins in his hands.

But he knew his climb would be worth his efforts. Come daylight he would have a full view of the trails below and anyone traveling on them. With Apache traveling the trails—drunk or sober— he needed every advantage he could take for himself.

At dawn, Ian Pusser and Bernard Stevens lay atop a flat rock looking down on a switchback trail below them. At some time during the night they had heard the faintest sound of horses moving along the hard, stony trail. But with their bellies full of warm horse steak, neither had dragged himself from sleep long enough to investigate.

"Do you see what I see?" Pusser whispered, barely keeping his excitement from showing.

"I'd be blind if I didn't," said Stevens. The two of them stared down at five sleeping warriors stretched out on the rocky ground over two hundred yards away. Three warriors were loosely wrapped in blankets. Two were spread-eagle on the ground, shirtless, like two men staked to the earth to keep from falling off. A sixth warrior, sitting guard, had fallen over onto his side atop a tall boulder. His rifle lay ten feet away.

"I've never seen a heathen Apache sleep till daylight," Pusser said, staring as if in disbelief.

"You likely never will again," Stevens said. As he spoke he checked his rifle, raised its long-distance sights and placed the butt to his shoulder. He looked down the barrel.

Pusser clamped a hand around the rifle chamber, blocking Stevens' aim.

"Wait!" he said. "The hell are you doing?"

"What any natural man would do when a half dozen scalps fall into his lap—I'm skinning them." He gave Pusser a shove. "Don't ever grab my rifle."

"What about the Ranger?" said Pusser. "We're supposed to be tracking him."

"What about him?" said Stevens. "If he shows up I'll skin him too." He looked Pusser up and down. "Are you getting weak on me? If you want any of this, you best be shooting while I'm shooting. Otherwise I'm keeping the whole bounty to myself."

"They're too far away," Pusser said. "Listen to me." As he spoke he reached around to his side and picked up his rifle. "This far off if any of them gets away, we'll be all morning tracking them down."

"I'm not letting a chance like this get away from me. I don't expect they'll walk up here and scalp themselves," said Stevens.

"I say we need to get closer, make sure when we strike, we leave none standing," Pusser said, getting his fill of Stevens. "I was only trying to prepare us for what could happen."

Stevens considered it.

"Maybe you're right, we need to get closer," he said.

"Now you're talking. Let's get down on the trail and hit them head-on. With surprise on our side, they won't stand a chance in hell," Pusser said. He reached back and drew a big bowie-style knife from its sheath behind his back and gripped it in his hand. "Any luck we'll go back to Bigfoot with six scalps on our saddle horns."

"Yeah, and the Ranger hung over his saddle," Stevens said. He gave a sharp grin and scooted back away from the edge of the boulder. "He'll see who knows how to kill these heathen Injuns."

Chapter 15

From the cover of a scrub pine on the high path where he and his horses had spent the night, Sam watched the two scalpers through his outstretched telescope. Farther below them he saw the Lipans rise from their drunken sleep and stagger over to where their horses stood hitched to a rope line. These were the Indians who had passed him in the night. He was sure of it. Looking away from them back to the two mercenaries, he saw the rifles in their hands. He'd watched one of them draw his big scalping knife from its sheath behind his back. When he saw them stand and step toward their horses a few yards away, it was plain to him what they were up to.

All right, it's between them and the Lipans, he told himself. He collapsed the telescope between his palms and walked to where his two horses stood warming in the early-morning sunlight.

"Good news," he said, unhitching them, gathering the dun's rein and the barb's lead rope. "Looks like we've got a clear trail toward Ozzie Cord . . . for a while anyway."

He swung up into the saddle and rode off along

the trail in the opposite direction of the Lipans and the scalpers. An hour passed before he heard the gunshots resound high up on the hill line behind him. He didn't bother looking around. Instead he followed the tracks of the many shod horses he'd followed off the hill trail and down along the edge of the sand flats.

At noon when the sun had turned the sky white and waves of heat danced languid across the desert floor, Sam put the horses in the shade of rock and cactus along the belly of a dry creek bed. Using his upturned sombrero, he watered the animals from a canteen, poured a trickle of water on his neck and wiped a small palm full around on his face. An hour later he was back in the saddle, following the hooves of the same group of riders he'd followed since leaving the burned-out village. Now the hoofprints turned out across the sand flats.

"Hate to do it to you," he said to the dun and the barb. Then he pulled his bandanna up over the bridge of his nose, tugged his sombrero down and rode on.

Nearing dark he'd left the hot desert wind behind him and moved the animals off the sand flats. Picking up the hoofprints he had lost for only a few minutes in the stir of sand, he followed a calm meandering path at the base of a rocky foothill until the horses grew restless at the scent of water. Seeing that the hoofprints he followed also turned up onto the sloping hillside, he let the horses lead him upward among cactus and brush to the edge of a stone-lined water hole.

"Good work," he said quietly to the horses as he stepped down from his saddle and let them walk forward and drink their fill.

While the two animals drank, he picked up a pointed wooden trail sign from the dirt, shook it off and read it in the failing evening light.

Casa Robos. . . .

He looked all around in the grainy darkness and twisted the pointing sign back and forth as if to discern its intent. Then he dropped it back to the dirt and let his eyes follow the hoofprints of the Perros Locos away from the water hole where they too had slaked their thirst.

"Wherever you're headed, I'm right with you," he said quietly. He took off his sombrero, pitched it to the ground and walked to the water's edge. He took two canteens down from the dun's saddle horn and sank to his knees by the dun's hooves.

As the canteens lay filling, he lowered himself onto his palms and sucked in a mouthful of water, swished it and spat it on the ground beside him. He took another mouthful and swallowed it, feeling the cool wetness surge in his chest. As he started to take another mouthful, he heard a sound in the rocks behind him and swung around, bringing his Colt up from its holster cocked and ready in his wet hand.

"Please, *señor*, don't shoot," said a gruff, wheezing voice. "I will tell no one what you and your *compañeros* did, I swear to you on the Blessed Virgin!"

Sam saw an old man and woman step out of the

brush where they had been hiding. They held their hands chest high.

With his free hand Sam wiped his lips.

"What is it you saw me do?" he asked.

"Nothing! Nothing, *señor*, like I told you," the old man replied nervously.

"Take it easy," Sam said. "I'm not who you think I am. I'm an Arizona Ranger tracking a killer this side of the border."

"A Ranger?" the old man said with relief. "Then thank God it is you instead of another of the Perros Locos chasing us."

"Come in closer. Let me see you," Sam said, looking all around in the darkness. "Why are the Perros Locos chasing you? Where are they?"

"We are from Casa Robos," said the old man, stepping closer, the old woman right beside him. "I am Miguel Bovier. She is my *esposa*, Josefina — she does not talk so much. We have escaped with our lives, when so many of our people did not." He lowered a hand enough to cross himself; the old woman did the same.

"One of the Perros Locos pursues us. God forbid what he will do if he catches us."

Seeing how excited the old man was, Sam gestured toward the water. "Both of you have some water, sit down and rest. Nobody's going to bother you here."

"*Gracias*, Señor Ranger," Miguel said. "He is a devil, this one. He chases us so hard we have to leave our cart, our poor donkey behind. He would already have caught us, except . . . he keeps falling from his horse."

"Falling from his horse?" Sam said.

"*Sí*, from his *horse*!" the man said as if having a hard time believing it himself. "They come to Casa Robos and drink everything in the cantina. They kill our goats and eat them. They rob all of our stores—chase the women. Then they set fires and leave."

"How far back is he?" Sam asked, looking out along the dark trail.

"He is not far," said Miguel. "The last place we see him, he was chasing his horse and cursing it—"

"Shhh . . . hold it," Sam said, silencing him. They listened toward the faint sound of a horse's hooves clopping on the hard path leading to the water hole. "Get back in the brush," Sam whispered. He backed away to the dun as the old couple took cover. Not wanting to fire a gun unless he had to, he slipped the Winchester from his dun's saddle boot and moved to the edge of a large rock standing alongside the path the hooves were walking in on.

As the sound of the hooves grew nearer, Sam stepped higher onto the rock and drew back the rifle for a hard jab when the rider came into sight. Yet, when the horse appeared and walked past him toward the beckoning water hole, Sam lowered the rifle, stepped out and looked back along the trail. In the grainy moonlight he saw a huge Mexican staggering forward on foot carrying something in his hand. Sam could hear him cursing to himself in Spanish.

At the sight of the big Mexican, the mute woman, Josefina, grew terrified and let out a high, tortured shriek before her aged husband could grab her and stop her.

"Ah, so there you are, you little piglets, you," the Mexican said, staggering in past the rocks where Sam stood ready to deliver a blow with his rifle butt. "You have caused me so much trouble that now I have to kill you!" He drew a big pistol from his holster, and pitched the object he carried onto the ground. Sam recognized it as a broken saddle stirrup.

"Por favor! Por favor, señor!" Miguel said, holding his wife pressed tight against his side. As he pleaded, the Mexican thought the old man was pleading to him for his life. In reality the old Mexican was asking the Ranger to make his move. Which he did.

"It will do you no good to beg," the big Mexican said, spreading his feet, getting ready to raise the pistol toward the old couple.

"Hey, over here!" Sam said, moving quickly from the side, getting the Mexican's attention. As the big lumbering man turned to face him, Sam unleashed a hard, stabbing blow with his rifle butt to the man's forehead. The big Mexican dropped back a step; the gun flew from his hand. But then he caught his balance just as the Ranger stepped in and delivered another blow that sent him sprawling on the ground.

"Oh, Señor Ranger, *gracias, gracias*!" the old Mexican said, still holding his sobbing, frightened wife. "This man would kill us for no reason except that we fled Casa Robos to *keep from* being killed. What is wrong with people like this? Do their souls belong to the devil?"

"Maybe that's it," the Ranger said, realizing that he himself had no better answer. He stepped over, picked up the big French revolver and stuck it down behind his belt. He reached into the man's boot well and pulled out a long sheathed dagger. He pitched the dagger to the old man.

"Gracias," Miguel said, turning his wife loose. He slid the knife from its sheath and examined it. "What — what about his gun, *señor*?" he asked haltingly. "May I have it?"

"In a minute," Sam said, hearing the Mexican already starting to groan on the ground. Looking down, Sam saw the man shake his large head and try to focus his eyes — eyes that appeared too large and shiny in the moonlight. He started to try to raise himself, but the Ranger clamped a boot down on his chest.

"Lie still, big fellow," he said, holding his rifle ready in both hands. "I'll give it to you again."

"Who . . . the hell . . . are you?" the big Mexican said in a thick, deep voice, staring up through eyes that the Ranger could now tell were lit and fueled by cocaine.

"Arizona Ranger Sam Burrack," Sam said. "Where are the Crazy Dogs headed?"

"Perros Locos . . . ?" the man said as if having to let his mind catch up to him. "I don't know . . . we — we are robbing villages?"

"Yes, that would be my guess too," Sam said, helping the man's memory a little. "But where are you headed next?"

"Arena Grande?" the Mexican said, still unsure of himself.

"He says they head to *Big Sand*, Señor Ranger," the elderly Mexican said.

"I heard him," Sam said. He turned to the elderly couple. "How far back is your mule cart?"

"Three . . . four miles," the old man estimated.

"You've got a horse, a knife and a gun." He lifted the French revolver from his waist and held it out to the old man. "Ride back and get your cart. Take your *esposa* and lie low somewhere."

"You don't take *my* horse!" the big Mexican shouted, making a grab for Sam's leg, pulling himself quickly onto his knees. Sam drew back the big revolver, but before he could swing it he saw the aged man drop down onto the big Mexican's back like a dark spirit. He saw a glint of steel in the moonlight as the big knife moved around quickly and sliced the big Mexican's throat ear to ear.

Sam took a step back as blood spewed. The old man stepped back too, the knife hanging in his hand. The Mexican clasped both hands to his throat; blood gushed between his fingers. He gagged. He fell to the ground and wallowed and thrashed. Then he appeared to relax. He fell silent and still.

Sam gave the old man a look.

"Is it wrong what I do?" old Miguel asked.

Sam didn't answer. He stood with his rifle in one hand, the French revolver in the other. The dead

Mexican's horse had clopped over and stood at the water's edge, drinking side by side with the dun and the speckled barb.

In moments, the Ranger and the old man had dragged the dead Mexican into the brush and stacked a few rocks over his body. They'd finished watering the three horses and mounted and ridden away in the moonlight toward Casa Robos. Josefina sat behind her husband with her hands clasped together around him. The big French revolver stuck up from behind the old man's waist. Two miles down the trail they heard the squeaking of a wooden cart wheel and stopped short for a moment, listening.

"Ah yes, it is my cart," Miguel said, relieved. He looked at Sam in the moonlight. "A man who is truly a man knows the sound of his own cart, *sí*?"

Sam only nodded. He nudged the dun and led the barb forward until the donkey stopped the cart in the trail facing them. Beside him, the old man and woman stepped down from the dead Mexican's paint horse and hurried to the donkey.

"See? I told you it's my cart," the old man said.

Sam stepped down from the dun and helped Miguel and Josefina turn the donkey around on the trail and point it in the direction of Casa Robos. As soon as the cart was righted, the old woman scrambled over its side and took up the donkey's reins. She smiled at her husband and nodded vigorously.

"And now she is happy again," the old man said, his hand resting on the French revolver in his waist.

Back atop the horses, Sam and the old Mexican

rode alongside the woman and the donkey cart. In the distance several thin glowing firelights seemed to rise from the earth and dot the darkness of the domed purple sky.

As they rode, the old Mexican looked down at the gun in the waist of his peasant trousers and laid his hand back on its butt.

"I can only imagine what it must feel like to live in a country like yours where all men have guns with which to protect themselves and their loved ones."

"It can be a blessing and a curse," Sam replied, looking ahead toward the firelights in Casa Robos, knowing the Perros Locos would be gone by the time he and the elderly couple arrived there.

"A blessing and a curse . . . ? No, Señor Ranger, it must be a wonderful thing to stand boldly and demand that such men as *that one* back there go away and leave you alone."

"But in my country men like *that one* have guns too," Sam said.

"Ah yes, but all you must do is take the guns from the bad hombres and give them to the good and honest people, to hunt their food and protect themselves."

"Sounds simple enough when you put it that way," Sam said. He decided not to go any further on the matter. Instead he gazed forward, wondering where Ozzie Cord and the Perros Locos might be headed next. "Any idea where the Crazy Dogs might've headed when they left Casa Robos?"

"*Sí,*" Miguel said, "they go to the French mines."

"You heard them say this?" Sam asked.

"*Sí*," said Miguel. He shrugged. "They speak boldly of robbing the French. But it is no secret that every bandito wants to rob the French mining companies. It has been this way ever since the French invaded my poor country. What their army did not loot from us at gunpoint, their businesses and government leaders take from us these many years with their mineral contracts."

"I understand," Sam said.

They rode across the sand flats toward the fire-lights of Casa Robos until the sun revealed its thin silver-white wreath on the eastern horizon. When they drew closer and the flames of the campfires were recognizable, as were the outlines and faces of people gathered around them, a few men with ancient rifles, machetes and farming tools moved in closer and stared coldly at them. Behind their camp-fires, smoke still rose and drifted from the remnants of buildings the Perros Locos had set aflame.

"*Vecinos*," Miguel called out from his saddle, "it is us, Miguel and Josefina. The Perros Locos did not catch us, as you can see!"

The armed village men moved in even closer, this time hospitable, recognizing two of their own.

"The Ranger found us just in time, before the Perros Locos came to kill us," the old Mexican called out across the campfires. He gestured a hand toward Sam. "Let us make him welcome."

Sam nodded and tipped his sombrero as the people cheered. But he knew that as soon as his horses were rested and grained, he would be on his way. This was not the time to stay long in one place on the trail. He was getting closer to Ozzie Cord with every mile. As soon as the villagers pointed him in the direction of the French mines, he'd be back on the trail.

PART 3

PART 3

Chapter 16

Bigfoot Turner Pridemore stood out in front of the Mockingbird Cantina's new home, the building where Pancho Mero's cantina used to be. Three days earlier the bright red-and-green sign reading PANCHO MERO'S CANTINA, had come down and been painted over. The only place Pancho Mero's name could be seen now was on a wooden grave marker stuck in a fresh mound of earth in the town cemetery. The big colorful sign now read BIGFOOT'S MOCKINGBIRD SALOON.

"You know what might make me happy, Big Darlin'?" Pridemore said to Bertha Buttons, who stood beside him, his arm looped over her shoulders, a cigar hanging between his fingers.

"What would that be, Bigfoot?" she asked. Her black eye had mended, except for a dark half-moon smudge against the side of her nose.

"I'd like to take this pissant country over, see what I can make of it."

She just looked up at him.

"I mean it," he said, looking out along the trail to the hill country, the direction his three men had taken to follow the Ranger. "These jelly-headed Mexes have no idea what to do with this place. Neither did the French, nor the Germans."

Before replying, Bertha glanced at the pine board leaning against the front of the building beside the open doors. The curing, round, bearded face of Diamond Jim Ruby stared out through eyes someone had drawn in with a charcoal pencil. Someone, the same person perhaps, had stretched the lips open in a grotesque grin and penciled in a large row of teeth.

"That's real ambitious, Bigfoot," she offered warily, not sure what might set her new mate into a killing rage.

Pridemore gave the idea some more thought, then lifted his arm from around her and stuck the cigar into his mouth and bit down on it.

"Hell, I'm talking crazy," he said. "I wouldn't know no more what to do with this place than the Germans or the French." He let out a breath. "Since I started scalping I ain't used to sitting around this long. I'm just getting restless now that Iron Point is being run the way it should. I need to find some scalps and ply my trade."

"What about when the *federales* come calling?" Bertha asked.

"Don't worry about them," Pridemore said. "We've got enough money coming in. We can keep buying them month after month. That's all you ever get from any government—whatever you can buy from them."

Bertha only nodded.

"How's Ria and her very young 'daughter' working out?" he asked with a grin.

"Ria got all the sewing caught up. She wants to start tending bar, get herself a dice game going," Bertha said. "I told her *maybe.* First I want her to go home, hire some more *'very young daughters'* and bring them back here." She smiled. "These French and Cornish miners can't get enough. Said Ana turns down marriage proposals every night."

"I don't doubt that. She's the youngest-looking whore I ever seen," Pridemore said, drawing on the cigar. "How old you say she is — twenty-five, thirty?"

"I won't guess," said Bertha. "What do you care anyway? You've got all the woman you need right here." She hugged in close beside him.

Pridemore stared out again toward the distant hills. "My three men should have been back by now. So should Fox unless he's found something that's got his interest up."

Bertha looked up at him, reached her nails between the buttons of his shirt and scratched easily.

"It's good what we've got here, Bigfoot," she said, sounding believable. "Don't go thinking about leaving me."

"You don't want to be telling me what to do and not do, Big Darling," Pridemore said with a warning in his tone.

"I'm not," said Bertha. "I know better than to try. It's just that I've gotten used to you, Bigfoot. Who would I ever find to take your place?"

"Well . . . I expect I see your point there, Big Darling," Pridemore said. "I would be damn hard to replace." He gripped a hand on her buttocks. "But I might have to ride out and stir something up, see what's keeping Fox and the men. With the Wolf Hearts lying low, a man needs something to scalp or skin." He looked off toward the well where Darton Alpine and Ohio Phil walked along with their rifles under their arms, returning from scouting the trails.

"Both of you come over here," he called out. "I'm wondering what's become of my boy."

Bertha kept herself from smiling. If only she could get rid of him. If only something or someone would kill him—the Apache, the Ranger or, she didn't care what, a bear, a rattlesnake bite.

"What will I do while you're gone?" she said with a pout.

"Keep these big sweet legs crossed if you know what's good for you," Pridemore said as Alpine and Ohio Phil walked over to them.

Bertha smiled and pulled away from him.

"I'll just leave you fellows to talk," she said, turning to the open saloon doors.

"Get our horses ready, Dart," Pridemore said as Bertha walked inside the big saloon. "We're going to look for Fox and that idiot Ozzie—see if we can't find some hair to cut on our way."

Fox Pridemore, Ozzie Cord and Silvar Stampeto sat atop their horses looking out and down onto the large mining complex that took up an entire terraced hillside a half mile below them. Terese Montoya sat on her paint horse beside Fox. The

Mexican gunmen and their horses stood a few yards behind them, all of them feeling better after Fox had decreed a night of drinking whiskey and cocaine after a day of pillaging.

Upon leaving Casa Robos, they had burned the stores, cantinas and businesses to the ground. At Ranchero Casa Robos, a large spread just north of the village, they had killed four unsuspecting vaqueros and stolen enough fresh horses to make a fast getaway after robbing the mine payroll.

"So far you've done good, Silvar," Fox said to Stampeto.

"Yeah, so far you've done good, Silvar," Ozzie echoed, giving Stampeto a sharp stare.

"Everything has been just the way you said it would be," Fox said.

"Yeah," said Ozzie Cord, "everything has been the way—"

"All right, that's enough, Oz," Fox cautioned his friend, cutting him short.

Ozzie fell into silent brooding.

Fox looked all around.

"What do you suppose happened to Paco?" he asked. "By now he should have killed them old folks, or stopped chasing them."

"Paco gets too much cocaine, he is like a bulldog," said Stampeto. "He can't turn something loose. He no doubt is still chasing the old couple."

Fox gave him a cold stare.

"Maybe you made a mistake sending him," he said.

Ozzie started to repeat his words but caught himself and stopped.

"Want me to ride back—see if I can find him?" Ozzie said.

"No," said Fox, still staring at Stampeto. "If anybody goes back it'll be Silvar here. And if he ain't back when we rob these French, Paco ain't getting paid. Fair enough, Silvar?"

"Yes, it is fair," Silvar said, his dark eyes lowered as if in shame. "When Paco joins us, he will answer to me."

"He better," Fox warned. He nodded down at the valley floor far below them where a flatbed Mexican ore wagon made its way around the winding dusty trail. Men in straw sombreros and narrow Cornish mining hats lined the wagon's sides, their legs dangling in a stir of dust from the rolling wheels.

"Who's these flatheads?" Fox asked Stampeto.

"These are men who work claims outside the main yard," he said. "The wagon brings them in on payday. They get their money and spend it on everything the company brings here to sell to them." As an example he pointed off to a large tent being set up inside the yard.

"I see." Fox nodded as he looked at women lounging half-dressed on blankets spread on the ground while they awaited their facility. A long plank bar was being set up near a small payroll shack. Crates of whiskey and wooden beer kegs sat stacked and ready in the shade of a canvas overhang.

"At noon the guards will escort the paymaster and his assistant to that table." Stampeto pointed to a long wooden table out in front of the payroll shack. "The paymaster will blow a whistle. Everybody will stop work and get in line for their pay."

Fox smiled a little to himself.

"You've been watching this place for a while, Silvar," he said quietly.

"I have spent many hours on this spot, seeing this month after month. We all longed to rob it, but our leader was too lazy to allow us to do so," Stampeto said. "When we leave here with the money, the *federales* will hear of it and come after us. But they will not try too hard to catch us. They hate the French, like everybody else." He smiled.

"Anything else you need to tell us?" Fox asked. "I don't want anybody surprising us once we get started."

"No surprises," said Stampeto, gazing down on the large rocky mining yard, the armed rifle guards walking back and forth inside a set of open iron gates. "Our only problem is to get inside. When they see us coming they will try to close the gates."

"We won't let them do that," Fox said, closely studying the scene on the hillside below them. "How many men will be standing in the line when the pay gets started?"

"I've seen the line stretch thirty, maybe forty men long," said Stampeto.

"Not counting the ones already at the bar and inside the whore tent once the paying gets started," said Fox.

"That's right," said Stampeto, "not counting all the whores and drinkers." He looked at Fox curiously. "Getting any ideas how we need to do this?" he asked.

"Yeah, I got it all worked out," Fox said, backing his horse and turning away from Terese, Stampeto and Ozzie. "Break up your Perro Locos, have them meet down as close as they can to the gates without being seen. When Oz and I come riding through, all of you fall in beside us."

Stampeto just stared at him for a moment.

"And that's it?" he asked finally.

"Mostly," Fox said as if brushing the matter aside. "We go in shooting. You stick with Oz and me while the Perros Locos mix into the drinkers and the whores. The guards won't be so quick to take a chance shooting their workers." He turned his horse and put it forward at a walk, leading Terese on her paint horse beside him.

"There you have it," Ozzie said as Stampeto looked around at him. "You stay close to me, and do everything I tell you."

"That's not what he told me," Stampeto said.

"That's what *I'm* telling you," Ozzie said, thumbing himself on the chest. He nodded toward the Mexican banditos. "Now let's go talk to the Perros Locos, get this thing under way."

The leader of the mine guards, a big Norwegian named Arvid Asp, stood out in front of the payroll shack watching the line of employees move along in an orderly manner. He smoked a cigar as he twirled a two-foot-long hickory club by a leather hand strap looped around his wrist. But he stopped twirling the club when he saw one of his gate guards running up to him. Asp stood watching him curiously until the man slid to a halt with a concerned look on his face.

"Why are you running, Henri?" Asp queried in a stern tone, always striving to keep things orderly in the yard, especially while payroll was being distributed.

"We have two riders coming to our facility at a hard run," Henri Deloof said, out of breath, having sprinted all the way from the front gates.

"Are they being pursued?" Asp asked. As he spoke he craned his neck and stared toward the front gate.

"I—I don't think so," said Deloof. "But they are in a big hurry. We thought you should know."

"Yes, of course, Henri," said Asp. He started twirling his club again. "But settle down. We don't want our miners to see you so excited over two riders, do we?"

"No, we do not," said Deloof, calming down quickly now that he saw his superior was not too concerned with the news.

As the two spoke, a Texan guard named Jep Rayburn came trotting from the gate.

"Now what . . . ?" said Asp. The club stopped twirling.

"Boss," the Texan called out in a drawl, "we best shut the gates. There's three more fell in with them! Looks like an attack coming this way!"

Asp and Deloof looked at each other. The employees in line fell silent and looked off in the direction of the open gates.

"Yes, Jep!" Asp shouted, jerking the cigar from his mouth. "Tell Lobeau to shut the gates immediately!"

"You best come a-running, Asp," said Lep. "Lobeau don't listen to nothing I say."

"Consorn it all" said the big Norwegian. He and Deloof ran toward the front gates, Jep Rayburn falling in with them on their way. "What kind of imbeciles would attack a well-armed facility such as ours?"

"Folks will do most anything these days, boss," said Rayburn, he and Deloof giving each other a look.

At the gate, the senior French guard, Dillus Lobeau, saw the three guards coming and pointed out at a roiling cloud of trail dust on the trail leading straight to the gates.

"There's more of them now, Asp!" he shouted. He'd already walked over to the large iron wheel and started turning it, drawing the iron-barred gates shut. "Must be some kind of suicide riders, is the best I can make of it."

"Suicide, *ha*!" shouted Asp. "We'll show them *suicide* if that's what they're looking for!" He leaped up onto a stone column beside the left gate and climbed a ladder to the top, fifteen feet up.

"*Jesus!*" said Rayburn, looking up at Asp. "What the hell's he doing?"

"Stop this at once!" Asp shouted at the riders thundering toward the gates of the mining facility. "This is the property of the sovereign nation of—" He stopped short as a volley of gunfire ripped through him and flung him backward off the column and onto the ground with a heavy thud.

"Oh yeah, we're in trouble," Jep Rayburn said, grabbing his rifle from where it leaned against a low stone wall.

Stunned by seeing Asp fall dead on the ground, Lobeau froze with his mouth gaping. He stopped cranking the gates shut, crouched low and ran to the cover of a nearby freight wagon as more gunfire erupted from the riders.

"For God sakes, Lobeau!" Rayburn shouted at the fleeing guard, seeing the gates still open ten feet wide. "Henri! Close the damn gates!" He raised his rifle to his shoulder, returning fire.

Deloof made a stab at cranking the gates shut, but the riders had gained so much ground that he saw he would never get the task completed.

"These are Mexican bandits!" he shouted at Rayburn as bullets banged and thudded against the partially closed gates.

"I don't give a damn if they're Chinese laundrymen!" Rayburn shouted in reply. "Get the gates shut!" Even as he made his demand, he saw for himself that the riders had gotten too close too soon. As bullets sliced through the air, Deloof had to abandon his task and make a run for cover. The riders were so close now that they were riding back and forth twenty feet from the gates, firing at will.

"Holy jumping cats!" shouted Rayburn, seeing two riders throw out lariats from their saddles and loop the gate handles and hold them open. "Get to the pay shack and hold them back from there!" he shouted, seeing the two riders loop the lariats around their saddle horns and begin to pull the big gates farther open.

In the yard miners ran wild, some taking cover, other racing to their shacks for guns and weapons. Shrieking whores took cover behind the bar. The payroll clerk had scooped up his paperwork and made a run for it.

"Jesus, we're dead, boys," Rayburn murmured, firing as he moved backward toward the payroll shack, stunned by the relentless speed and fierceness of the outlaws.

Chapter 17

───────

As the two riders pulled the gates open wider with their lariats, Fox Pridemore led the Perros Locos inside, firing and trampling into the crowd of drinking miners and scantily clad women. Guards, joined by a few miners with guns, took positions in the payroll shack, ready to defend the large amount of cash on hand. But instead of attacking the shack straight-on, Fox led his bandits into the crowd and began herding them into a tight circle like cattle being prepared for slaughter.

"The hell are they doing now?" Jep Rayburn said to anyone listening inside the payroll shack. As soon as he asked he saw a miner fall from one of the guard's bullets that had sliced through a bandit's arm and hit the hapless miner in the chest.

"Got one!" shouted the guard, firing from an open window. He quickly levered a fresh round into his rifle chamber.

"You hit one of ours!" Rayburn shouted above the roar of gunfire. "Good God, men, stop shooting!" He waved a hand up and down in the looming gun smoke. Another miner fell on the street even as the shooting inside the shack halted.

As the firing from the shack stopped, so did the shooting from the bandits, except for Ozzie Cord, who had dragged a half-naked woman up onto his lap while she screamed and kicked.

"Easy, woman, easy," Ozzie said into her ear. "Don't make me start whittling on you." He reached his free hand around and plopped his big scalping knife across her naked lap.

The woman settled, trembling but under control.

"That's good," Ozzie said. He slipped a hand around, cupped her exposed breast. "Every time I shoot, you scream, else I'll clip the noses off your puppies and use them for earplugs."

The woman gasped, believing he'd do what he said.

Holding her against his chest as a shield, Ozzie continued firing, spacing his shots to every fifteen or twenty seconds, his rifle resting on the woman's bare shoulder. Every time he fired the woman screamed as if being tortured.

"Hold your fire!" Rayburn shouted, jerking a white handkerchief from his lapel pocket. "We're not shooting back! See?" He stepped into full view in the open window and gestured the white hand-kerchief back and forth.

This is how easy it is robbing a payroll, Fox told himself. He gave a slight smile, his horse restless, stepping back and forth among the miners and the women. Every few seconds Ozzie fired another round into the closed door of the shack. With every shot the woman on his lap screamed loudly.

"Jesus, I can't stand much more of this," Rayburn said to the men nearest him.

"Then lucky for you I'm here," said the gruff voice of the head mine engineer, Harvey Gatts. He stood up from behind an overturned desk in front of a large safe that he had closed and locked as soon as the shooting started. "I'll get this nonsense organized." He walked to where Rayburn stood in full view. He jerked the handkerchief from his hand and shoved him aside.

"See here, you rapscallions," he shouted out at Fox. "Have your man stop that infernal shooting this instant! I won't even speak to ill-mannered saddle tramps."

Ill-mannered saddle tramps?

Fox grinned. He still sat alone atop his horse while the rest of the bandits had grabbed miners and women for shields.

"I can't stop him. He likes shooting at you," he called out to the engineer. Around him the Perros Locos gave a laugh as Fox continued. "You know what we're after. Give it up. Else we start killing everybody out here."

Fear stirred among the crowd. The miners and the women surged, but the riders held them herded in.

"I'm afraid you're in for a disappointment," Gatts said confidently. "You have killed the only man who knows the combination to this safe." As he spoke he looked shrewdly at Rayburn.

"Don't fool with these men, sir," Rayburn warned. "He looks like one of them scalpers—"

"Oh, shut up, Rayburn," said Gatts, cutting the Texan off. "Had you and the guards done your job, we wouldn't be in this pickle."

Rayburn just stared at him. *All right, son of a bitch. . . .*

"You're the one in for a disappointment," Fox called out to the shack window. A shot resounded; the woman screamed. "Give over the money or we will blow the shack up . . . all of you with it."

"All right, I've got him talking," Gatts said under his breath to Rayburn. He kept the white handkerchief waving in his hand. "Stop the shooting, put the woman down and let's talk," he called out to Fox.

Instead of answering Gatts, Fox called out over his shoulder to Silvar Stampeto, "Hey, *segundo*, get over to the dynamite shack. Bring us back, say . . . five or six sticks—some fusing too." He turned and grinned at the engineer waving the handkerchief in the window. "We'll blow up the shack, then the safe."

"That will do you no good," Gatts called out. "You'll blow up the money when you blow up the safe. You still won't leave here with any money."

"So?" Fox shrugged. "We didn't come here with any." He gave Ozzie a look as Ozzie sat with his rifle cocked and ready on the woman's bare shoulder.

"That would be the most idiotic, mindless, irresponsible thing you could possibly—" Gatts' words stopped as a shot exploded from Ozzie's rifle, followed by the woman's scream.

Gatts' blood splattered all over Rayburn as the shot flung the engineer backward, leaving the handkerchief hanging suspended in the air for a second. Rayburn grabbed the handkerchief in reflex as Gatts flew backward across the shack, across the overturned desk and slammed against the big locked safe door. A misty streak of blood trailed in the air behind him.

"Anybody here feels like getting blown up today, raise your hands," Rayburn said democratically, wiping Gatts' blood from his eyes with the handkerchief he'd retrieved on the fly.

The miners and guards looked at each other and shook their heads.

"That's what I thought," said Rayburn. He waved the blood-smeared handkerchief in the window and called out to Fox, "You've got it all, mister! We're giving it up."

"Throw out your guns," Ozzie called out. He whispered into the woman's ear, "See . . . ? You get to keep those puppies, nose and all."

Fox smiled and looked around at Stampeto and the Perros Locos. He motioned for Terese to move her horse over beside him. She had ridden in wearing a large sombrero like one of the bandits. Joining Fox, they watched rifles, shotguns and revolvers fall out of the window onto the rocky ground. A small Uhlinger pocket pistol slid over by her foot. She stepped down from her horse and stretched her back and stood watching for a moment. Before stepping back into the saddle, she managed to pick the small pistol up and hide it in her clothing without being seen. A moment later the shack door opened and Jep Rayburn stepped out, the men filing behind him, all of their hands raised chest high.

"You'll have to blow open the safe door," Rayburn said. "The engineer was right about none of us knowing the combination. He knew it. So there's that, unless you can raise the dead." He gave a shrug.

Fox cocked his head slightly.

"Are you sure you don't know the numbers?" he asked.

"If I did, it's possible I would have robbed it myself," he said. "I once went so far as to figure the miles between here and every water stop on the way to the Guatemalan border." He stared at Fox. The bandits gave a hearty laugh.

"You seem like a cool hombre," Fox said. "Play your cards right, you won't have to die here before we leave."

"You get the money you come for," said Rayburn, "why does anybody have to die?"

"See what I mean?" Fox said, wagging a finger at Rayburn. "That sounds like a man who's looked down a gun barrel from both ends."

"I'm not admitting nothing," Rayburn said calmly to Fox, noting the eyes of the miners on him.

"Why don't I shoot him, Zorro?" Ozzie blurted out for no reason, butting his horse through the crowd over beside Fox.

Fox looked at him curiously.

"Easy, Oz," he said, surprised by Ozzie's sudden outburst. "The man and I are speaking civilly here."

"Zorro . . . ?" Rayburn ventured to ask.

"It's a long story," said Fox, brushing it off.

Ozzie settled but stared coldly at Rayburn. Fox noted that instead of cowering under Ozzie's stare, Rayburn gave it right back to him.

Nodding at the bar, the crates of whiskey and the kegs of beer, much of which had been overturned in the melee, Fox said to Rayburn, "I don't suppose you'd object to my men having a drink?"

Coolly, Rayburn looked back and forth at all the Perros Locos staring at him from among the women and the miners.

"Not at all," he said. "In fact, have one yourself while the miners blow open the safe." He offered a thin, wry smile. "I'll even have one with you."

Silvar Stampeto and the Perros Locos looked on while two Cornish miners prepared an adequate proportion of dynamite to take the heavy door off the safe. Out in front of the shack, Fox, Ozzie and Jep Rayburn sat atop a freight wagon load of desks, chairs and other burnable wooden items. Terese Montoya sat at Fox's side. As they waited for the safe to blow, they passed a bottle of mescal back and forth between them. Ozzie sat brooding silently while Fox and Rayburn talked.

"Sure, I remember Pridemore's trading post," Rayburn said, having heard about how the Apache had burned the trading post to the ground. "Been a while since I was by there." He raised a drink from the mescal bottle and wiped a hand across his lips. "I recall Bigfoot had two sons. . . ."

Fox looked around at the miners and women who sat cross-legged on the ground in the mine yard. One of the Perros Locos stood guarding them with his rifle.

"Yeah," Fox said. "But the heathen Apache killed my brother, Lucas."

"Damn heathen Apache," said Rayburn, passing the mescal bottle to Fox.

"And I was there when it happened, so don't tell me," Ozzie put in quickly, pounding himself on his chest as if proving something. He fell silent again when Fox and Rayburn both looked at him curiously.

"Here she blows, Zorro!" shouted Stampeto, he and the others running out of the shack, the two Cornish miners right behind them.

Fox only hunkered down a little and put a hand atop his battered hat. As did Rayburn and Ozzie. The people seated in the yard hugged the ground. When the dynamite exploded, the earth beneath the freight wagon shook violently. The remaining shards of glass in the shack windows blew out. A black plume of smoke erupted from the windows and doors, even through cracks in the plank walls.

Fox stood up on the freight wagon and fanned the smoke and dust. Rayburn and Ozzie stood up beside him. Fox reached down and pulled Terese to her feet. She rose reluctantly.

"When you leave here, what say you take me with you as hostage in lieu of killing everybody?" Rayburn asked, just between him and Fox.

Fox appeared to consider it as he stepped down from the freight wagon and lifted Terese down beside him.

"All depends," he said to Rayburn.

"On what?" Rayburn asked.

"On whether or not I see a ton of money in that big ol' safe," Fox said.

Rayburn nodded to himself, having seen all the payroll money stacked inside the safe right before Gatts shut the door and twisted the dial.

"Sounds fair to me," he said to Fox.

"Are you wanting to join us?" Fox asked on their way to the shack thirty feet away. He kept his voice low and guarded, against any of the miners hearing him.

"I'd join you, sure enough," Rayburn said. "Soon as this is over, it's a sure thing my job here is over."

Fox just looked at him, knowing there was more.

"All right, the fact is I'm through going straight," Rayburn said. "I need to get on the other side of the law . . . where the money is." He gestured Fox inside the shack where the Perros Locos stood staring through the smoke at the payroll money.

"Now, right there is some serious money," Fox said, staring as if in awe for a moment.

"Holy Moses!" said Ozzie, staring wide-eyed at the stacks of cash. "We could buy us a whole string of Chinamen and use them for target practice. Drink whiskey . . . shoot Chinamen, all day long," he added as he visualized it.

"Huh-uh. This is just the start, Oz," said Fox. "We're going to be doing a lot of this from here on out."

"Whoo-ee! I'm good with that too," Ozzie said, barely containing himself.

Jep Rayburn stood watching, listening, figuring his best chances at staying alive.

"Well, the money's all there," he said to Fox. "Where does that put us?"

"You really want to ride with us?" Fox said, studying his eyes closely.

"I don't say things I don't mean," Rayburn replied. He held Fox's without wavering.

Fox considered it; then he looked around at Ozzie, Stampeto and the Perros Locos where they stood waiting to pull out the stacks of money and sack it all up.

"Everybody, listen," he said. "This Texan, Jep Rayburn, is going with us when we leave here. Don't none of you go shooting him thinking he's following us. He's on our side. All right? Everybody got that?"

The men stifled a laugh. They all nodded in agreement except for Ricardo Mirano, who stood holding a hand to a bullet wound in his lower side.

"How bad are you hit?" Fox asked.

"I'll . . . be all right," Mirano said with effort.

"Then stick a rag in. If you slow us down we'll have to finish you off," Fox said with no compassion.

"I will watch about him," said Sergio Sega. Fox only turned away.

"*Segundo*," he said to Stampeto, "get the money bagged and bring it out. "We're going to run off all their horses and burn this place to the ground."

"And I get to kill all these fools—right, Zorro?" Ozzie called out.

"Not this time, Oz," said Fox. He turned and held his hand out to Rayburn; the Texan raised his Colt from its holster and laid it in Fox's hand. Fox nodded at the front door and followed Rayburn out onto the street.

"All of you listen good," he called out to the miners. "We're not going to kill you. Instead we're taking your horses and leaving you with a fire to put out." He gave Rayburn a shove toward their horses. "We're taking this one with us. I see any sign of you following us, I'll stick his head on a rock and leave it for you."

The miners stood dead silent. Fox looked at one of the Perros Locos, Otis Seedy, guarding the miners and said, "Take him to get his horse. Watch him. He's one of them *slippery* Texans." He gave Rayburn a wry half grin when Rayburn looked at him.

"Let's get the hell out of here, Zorro!" Ozzie shouted, he and Silvar Stampeto walking out of the shack, each with a large canvas bag of money on his shoulder.

Chapter 18

The miners and the women stood watching as the bandits' horses thundered through the open iron gates, out of the mining complex. Fox Pridemore rode at the head of the group, Terese Montoya beside him. Ozzie, Stampeto and Jep Rayburn flanked their leader, Ozzie and Stampeto carrying the canvas money bags tied down behind their saddles. Behind them the Perros Locos herded along every horse and mule and cart donkey the mining company owned. Flames licked and swirled on every building in the complex.

"Zorro, huh?" said a bald miner with a purple gun barrel welt atop his head. He spat on the ground in contempt as the riders thundered out of sight in a rising cloud of dust. "I'd walk forty miles to see them hang real slow."

"What about Jep Rayburn?" another miner asked. "Reckon they'll kill him when they get where they're going?"

"I wouldn't worry about Rayburn if I was you," the bald miner said. "This bunch will be lucky if he don't kill them and take all the money for himself."

"Yeah, *our* money," the other miner said, staring out at the dust drifting on the air.

"Damn right, *our* money." The bald miner stared at the dust with a bitter twist in his lips. "I expect we'll never see any of it again."

Once out on the trail, Fox Pridemore led the riders at a hard, fast pace for the next half hour. When they arrived at the place along the trail where they'd hidden the fresh horses they stole from Ranchero Casa Robos, they dropped from their tired horses' backs. They immediately switched their saddles and gear over onto fresh mounts and prepared to ride on. Jep Rayburn managed to strip his saddle and bridle from his tired horse and grab one of the mine horses before Ozzie and Stampeto shooed all the animals away into the hills.

"Where we headed now?" he quietly asked Terese Montoya, who stood saddling her fresh horse beside him.

"I don't know. Don't talk to me," she whispered nervously, casting a glance in the direction of Fox and Ozzie Cord. "If my husband sees you he will kill us both."

"Your husband, ma'am . . . ?" said Rayburn, his voice also at a low whisper. "You don't remember me, Terese, but I remember you from Poco Aldea." He stared at her. "Your husband was a fellow by the name of—"

"Carlos Montoya," Terese said, finishing his words for him.

"That's right, Carlos Montoya," said Rayburn. "A big tough hombre as I recall. What happened to him?"

"What do you think?" she said with a snap, gesturing a glance toward Fox. "Shut up before you get us killed."

"You mean ol' Zorro there killed Carlos?" he said as if in disbelief. "Had I known Carlos was that weak, I wouldn't have paid him that night."

Terese looked at him closer. "You mean, you and me? We . . . ?"

Rayburn chuckled and shook his head.

"I swear you gals have a short memory," he said.

Terese started to grab her horse's bridle and walk away, but Rayburn also grabbed the bridle and stopped her. "I'm not here long, honey, so listen to me," he said quickly. "If you want to leave here with those bags of money, be ready when I make my move." He turned loose of the bridle and took a step back. Terese stood staring at him without reply, but Rayburn saw an answer in her dark eyes.

"What the hell's taken you so long, Rayburn?" Ozzie called out from atop his fresh mount twenty feet away. "How long does it take a Texan to get saddled?"

"You don't want to be telling me how to saddle a horse, *mi amigo*," Rayburn said with a threat to his voice.

Ozzie turned his horse angrily to step it toward him. "I will tell you any gawd-damn thing I please —" He stopped short as Stampeto put his horse between the two of them.

"Zorro says *let's ride*," Stampeto reminded Ozzie, who had stopped a little too easily, Rayburn noted.

"Yeah, *Zorro* says ride, let's ride," Rayburn said,

a thin smile of contempt for Ozzie on his face. He cut a quick glance to Terese, who sat atop her fresh horse watching. He gave her a guarded look to make sure she understood he wasn't afraid of anybody here. *Look at me. I'm the best chance you've got,* his eyes told her before she turned her horse away and took her place beside Fox.

"What's going on over there?" Fox asked her as she sidled her horse up to him.

"I don't know," she said, shaking her head. Then she lowered her voice and said, "I think your amigo, Ozzie, starts trouble with everyone."

Fox chuckled as the men gathered atop their horse to fall in behind him.

"So you don't like Oz, huh?" he said. When he saw her turn silent on the matter, he said, "It's all right, you can tell me. I won't say anything."

"I do not like him. I do not like the evil way he looks at me," she said.

"You're a whore," said Fox. "What do you care how he looks at you?"

"It is true I am a whore, and because of it I know when a man likes to hurt women. This one likes to hurt women—he likes to hurt *anyone* he can. He has evil ways." She nodded toward Ozzie, who sat with a hand resting on a bag of money tied down behind his saddle.

Fox gave a short laugh.

"Evil ways, huh?" he said. "You might want to get used to his ways. He asked me if he can be your husband when I get through with you."

Terese looked stunned and frightened.

"What—what did you say?" she asked in a shaky voice.

Fox shrugged and stepped his horse forward. "I told him we'd have to wait and see."

"But you won't do that, will you . . . give me to him?" Terese said, her voice weakened at the very thought.

Fox shrugged.

"I haven't decided yet, little darling," he said. "But it's always hard to say no to a friend."

Terrified, Terese stared to reply, but before she could Jep Rayburn rode on Fox's other side.

"Drop back now," Fox said to her. "I want to talk to this slippery Texan—man talk," he added with a half wink.

Rayburn gave the woman another look as she reined her paint horse back from beside Fox. He had no idea what they been talking about, yet something told him she had suddenly decided to give his offer closer consideration.

"What went on back there between you and Oz?" Fox asked him when Terese was back far enough to not hear them.

"Not much," Rayburn said. "Just your pal Ozzie wanting to crowd a new man." He paused and then said, "I'm glad to be riding with you, Zorro . . . especially glad to see how you set it up to the miners. For a minute there I was thinking I was a hostage." He gave a slight chuckle.

Fox only looked at him.

"Everybody's a hostage," he said flatly.

Rayburn didn't know how the young bandit leader meant it, but he let it go. He wasn't worried. Living or dying never worried him. He'd been around enough to know that most bad hombres were only as bad as their opportunity allowed them to be. Fox was testing him, seeing how he responded.

So take this, Zorro, he said silently to himself.

"Good way of looking at it," he said casually. "I've been trying to recall . . . no offense, but didn't your pa have one son who was a little slow?" He said it matter-of-factly. "I take it he'd be the one the Wolf Hearts killed?"

Fox just looked sidelong at him.

"Yeah, he would be," Fox said, "unless you're thinking I'm slow-witted."

"No," Rayburn explained. "For all I know you could have had a third brother. Anyway, I said *no offense.*"

Fox nodded and gazed ahead toward a distant hill where a trail would swing them around and put them back toward the village of Big Sand.

"None taken," he said. "It was Lucas they killed. I always looked out for him best I could. He put up a good fight, but in the end they got him—nothing I could do."

"Sorry to hear it," said Rayburn. "But I'm glad I asked. I was starting to think maybe Ozzie was your brother." He studied Fox's profile, trying to see how he would take that.

Fox chuffed and said, "So you think Ozzie Cord is slow-witted?"

Rayburn didn't answer.

"I can see how you might," Fox said. "Ozzie was riding with his uncle's mercenaries. I met him the day Lucas got killed. We became friends after that."

"All right, that explains it," Rayburn said.

"Explains what?" Fox asked.

"Why you let him think he's your *segundo*," Rayburn said. "Nothing against him, but he's got as much business being your *segundo* as I have being president." He paused and waited, unsure of how Fox would take it.

Fox gave a slight grin, staring ahead.

"Stampeto is my *segundo*," he said. "Ozzie just keeps an eye on him for me."

"Neither of the two could count to ten if he ever lost a finger," Rayburn said.

"You've got guts for a new man, Rayburn," Fox said, giving him a harsh sidelong look. "I'll give you that."

"I'm glad to be riding with you, Zorro," Rayburn said. "I want us to make lots of money without one of these fools getting us killed."

"These fools just put your mine out of business," Fox said coolly.

"It was *you leading* that made this robbery work," said Rayburn. "I saw it all from the other side. Without you this bunch would never have made it through the gates."

Fox fell silent for a few seconds.

"We've just got started, Rayburn," he said finally. "I've seen you've got guts. That's why you're still alive. Now let's see if you've got brains to go with them."

It was afternoon when the Ranger rode into the mining camp. After following the hoofprints on the ground and the steady rise of black smoke for the past seven miles, he wasn't surprised to see the burnt buildings or the dead miners lying in a row covered with canvas tarpaulins. No sooner had he arrived inside the gates than an assistant mine engineer named Doyle Paulie walked up to him carrying a telescope, flanked by three armed miners. The assistant looked relieved by a closer sight of Sam's badge.

"Don't think we didn't see you coming, Ranger," Paulie said, gesturing at the telescope in his hand. "I spotted the badge from a long ways off." He nodded at the ashes, the debris, the skeletal shells of charred wooden structures, still smoking. "Believe me, we're watching anything that moves out there."

"Arizona Ranger Sam Burrack," Sam said, stepping down from the dun, the barb's lead rope in hand. He took off his dusty sombrero as he looked over at the row of bodies. "Anything I can do to help here?"

"Engineer assistant Doyle Paulie," he said, touching the brim of his dusty bowler hat. "We're grateful for your offer, Ranger Burrack. But I believe we've got everything under control here." He gestured a hand around toward where the payroll shack had stood. All that remained standing now was the big safe, its thick door hanging open, its insides empty and blackened from the dynamite blast and the following fire.

"I'll tell you something you can do, Ranger," said a half-hysterical voice of one of the women.

"Please, Molly," said Paulie. He reached a hand out and stopped her from stepping any closer to the Ranger. But it didn't keep her from speaking her piece. "You can get that *idiot* the leader called Oz, and bring him back here to me. I'll see to it he never pees standing up again!"

"Please, Molly," the young assistant engineer repeated.

"Oz . . . ," the Ranger said. "That sounds like Ozzie Cord, the man I'm after."

"He threatened to cut off my—" Molly stopped short for modesty's sake. She glanced around at the miners and held two fingers at the tip of her breast as if wielding scissors. "Do I have to say it?"

"No, ma'am," Sam said, "I understand." He turned back to Paulie and asked, "How far are they ahead of me?"

Paulie looked around at the others as if for affirmation, then said, "Three hours . . . four at the most?" When the miners nodded their agreement, he looked back at Sam.

Four hours. . . . He was getting closer. He breathed a little easier just realizing it.

"If there's nothing I can do here, I'll be getting back on their trail," Sam said.

The man nodded and said, "We've got grain and

water for your horses and the women have fixed some food. You and your horses might move faster with some food and water in your bellies."

"Obliged," said Sam.

Within a half hour the Ranger was mounted and back under way, after a hot meal of roasted elk and gravy with red beans and peppers. Before riding out he had changed his saddle and gear from the dun to the spare horse and gotten rid of most of his supplies—traveling lighter now that the end might be coming into sight. On the ground the hoofprints he was following were fresh and undisturbed. With no heavy rain or any hard sandstorms, he could have good trailing right up to Ozzie Cord's door, he told himself, wherever that door might be.

On a trail leading downward, he stopped long enough to raise his battered telescope and investigate a thin rise of dust on the sand flats below. Adjusting the scope, he brought the image into closer focus and recognized one of the scalpers he'd seen riding toward the Apache warriors two days earlier. As the rider drew closer, Sam saw dark blood on the rider's chest and a grisly string of scalps swinging from his saddle horn. Farther back at the edge of the sand flats, another rise of dust appeared.

The other scalper trying to catch up?

Sam sat on the speckled barb watching until at length he saw the second rider come into better focus and saw him raise a rifle and fire shots at the rider in front.

"It never stops with these men," he murmured to himself and the horses as their ears pricked toward the sound of gunfire.

For the next five minutes he watched through the scope, moving it back and forth from one scalper to the next. The one in front had drawn a big Colt and returned fire back over his shoulder. But as the bullets flew back and forth, the man with the rifle finally won out. Sam saw the front rider's horse go down and tumble in a roil of sand. The rider was alive, and struggled to his feet, jerking the string of scalps from his saddle horn while his wounded horse whinnied and thrashed on the ground.

Sam saw the man on foot hold his Colt out at arm's length and shoot the downed horse in the head, silencing it. But he realized it was not an act of compassion when he saw the scalper drop down and take cover behind the animal's body as the other rider rode closer.

Sam waited, watching, realizing the man behind the dead horse was letting his assailant get more and more into pistol range with every passing second. Rifle shots thumped into the dead horse; the man behind the fresh carcass held his fire, waiting. Finally when the horseman was in good close view, one pistol shot resounded and sent the rifleman flying backward from his saddle.

Sam shook his head and watched as the man stood up from behind his dead horse and walked toward the downed rider. He grabbed the reins to the downed rider's horse on his way. When he'd led the horse closer to the downed man, his big Colt appeared again at arm's length. Sam saw it buck once in his hand. He watched the man swing up onto the dead man's horse and ride off across the flats. "And there's that," Sam murmured. He turned his horses on the trail and went back to following the hoofprints on the ground. *Two down, one to go,* he told himself. He'd have to watch out for this last one. From what he'd seen of these scalpers, they were apt to pop up anywhere.

Chapter 19

In the evening light Fox Pridemore led his men around a rocky turn above the flatlands to the town of Big Sand. When he looked down to his right, he saw both *federale* and U.S. Cavalry troops riding into the desert town, and he waved his riders to a sudden halt behind him. But caught by surprise, Ozzie, horse and all, started sliding sidelong off the edge of the trail. Beside him, Jep Rayburn leaped out of his saddle and caught the unbalanced horse by its bridle. He and Ozzie goaded and wrestled the animal back onto the path and got it settled.

When horse and rider were safe, Ozzie jumped down from his saddle on weakened knees and looked down the three-hundred-foot drop that would have swallowed him and the animal had Rayburn not thought quick, grabbed the horse and gotten it moving forward off the loose gravelly earth and back onto the solid path.

"Man oh man! I was dead!" he said, rubbing his sweaty forehead, seeing loose gravel still showering down into the open chasm. He turned and checked the canvas bag full of money behind his saddle, then turned to Rayburn and looked him up and down as if with new eyes. "Obliged," he said almost humbly.

"Think nothing of it, Oz," said Rayburn, rubbing Ozzie's horse on its nose, settling it more. "I hope you'd do the same for me if it came down that way."

Ozzie looked at him for a moment as if considering it, then said, "I would now."

Watching it from the other side of Fox, Terese noted first thing that Rayburn had shot a glance at the canvas bag tied down behind Ozzie's saddle as he'd made his move. But she kept quiet.

Fox had grabbed Rayburn's horse when Rayburn leaped from his saddle. He handed the reins back to him now and said, "Fast thinking, Rayburn. Right, Silvar?"

"*Sí*, fast thinking, Rayburn," Stampeto said grudgingly, having been closer to Ozzie Cord than the fast-acting Texan, yet not making a move when the horse had slipped.

Ozzie just glared at Stampeto.

"Everybody stay back in these rocks while we see what we've got in Big Sand," Fox ordered.

The men backed their horses on the high, narrow trail. Fox, Ozzie and Stampeto eased upward atop a boulder and lay looking down on the town, Fox with a battered telescope to his eye.

"Yep, just like I thought," said Fox, scanning the streets of the town, its cavalry and the Mexicans. "My pa was afraid this would happen." He lowered the scope and handed it sidelong to Ozzie.

"What's it all mean?" Ozzie asked, taking the

battered lens and looking down through it, seeing sweaty, dusty horses lined up riderless in columns of twos along the narrow streets of Big Sand.

"It means the U.S. and Mexico have joined together to get rid of the Lipans and Mescaleros on both sides on the border," said Fox. "The governments palavered about it a long time. Now here it is."

Stampeto nodded, watching the streets with his naked eyes.

"If they are united to kill Apache, what will stop them from killing us too?"

"All right, let's not get crazy over it," Fox said, scooting back from the boulder's edge and standing. "I'm just glad I spotted them before we rode in with these bags of money strapped down behind us." He gestured toward Ozzie's and Stampeto's horses standing below the boulder on the trail. "Except for all that money, we're just good ol' scalp hunters, out to kill the heathen Apache. I'll say I came all this way and recruited you men to work for my pa's mercenaries." He grinned. "Hell, they'll want to buy us all a drink."

"We're riding in, Zorro?" Ozzie asked.

"Some of us," Fox said, "but not you and Silvar. You're both staying out of Big Sand. I want you keeping an eye on our money. I'm riding in and making an appearance in case we run into these soldiers out on the trail. I don't want us explaining who we are with a sword to our throats."

"Will you bring us back some whiskey?" Ozzie asked hopefully. "I figured it'd be all right to celebrate a little."

"You figured wrong," said Fox. "It's a long way

there and back. I'll be back by morning, but I'm not bringing no whiskey. There'll be no celebrating until we get somewhere and split up the money. Then you can get drunk as a one-eyed hoot owl, far as I'm concerned." He looked at Sergio Sega and Otis Seedy and said, "We rest our horses and ourselves a half hour. Then we ride."

The three of them walked away. Rayburn, Stampeto and the woman gathered wood and built a small campfire. They set a pot of coffee to boil. Ozzie turned sullen and drifted away and sat off by himself until the half hour had passed and Fox and the two Perros Locos walked back up from where they had rested, ready to ride. He only stood up after the three had ridden off along the first of a series of switchback trails leading down to Big Sand. Ricardo Mirano, tormented by the pain in his wounded side, stayed behind with Stampeto, Ozzie, the woman and Jep Rayburn.

As soon as Fox and the two Mexican bandits were out of sight, Ozzie drifted back and joined the others at the small campfire behind the cover of the large boulder. When he'd plopped down beside Stampeto, he let out a huff of breath.

"I know damn well they'll be drinking while they're in Big Sand."

Stampeto didn't answer; neither did Mirano. Ozzie sat brooding, staring into the fire.

Rayburn walked back from attending their horses and sat down across the fire from him. The two canvas bags of money lay just out of the firelight where Fox had put them earlier.

"Damn shame not being able to have a drink on a night like this," he said. As he spoke he pulled a bottle of whiskey from his saddlebags and stood it on a rock beside the fire. "I was going to pass this around tonight, sort of my way of saying obliged for letting me in."

"You mean for not killing you, Rayburn," Ozzie said. He gave him a flat half smile.

"That too, come to think of it," said Rayburn. "Either way it ain't going to happen now." He picked the bottle up and started to shove it back into his saddlebags. "Rules are rules."

Ozzie, Stampeto and the wounded Mexican stared at him.

"Not so fast, Rayburn," Ozzie said. He looked at Mirano and said, "How bad you hurting, Ricardo?"

"Damn bad," said the young Mexican in a pained voice. "My whole side is on fire." He stared longingly at the bottle of whiskey. "I can't see what harm one drink would do, as bad as I hurt."

Rayburn shook his head. "I shouldn't have pulled this out. I don't want to get nobody in trouble."

"Yeah, but this man needs it," Ozzie said. "Look at him. It's not right, a man hurting that bad, can't even have a drink of whiskey."

"Not much we can do about it, though," Rayburn said. "Zorro says no drinking. I don't want to take the chance and have somebody tell him about it." He looked back and forth from one shadowed face to the next.

"The thing is," Ozzie said, "if we all take a drink,

nobody can tell Fox without getting himself in trouble."

A big stupid kid, Rayburn thought listening to him.

Ozzie looked around then at Mirano, then at Rayburn holding the bottle.

"I'm giving this poor sumbitch a drink, and then I'm passing the bottle around." He reached for the bottle. "Any objections?" he asked in a menacing tone. Rayburn handed the bottle over without another word.

Ozzie helped Mirano raise the bottle to his lips and take a drink. Then Ozzie took the bottle, raised it, poured down a long gurgling swig and let out a whiskey hiss.

"Here, Silvar, take a drink and pass it to her." He nodded toward Terese, who sat watching in silence. "Everybody drinks." He gave Terese a dark look.

"Don't worry about running out. I've got more," said Rayburn. He reached into his saddlebags and pulled out a second full bottle. "I grabbed them when I saw we were leaving the mines."

Ozzie took the bottle back after Terese took a modest sip. He poured another long swig down his throat before passing the bottle to Stampeto. Rayburn sat back and watched.

In the middle of the night, Terese had dozed for a moment as the drunken back-and-forth talk among the men waned into snoring around the small fire. She awakened with a start when she felt a hand take her by her forearm. But when she opened her eyes, she saw Rayburn stooped beside her. He whispered, "Let's go," and it immediately came back to her what they were about to do.

Rayburn assisted her to her feet and she looked around the fire at the three passed-out men. Their holsters were empty; their rifles were gone. So were the two canvas bags of money. Yet, upon seeing a big knife stuck in the ground by Ozzie's side, she started to step toward it.

Rayburn's hand on her arm stopped her. She looked at him in the light of the three-quarter moon and saw him shake his head no. He gestured toward their horses, standing only a few feet away, saddled and ready to ride, the canvas bags both tied down behind the saddle on Rayburn's line-back dun. She started to speak, but he touched a finger to her lips and ushered her away from the sleeping men.

When they had gathered the two horses and led them farther away, Rayburn reached out with the knife from his boot well and cut the rope line holding the other horses. He gave one horse a shove on its rump and watched the animals turn and walk away quietly.

"We must kill these men in their sleep," Terese said as Rayburn handed her the reins to her horse.

"No," said Rayburn, "let them face Fox when he gets back. Every second they waste here is a second we gain getting ahead of them. If they start killing each other, so much the better."

Terese nodded.

They led the horses away a few yards, then stepped into their saddles and rode off into the purple night as quiet as ghosts. Behind them two of the three loosened horses milled and nipped at blades of pale wild grass until the trail of their grazing led them away from the sleeping campsite.

The third horse—Ozzie Cord's smoky dun— milled and sniffed and stood around for a few moments like an animal lost. Finally, in its wandering, the animal made its way fireside, stood over Ozzie and stuck its muzzle in his sleeping face, letting out a blast of wet breath. When Ozzie only stirred but didn't awaken, the smoky dun raised its lip, opened its mouth, took a hard bite on Ozzie's nose and shook its head back and forth mercilessly.

Ozzie let out a drunken nasal yelp, swinging both arms, striking the animal. The smoky dun turned Ozzie's nose loose and bolted away ten yards, then stopped and looked back at its staggering owner.

"You gawd-damn flea-bitten, slab-sided son of a bitch!" Ozzie raged and sobbed, his left hand cupped to his bleeding nose. His right hand tried to grab his gun from its holster but found the holster empty. "God Almighty, Silvar! Wake up!" He kicked at Stampeto's shoulder, but Stampeto only grumbled and rolled away onto his other side.

"He's bit my nose off!" Ozzie sobbed. He looked toward the dun with watery eyes. Why? *Why?*

Sobbing overcame his rage as his fingertips

found the sharp edges of bloody severed cartilage hanging between his eyes. The dun stood watching with disinterest outside the small circle of firelight.

Ozzie looked all around on the ground for his Colt, as if he might have lost it in his sleep. When he couldn't find it he looked for his rifle. Nothing. He loosened a bandanna from around his neck and pressed it to his bleeding nose. *This is bad.* Sobering up quickly, he looked around for the canvas money bags. They were gone too! He looked around for Rayburn and the woman, seeing no sign of them. Horses lose . . . money gone.

Oh no!

"Stampeto, you damn drunk, *wake up*! Rayburn's robbed us!" he shouted. Still no response from Stampeto.

Think! Think! he told himself, pacing back and forth, realizing what Fox would do when he got back and found the three of them drunk, the money gone!

"Stampeto, Mirano, wake up!" he shouted. Neither man stirred. He started to kick Stampeto again. But he stopped and fell silent for a moment as an idea started forming. *All right. . . .* He looked all around, saw his knife standing stuck in the ground beside his spot, and reached down and picked it up.

"You should have woke up, fools," he said, looking back and forth at the sleeping men. He quickly rolled up the bloody bandanna and tied it around his face, making sure it pressed his nearly severed nose back in place. His whole face throbbing in pain, he stooped over Stampeto, put a hand down to hold him and slit his throat deep and wide.

The doomed man bucked and kicked, but only for a moment as his lifeblood spewed in every direction. Rising when he felt Stampeto fall limp to the ground, Ozzie walked over to Mirano and methodically did the same thing.

"That'll teach you both for drinking against Zorro's orders," he said in earnest. Wiping the blade on the dirt, he picked up both bottles, one of them empty and the other nearly so. He turned up the one with some whiskey in it and gulped it down. "Waste not, want not," he said.

He walked outside the circle of firelight and threw the bottles off into the brush. The story of what happened here began to assemble itself in his mind.

"That slippery Texan and his pals caught you two off guard, but not me," he said to the bloody bodies on the ground, making it up on the spot. *I was off relieving myself when some men slipped and took these two by surprise. I come running, but something hit me over the head—woke up, this is what I found. . . .* He rummaged through his saddlebags as he constructed the story, even reaching up and rubbing the imaginary knot on his head. Right now the story was full of holes, but he'd work on it along the trail.

He took out a lightweight Navy Colt and slipped it into his holster. Picking up the saddle, he walked to the smoky dun, who still stood watching him.

He saddled his horse and rode away, leading a

spare horse beside him. Behind him the low flames
flickered eerily on the recent dead. The campfire
lay shrouded in the silence of death. At length the
two loosened horses wandered back in from their
night's foraging and prowled about aimlessly until
they finally stood sleeping in the silvery hour of
dawn.

They awakened and pricked their ears at the
faintest sound of the Ranger as he crept up a path
leading behind the boulder. In his left hand Sam
carried his Winchester rifle, pistol-style, cocked and
ready. In his right hand he carried his Colt, hammer
back, his thumb over it, ready to fire. Yet he sensed
something was wrong as he stepped closer to the
low, glowing campfire.

His first indication was the horses standing a few
feet away from the two men on the ground, no lead
rope, no hobbles, nothing. The horses continued to
stare at him curiously as he took a few more silent
steps toward the waned campfire. Then he stopped
again, suddenly. His gun hand tensed as he saw one
of the men's eyes staring straight at him. But he un-
coiled his grasp when he saw the curtain of dark
blood down the man's chest, the open gap in his
throat.

He let out a tight breath. He looked at the other
man and saw the same gruesome handiwork, only
this one with his eyes half-closed staring off at the
pale morning sky.

Chapter 20

The Ranger inspected the campsite in the grainy morning light. He first pressed a hand to each of the dead men's foreheads. He took note of the blackened blood, the slight congealing of it. Next, he stood up and walked all around the campsite. The loose horses followed him as he tried to construct an idea of what might have gone on there on that isolated hillside in the dead of night. But no clear picture came to him. He found the horses' rope line cut and lying on the ground; he found hoofprints leading away from the rope line in opposite directions. One group of prints led to the trail headed down toward Big Sand. Hooves in the other direction led toward any number of narrow paths and game trails leading back in the general direction of the Mexico-France Consorta Mines.

Three sets headed back that way . . . why?

He gazed out across the hill line and the sand flats below. Regardless of the condition the robbers had left the mine company in, he was confident that by now the miners would have gathered horses and arms and put together some sort of search posse. Who would ride back that way?

Finally he pushed up the brim of his sombrero and walked back to the path leading down to where he'd hitched his horses. He'd slipped his Colt into its holster and started to loosen their reins from the juniper when he heard a voice from the brush and rock behind him.

"Leave them where they're standing, mister. You're not going anywhere," the voice said confidently.

Sam heard the slow cock of a rifle and knew it was meant to get his attention. It did. His hand froze for a moment at the hitched reins, then pulled back slowly and rose chest high. He turned to face Fox Pridemore and two Perros Locos, all three with rifles aimed at him.

"Well, now," Fox said, seeing the badge on Sam's chest. "You must be the Ranger who's been dogging my pal Ozzie."

"I am," Sam said, managing to ease his cocked rifle around, his right hand raised but his left holding the rifle aimed and ready at Fox's belly. "Where is he?" he asked, as if not realizing the men were any real threat to him.

"Where is he . . . ," Fox chuffed, and said to his two gunmen, "Can you believe this man?" He said to Sam, "Drop the rifle. We'll go tell him howdy."

Sam ignored dropping his rifle.

"He's not up there," he said. "But two of your men are, with their throats cut."

Fox's stare hardened.

"Get up there, Otis. Check it out," he said to Otis Seedy. As the gunman hurried away along the path to the boulder, he said to the Ranger, "If Ozzie's dead, you'll be joining him in hell."

"I told you Ozzie Cord's not up there," Sam said. "If he was, he'd be in cuffs right now, or dead."

"Keep lying," said Fox. "I've always wanted to kill one of you five-pointed fools." He nodded at the five-pointed Ranger star badge on Sam's chest.

"Jesus, Zorro! They're dead up here!" Otis Seedy shouted down from behind the boulder.

Fox glanced up the path. He hardened his stare as he turned back to the Ranger.

"What about the money, Otis?" he called out.

"There's no money," Sam said.

"Shut up, Ranger," said Fox.

"The money's gone, Zorro," Otis called out.

"Our money is gone?" said Sergio Sega. He stepped forward heatedly, his cocked rifle tight in his hand. "Let me kill this one!"

"Stand down, Sega!" said Fox, shoving the rifle barrel away angrily. "Kill him when the time comes. First let's see about the money."

"He has it!" Sega said, his temper raging out of check.

"Get up there, Sega!" Fox said. "Before I shoot you where you stand."

As the hotheaded bandit turned in a huff, Fox gestured up the path. Realizing it was too late to even try making the Ranger drop his aimed and cocked rifle, Fox sidestepped along with him. Sega rushed on ahead of them.

"Don't even think of trying anything, Ranger," Fox said, the two of them ascending the path by themselves.

"I'm not going to try anything. I'm curious about all this," Sam said, walking on, his rifle steadily aimed at Fox as if he'd had the drop on the three all along.

"Jesus, Zorro, look at this!" Otis Seedy said as the two walked into sight around the boulder. Sega had kneeled over Stampeto's stark pale corpse.

Fox lowered his rifle an inch. Sam noticed, but kept his level and ready.

"Feel his face, Sega," he said.

Sega gave his leader a strange look and started to stand up toward Seedy.

"Not Otis' face, gawd-damn it," said Fox, "Silvar's!"

Sega kneeled back down quickly and placed a hand on the pale face of Silvar Stampeto. He gazed at Fox, awaiting further orders.

Fox let out an exasperated breath, glanced at Sam, then said to Sega, "Is it cold?"

Sega looked all around as if checking the weather.

"No! *Gawd-damn* it!" shouted Fox. "You stupid son of a bitch! Is Stampeto's *head* cold?"

"*Jesus.* . . ." Otis Seedy shook his head and looked away.

"*Sí*, yes," said Sega, finally getting it. "His head is cold." He gave a shrug. "Cold and dead."

Fox looked at Mirano's corpse. "They're both cold. Whoever killed them did it earlier in the night. They were dead when I got here."

"Save your breath, Ranger," said Fox. "I know you didn't do it. We spotted you on the trail before you headed up here. You didn't have time." As he spoke he lowered his rifle a little more.

The two gunmen walked back to Fox and stood awaiting what he had to say.

"Looks like the three of them killed these two and took off with our money," he said. He looked off along the hill trail leading back toward the mines. The other two looked off in the same direction, their rifles slumped in their hands.

Sam knew the money he was talking about was most likely the mine payroll money. But the payroll money wasn't why he was here. The man he was after was still somewhere ahead of him. He had to catch him before the trail between them grew longer. While the three stood looking away, he eased his Colt from his holster and held it leveled at them in his right hand. Now he didn't have to act as if he had the drop on them—he *had it*.

"You want to hear what I think?" he said quietly. Even with the upper hand, he didn't want to spark a gunfight if he could keep from it.

The three turned toward him. First thing, their eyes went to the Ranger's rifle and Colt pointed at them, both guns cocked and ready.

"Easy, fellows," he said calmly. "I'm not your enemy. I don't want your money and I don't want to kill you unless I have to."

Fox let out another breath and glared at his two men, as if they had allowed the Ranger to take over.

"All right, Ranger, what you figure happened here?" His rifle slumped more; he gestured his men to lower theirs.

"Your pal Ozzie killed your men and took your money," Sam said.

"There were two others here," Fox offered. "Ozzie might not have been in on it."

"If he wasn't, he is now," Sam said. "Either way we're after the same man . . . for different reasons."

"That don't make us partners, Ranger," Fox said.

"I'm not saying it does," Sam said. As he spoke he took a step back toward the path to his horses. "All I want is to get out of here without a gunfight. I'm going after Ozzie. I know you are too. I'll stay out of your way if you'll stay out of mine."

"Problem is, I'm not out to kill him . . . leastways not until I know he's done us wrong," said Fox.

Sam took another step back.

"I'm not out to kill him either," Sam said, "unless he pushes me to it."

"You're known as a hard-boned killer, Ranger," Fox said.

Sam replied, "I'm taking him back."

Fox took a step forward as Sam took another step back.

"Ranger, you take Oz back across the border, they're going to hang him," he said.

"I don't care," Sam said. "I don't care if they hang him every day for a month. That's up to a jury. He killed a sheriff." He took another step back. This time Fox stopped and made no effort to keep him from leaving.

When the Ranger was out of sight around the boulder, Otis Seedy started to hurry forward, but Fox stopped him.

"Leave him be," he said.

Seedy and Sega looked at him.

"I don't care what he said. He'll kill Ozzie," said Seedy.

"If Ozzie and Rayburn stole our money, I don't care if this Ranger kills them both, long as we get the money back," said Fox. "Either way, wherever this Ranger goes we'll be right behind him."

"What about the woman?" said Sega.

"Forget about Terese," said Fox. "Whoever's got the money gets the woman. My pa taught me about *putas* a long time ago."

In the morning light Rayburn reined his horse to a halt and sat closely studying the distant sky west of them. At the far edge of the sand flats, dust rose and swirled. To their left the Mexican hill lines lay strewn out in endless rows one after another. To their right a world of heat, sunlight and sand stretched for twenty miles or more, a land filled with dry washes, cactus and stone. The woman had been afraid that at any moment Rayburn might tell her they had to cross that inferno. But he didn't.

"Looks like we're in luck," he said, craning upward in his saddle. "I'm betting this will be the miners coming. If we're lucky we'll meet them straight-on."

"What?" said Terese, taken aback by his words. "You—you want to run into the miners?"

Rayburn stared straight ahead toward the white distant sky.

"I sure do," he said. "I know it's going to take some explaining. But once they understand, they'll be grateful to get their money back."

Terese shook her head, as if to clear it. "But I thought—" She gestured a hand toward the bags of money stacked and tied down behind Rayburn's saddle. "I thought we would keep the money, the two of us. You even said, *How would I like to leave with the money?*"

Rayburn looked around at her, then back out at the dust.

"Yes," he said. "I figured you'd get some satisfaction taking it, after the way you've been treated by Fox."

Terese just stared at him.

"I figured you'd know I meant to return the money to its rightful owners as soon as I found a way to do it," he said.

"I thought you meant you and me, all this money . . ." Terese let her words trail.

"I didn't mean to give you any wrong ideas, ma'am," said Rayburn. "I thought you wanted away from those Perros Locos, before they started passing you around when Fox got tired of you."

"I did," Terese said. "Of course I did." She gestured at the canvas bags. "But the money, the two of us . . . ?" She paused to let the vision sink in. "I could make you so happy for saving me."

"I bet you could, ma'am," said Rayburn, turning away and putting his attention back toward the far-distant riders. "But you've got to understand—I'm a guard. My job is protecting people's money. I take my responsibilities very seriously." He smiled toward the far horizon in satisfaction. "My whole life I've been a bank guard, a shotgun rider . . . a lawman of some sort, off and on. For a time I even considered—"

The sharp crack of the small Uhlinger pocket pistol resounded behind him. His words stopped short; he jerked upright in his saddle. His hand went around to the small of his back and felt the warm blood oozing from the wound.

"You—shot me," he said haltingly. As he said it the small pistol fire cracked again. He stiffened more. The second bullet hole was only a few inches from the first.

Without wasting time, Terese gigged her horse over beside him, jerked his Colt from its holster and aimed it at him. Rayburn stared at her, his face frozen.

"Why?" he said in a failing voice. Even with a bullet in his back he managed to keep his spooked horse under control.

"Why?" said Terese. "Are you kidding me? For the money, you *idiota*." She cocked his Colt at him. "I am a *puta*—a whore. Do you think I have never been passed around before?" She started to pull the trigger, but before she could, Rayburn fell sidelong from his saddle onto the scorching-hot sand.

So much the better. . . .

Before Rayburn's horse could bolt away, she grabbed its reins and yanked it over beside her.

"Give me any trouble and I will shoot you too," she warned the nervous animal. She looked at the canvas bags as though to make sure they hadn't disappeared in their melee. She managed a dry, tight smile in spite of the toll the desert heat had taken on her face, her lips.

With Rayburn's heavy Colt hanging in her hand, she rode away toward the distant rising dust, leading Rayburn's horse—and the bags of money. Knowing she'd have plenty of time to veer over across the flats and avoid whoever was coming, she rode straight ahead for now. She knew of a small village hidden off a hill path that lay only a few miles ahead, a place none of these gringos would know about.

She smiled to herself, lying low on the running horse. Anyway, she told herself, whoever was coming, her life could be in no more danger running into them than it would be facing Fox and his men once they saw the money was missing.

Chapter 21

Riding hard, with a spare horse to shorten his time, Ozzie had made it close enough to hear the two sharp reports from the small pocket pistol. The sound sent him riding harder. So did the sight of dust roiling in the far-distant sky. He stayed on the hoofprints so closely that he almost rode past the spot where dark blood had soaked into the sand.

"Whoa, now!" he said, finally seeing the blood and reining both horses in a sharp circle back to it. He sat in his saddle looking back and forth between the drag marks where Rayburn had pulled himself out onto the flats and crawled up under a stand of low-hanging cactus, the hoofprints of two horses leading straight ahead. Not hard to figure, he told himself. Whoever had crawled out there—*shot*—either was dead by now or soon would be. Either way, the money was with whoever rode away.

Hope you die slow, whoever you are.

He gave a tight little smirk toward the flats, then batted his boots to the spare horse's sides and rode on, his own horse resting, galloping easily alongside him.

"*Adios!* Hope you like warm weather," he shouted out loudly across the hard, desolate land. *Warm weather, get it?* he said to himself. Chuckling at his mindless humor, he put his horses forward, fast and steady.

At midmorning he slowed as he looked far ahead and saw the lone rider veering diagonally up off the edge of the flats up onto a thin, rocky path. The woman? Yes, it was her all right, he told himself, a little surprised at first. But watching her, seeing her stop and climb down from her saddle, he saw her tie the reins of the horse carrying the money to the front horse's tail. She led the two horses up the rugged path as Ozzie gave the matter a quick thought and smiled to himself.

Hell, this could turn out better than he'd ever hoped for, he told himself as he put the horses forward, hoping she wouldn't see him before he got behind her on the bare lower slope and moved into the cover of rock higher up. Even if she did see him, so what? She was scared to death of him. He'd seen that every time he was near her.

Before he got to the path, he turned onto another thin trail leading upward, diagonally meandering across the hillside. *This will work,* he told himself. He kept the horses climbing instead of getting down and leading them.

When he got to where the two paths intersected on a terraced cliff side, he stepped down from his saddle and stood waiting midtrail, his Navy Colt in hand, as Terese climbed the path into sight.

"Well, well, *well — well — well*!" he said, overplaying his response to meeting her there. "I come out to take air and my, my, look who I find."

Terese jerked to a halt, startled, but she acted in quick reflex. Her hand went for Rayburn's Colt stuck down in her waist.

"Huh-uh," said Ozzie. He wagged his Navy Colt at her, the hammer cocked. "You don't want to do that, little darling." He grinned. "Ol' Oz here'll kill you dead."

Terese let her hand drop.

"All right, you've got me," she said. "What now?"

"What now?" Ozzie said. He walked in close and pulled the Colt up by its handles. "What now is whatever I want it to be." He looked at the bags of money, then back at her, standing so close she almost felt him against her. "I'm wondering whether or not I want to spend some time us getting to know each other, or wait until we've found some shade." As he spoke he bumped himself against the full length of her. "What do you think?"

"Listen to me, Ozzie," she said quietly. "I know how this looks, but I had nothing to do with stealing the money. Rayburn made me go along with him."

"That why you killed him?" Ozzie said with a grin.

"Yes, partly," she said, jutting her chin a little. "He is a terrible man who wanted to force himself on me. He would have had I not shot him. I kept telling him, *Please take me and the money back to Fox.* But he would not listen! I killed him, and I knew of nothing else to do but flee for my life!"

Ozzie nodded as she spoke, as if believing her quickly concocted tale.

"Go on," he encouraged her, putting the tip of his Colt up against her breast and jiggling it.

"I—I begged him to take back the money. I even told him I would do things to him. . . ." She paused, then said in a lowered suggestive tone, "Things that only a *puta* like myself knows how to do to a man." Now it was her turn to press herself against him. Her voice became a low wanton whisper. "Things that drive a man crazy with desire. Things that most men can only dream of."

"Yeah?" Ozzie wasn't completely buying it, but he wasn't opposed to the feeling her suggestions aroused inside him. "Like what?" He stood against her, but lowered the Colt a little, liking this fanciful game.

"They are things I cannot tell you about. They are things that I can only show you. Things that I can only *do*, if I really care for a man." She pressed herself more firmly against him.

Jesus!

He looked all around wildly, knowing he'd left his blanket roll behind in his haste. But what about a bed of pine needles, a flat spot on the cliff, in the shade, a downed log? Something . . . *anything!* He didn't care.

As he looked all around, Terese stared at the black bloodstained bandanna tied around his face. A fresh trickle of blood seeped down his upper lip.

"What has happened to your nose, Ozzie?" she asked.

"My horse bit if off," he said, still looking all around.

The woman grimaced.

"It is bleeding," she said.

"Yeah, yeah, I know," he said impatiently. "It's been bleeding all day."

"Does it hurt?"

"Not if I leave it alone," he said, looking down at her. "These things that you know. Does a fellow have to be lying down—?"

Before he got the words out of his mouth, Terese hiked a leg up behind her, slipped off her leather-soled shoe and began batting him on his wounded nose.

To get away from the hard repeated blows, Ozzie fell backward to the ground, screaming and thrashing, blood flying from under the bandanna. As he writhed and bellowed in agonizing pain, Teresa turned and ran, shoe in hand, and leaped atop her horse. Struggling to see through watery eyes, Ozzie pulled his Navy Colt and waved it back and forth, trying to focus on her.

But Terese had seen her chance and she wasn't stopping. Atop her horse, she batted the animal forward, grabbing the reins to both of Ozzie's horses on her way up the trail, the horse with the money bags reined nose-to-tail behind her.

"I'll *kill* you!" Ozzie sobbed and shouted. Staggering, trying to see through a watery veil of pain, he fired wildly in every direction until the Navy Colt clicked on an empty cylinder. Still sobbing, knowing he'd been left afoot, he sank onto a rock and sat slumped, Rayburn's loaded Colt hanging loose in his hand.

Fox, Otis Seedy and Sergio Sega had heard the gunfire in the distance only moments ago. They had pushed their horses along the Ranger's trail for a mile when Fox stopped short, jumped down from his horse and put a hand on its front shoulder. The other two men gathered close and looked down at the animal.

"What's wrong, Zorro?" Seedy asked.

"He's not riding right," Fox said. "I'm afraid he's coming up lame on me." He lifted the horse's front left hoof and twisted it back and forth slightly. The horse nickered a little under its breath. "Yep," Fox concluded, "I felt it no sooner than we left camp. Damn it!" he shouted. He set the horse's hoof back down.

"This is a bad place to be horseless," Sega commented, looking all around.

"I know it," said Fox. He breathed deep and kicked the sand, cursing his luck. Sega and Seedy looked at each other. "I was hoping I'd caught it before it had gotten too far along." He pushed his battered hat up on his forehead and looked all around as if expecting a horse to appear. "Of all the damn lousy luck," he cursed.

"You figure to stay off him awhile, see what that does?" Seedy asked.

"Yeah, I best," said Fox, gazing off in the direction of the gunshots they'd heard. "A couple of days he'll heal up. But damn all that. A couple days is too late with what we've got going on here."

"It can't be helped, Zorro," said Sega. "Do you want us to go on ahead and get the money?"

Fox stared off, considering it.

"If you do, we need to get going," Seedy added.

"Not so damn fast, neither one of you," Fox said. "You're too damn eager to get after that money."

Seedy and Sega looked at each other again, as if shocked by his accusation.

"Zorro," Seedy said. "We're just saying what it is we've got to do. If we don't stay after that money, its gone like a wild goose."

"*Sí*, Otis is right, Zorro," said Sega. "We are at a place where you must trust us."

"Trust you?" said Fox. "Here's an idea for you. Why don't one of you stay here with my horse, let me take yours? Soon as we've got the money I'll get right back here with it. Sounds fair enough, don't it?"

The two sat silent for moment; then Sega let out a sigh and started to swing down from his saddle.

"All right, take my horse," he said.

"Hold it," said Fox. He looked ashamed. "This is not good. I know how this works. It's my horse that's down. I'm the one has to drop back and wait."

Sega sat back down in his saddle.

"It's how things are generally done, if you don't mind my saying so," Seedy put in.

"Oh yeah?" said Fox. "Here's another way." His Colt came up cocked and pointed. He waved it back and forth. The two sat stone still. Finally he let the gun slump. "Damn it, go on, then, both of you!"

He turned away and stared out across the sand flats. The two started to turn their horses back to the trail, but Fox spun back toward them. He raised a finger for emphasis. "But if you try to double-cross me on this, as sure as there's a devil in hell, I'll find you and kill you!"

"We got it, boss," said Seedy. "You needn't worry. We'll be right back for you. You'll see . . . you can trust us."

"Get going," Fox said, dismissing the matter with a wild toss of his hand.

The two Perros Locos turned their horses and booted them out quickly before Fox could change his mind again.

As they rode along, Seedy said sidelong to Sega, "Now, there is man who has a terrible time trusting folks. I bet he goes to the jake one hand holding the door closed behind him."

"He still doesn't have this sitting just right inside his head. I can tell," said Sega.

"Well, that's too damn bad," said Seedy. "It's his horse going down, not ours." They booted up the horses' pace. "Let me ask you something," he said. "What the hell were you thinking, offering him *your* horse?"

Sega shrugged.

"It was foolish, but I wanted him to trust us," he said.

"Yeah?" Seedy grinned. "Well, what were you going to do if he took it and left you standing out here holding the reins to a lame horse?"

Sega thought about it.

"I don't know, kill him perhaps," he said. "Anyway, he did not take it, that's the main thing." They rode on, putting their horses up into a quick gallop toward the six gunshots they'd heard on the distant hillside.

"Two ways on this money when we get it?" Seedy said.

"*Sí*, two ways," said Sega. "You have my word on it."

"Yeah, that's what I'm afraid of," said Seedy. They both laughed a little and rode on.

The Ranger had also heard the shots in the distance. Hearing them, he'd looked up from under the low-hanging cactus where he'd found Rayburn taking shelter from the burning sun. He'd followed Rayburn's drag marks on the ground and upon finding him, he'd carried a canteen of water to him from his saddle horn. Now he sat watching the man replenish himself.

"Ranger Sam Burrack, I guess it goes . . . without saying I'm glad to see you," he said in a halting voice.

"Same here, Jep," Sam said. "Except under these circumstances. I hadn't heard anything about you the last couple of years. Figured you got that spread somewhere and settled down."

"Naw, that ain't going to happen, Sam," Rayburn said. "I took off my badge in Hayes City . . . left Texas. But after a while I took up guarding the mines down here." He adjusted himself and pressed the bandanna firmer against his back. "I never should have turned my back on one of these hard-baked *putas*. I blame myself more than her."

"What were you trying to do anyway, Jep?" Sam asked.

"Just what I figured . . . I was getting paid to do. I was still guarding the money." He gave a pained smile. "Even though it was in somebody else's hands. You know me, Sam . . . I'm like a bulldog. I don't turn loose easily." He took another swig of water. "You believe me, don't you . . . that I was taking the money back?"

"What do you think?" Sam asked.

"Aw, don't pay . . . no attention to me," Rayburn said. "Sounds like I might have been doubting myself."

"Not to me, it doesn't," said Sam. He took the canteen when Rayburn handed it to him. He capped it and laid it by Rayburn's side.

They both looked from under the cactus toward the sound of horses pounding along the trail in the direction of the recent gunfire.

"Perro Locos?" Rayburn asked.

"Yeah," Sam said. "I figured they'd be following me. But Fox isn't with them." He watched the two ride past in a rise of sand and blowing dust without even seeing that his horse's hoofprints had turned out onto the flat.

"You best get after them, Ranger Sam Burrack," Rayburn said with the same pained smile.

Sam laid a loaded Colt down beside the canteen.

"The barb is hitched out of the sun," he said. "I wish I had a saddle for you. Are you going to be able to make it across these flats and get some help?"

"I will . . . you bet," said Rayburn. "I'll wait the sun out and leave when it's cooling. Won't be the first time I rode with bullets in me. I know how it's done."

"I'll come back when I'm finished," Sam said.

"No need, Sam. I won't be here after this evening," Rayburn said. "You left me a horse . . . a gun and some water. What more does a man need?"

"Jep, that was some good work you did here," Sam said.

"Obliged, Ranger," said Rayburn. Again the weak smile. "I like to think I didn't do too bad . . . for a payroll guard."

"Not bad at all," the Ranger said. He nodded, scooted back from under the cactus shade, stood up and walked to his dun. Swinging up into his saddle, he looked west at the same rise of dust he'd been watching and speculating on his whole ride along the desert floor. The riders were getting closer now, he noted. Things were coming to a head.

But where's Fox Pridemore? he asked himself. Not that he cared, just that he didn't want to catch a bullet in his back the way Rayburn had done, when it came time to deal with Ozzie Cord. He turned his dun and put it forward in the hoofprints of the two Perro Locos. His turn to follow them for a change. . . .

Chapter 22

———

Sergio Sega and Otis Seedy had slowed their horses' pace by the time they reached the trail Ozzie had taken onto the hillside. They followed his horse's hoofprints until they spotted Ozzie on a cliff overhang walking on foot, struggling up the same trail Terese had left him on.

"Why is this idiot wearing a bandanna around his face?" Seedy asked, the two of them watching from a long way off. "Is he afraid somebody will *recognize* him up here?" He gave a chuckle and shook his head.

"I don't know," Sega replied humorlessly, "but I will be happy to blow the top of his head off and count the number of rocks in it." He started to turn his horse back to the trail.

Seedy had turned his eyes far up toward the top of the trail Ozzie was on.

"Whoa, hold on, Sergio," he said, stopping him. "We can kill him anytime. Look up there." He directed Sega's attention to the woman who was struggling upward with four horses, counting the one beneath her.

"Ah yes!" said Sega. "I see her. Now to kill this fool and go get her."

Seedy gave him a bemused look.

"Notice anything about her, Sergio?" he said.

Sega studied the woman for a moment, then nodded.

"Yes, I do," he said. He squinted; his voice took on a suspicious note. "Why does she have so many horses?"

"Jesus, I don't know," Seedy said, trying not to sound too disgusted. "What I'm talking about is that she has the money bags, not this idiot."

"Okay . . . ?" Sega said, prolonging his reply, as if expecting more on the matter.

Damn it. . . . Seedy gave him another look. "I'm saying, if we kill Ozzie first, do you suppose she might hear the gunfire and light out on us?"

"Oh . . . ," said Sega. "Yes, I think she might." He nodded to himself.

Seedy just looked at him again, still not certain he understood.

"Follow me, Sergio," he said in a patient tone. "Let's go take all that money from her."

"And we'll kill Ozzie afterward?" Sega asked as they both turned their horses.

"There you have it," said Seedy.

The bandits rode on to where the two trails intersected and turned upward in the direction of the woman and the money. They managed to travel quietly until an hour later when the trail leveled onto a broad stone shelf. There a row of crumbling adobe and weathered-plank *chozas* stood with

their thatched roofs long turned to dust and blown
out across the hillside.

At a bent iron hitch rail, the end dropped from
its stone anchor post, the four horses stood with
their heads bowed as if in prayer. The money bags
were gone. So was the rifle from the saddle boot on
Ozzie's smoky dun.

"Watch your step here," Seedy whispered sidelong to Sega, the two of them stepping down from
their saddles. He gave no response. Yet he shook
his head as Sega looked down and all along the
ground.

Fifty feet away, in the row of adobes and shack
dwellings, Seedy stared at the only place that had a
weathered front door still standing in place. He
drew his Colt from his holster and gestured the
barrel toward the small roofless adobe.

"Which one you think she's in?" he said quietly,
yet almost jokingly.

"How would I know?" said Sega.

"The only one with the door," said Seedy, as if
giving him a clue.

They took a step forward, then ducked quickly
as a rifle shot exploded from an open stone window
frame. In a crouch the two hurried behind the cover
of a low crumbling stone wall.

"Get on your horses and go away! This money is
mine!" Terese called out following her warning
shot.

Seedy looked all around for a better-covered position but found none.

"When have you ever known us Crazy Dogs to

go away when there's money on the line, Terese?" he called right back to her.

"I'll kill you both, the way I killed Rayburn!" she warned, not realizing that Rayburn was at that moment resting out of the sun preparing for his trip across the sand flats.

"Don't break ugly on us, Terese," Seedy warned in reply. "The only reason we stopped to talk about this instead of killing you is out of respect for Carlos." He paused, then added, "There'll be no talking once Zorro gets here. I think you know that." He looked at Sega and grinned slyly. "He's on his way right now."

"*Sí*, I know Zorro will kill me," said Terese. "But where was your respect for Carlos when this man Fox forced me to ride with him, to sleep with him — made himself my husband against my will?"

"All right," said Seedy, "we went along with that because we were told when one outlaw kills another he gets to own whatever that one had, *esposa* or whatnot."

"That is crazy," said Terese. "I never heard of any such thing, and I am a *puta*. I would know."

Seedy and Sega looked at each other for a moment.

"All right," Seedy said. "We might have been misled on that. Being part gringo, I should have kept up on how things are done on the other side of the border. But I didn't. That doesn't change nothing, though. You deal with us, or you'll deal with Zorro when he gets here." He gave Sega a wink and fell silent.

"Deal with you *how*?" she said after a short pause. "What are you proposing?"

Seedy took a deep breath and let it out slow and evenly. *Here goes.* . . .

"I'm proposing you give us the money bags and we let you ride out of here alive—*again*, out of respect for Carlos," he said.

"We'll look the other way when you leave," said Sega, "so we won't know which way you're—"

"Shut up, Sergio," Seedy said, cutting him off. "We're atop a hill here."

"What did he say?" Terese called out.

"Nothing," said Seedy. "He's a fool. Listen to me. We need to make a move here before Zorro comes up this trail."

"What did you call me?" Sega said with a surge of temper in his voice.

Seedy ignored him and called out to Terese, "What do you say, the money for your life?"

"You know what you can go do to yourself," Terese said without having to consider it.

"I'm going to be honest, Terese," said Seedy quickly. "I wouldn't have respected you much had you gone along with that. We're going to do an even split with you. But you've got to hurry it up. We've not got all day here."

A tense silence ensued. Sega stared sullenly at Seedy.

"You called me a fool," he said.

"Shut the hell up," said Seedy almost in a whisper. "Don't you see, once we get inside we'll take all the money. First we've got to get past this rifle—"

"All right, I'll do it," Terese called out.

Seedy spread his hands and smiled.

"See, now we're in," he said to Sega. "It's all ours now, sweet as a young cousin's kiss."

Seedy and Sega left the horses' reins hanging to the ground and walked slowly to the adobe.

"We get inside, let me do the talking, Sergio," Seedy said under his breath.

Sega looked at him with resentment.

"Why's that?" he said.

"Just let me," said Seedy, not wanting to start an argument.

"You had no right calling me a fool," Sega said, his temper still simmering over the remark.

Seedy ignored him. Reaching out, he slowly opened the heavy squeaking door. The two walked in, guns drawn, and saw Terese standing behind a thick weathered table by the back wall. She held Ozzie's rifle cocked and pointed at them.

"This is no way for us to start out doing business," Seedy said, acting a little surprised. He knew he needed the rifle out of her hands if he and Sega were going to shoot her and take all the money. The two canvas bags lay on the table in front of her.

"We're not *starting out*," Terese said. "We're finishing up." She gestured her eyes at the two bags. "They both look the same size. Take one and go."

"Hold on, Terese," said Seedy with a light chuckle. "This ain't how we're doing it. If we just wanted a loose count, and be gone, we'd've had you throw one out the window to us."

"Perhaps I should have," she said. "You come in with your guns drawn at me. I know what that means."

"Oh? And what about you? There you are with a rifle cocked on us," he said.

"All right, we are both armed," Terese conceded. "Take a bag and go, before Fox gets here."

"I'm drawing a knife from my boot," he announced. "Don't go nuts on me—"

"A *knife*? For what?" Terese asked quickly. Her hand tightened on the rifle.

"Easy, now. I just want to slice open a bag and see the money," he said in a calm, reasoning voice, his hand going down slowly toward his boot. "Then we take it and leave. Fair enough?"

"Bullshit!" said Terese. "Lay your gun down and loosen the tie on the bag if you want to see the money."

Seedy stopped; his hand came up away from his boot.

"All right, we can do it that way, now that you mention it," he said, calmly, looking a little embarrassed, Sega thought, watching him. "Here goes," he said. He laid his Colt down on the table beside the canvas bags.

Sega took a step closer, he and the woman watching Seedy closely.

Seedy loosened the knotted tie on one of the bags facing him and spread the top open. He grinned, raised the back of the bag and shook out the contents onto the table.

"What *the hell*?" He stared in stunned surprise.

Instead of stacks of money spilling out, two pine-cones rolled across the table, followed by pine needles, scraps of punk wood and dirty clothes.

"Damn!" said Sega. "We stole the miners' dirty wash."

"It's not the miners' wash, you fool!" shouted Seedy. "This is Zorro's!" He stared at a pair of dirty long johns on the table. Terese stood staring wide-eyed in disbelief. Seedy shook the bag again as if hoping money might yet fall out. But no, only dirty socks, a stiff wadded bandanna.

Sega gave a chuckle and grinned at Terese. "So you and Rayburn weren't so smart after all. You stole Zorro's dirty wash!" He cackled aloud, in spite of there being no payroll money for them.

Hearing him, Seedy gritted his teeth and snatched up his Colt from the table.

"I've had it, Sega!" He swung the Colt around at the laughing bandit. *"You stupid son of a bitch!"*

Sega, his own gun in hand, saw what was coming and turned his big Colt at Seedy. But he was too late. Even as his gun bucked in his hand, Seedy fanned two shots into his belly and sent him flying backward across the small adobe. Terese stood staring at Seedy, the rifle still up, still ready.

Seedy staggered back a step and pressed his free hand to his bloody chest. He stared stoically at Terese as blood oozed down between his fingers.

"That's the . . . stupidest son of a bitch . . . I ever seen," he said, wagging his Colt at Sega lying dead on the floor. "I'm glad I killed him." He managed to turn his Colt and fan it two more times at Terese as the rifle bucked in her hands. Even as she slammed backward against the wall and slid down beneath a wide smear of blood, the top of Seedy's head exploded. Thick blood, bone and soft tissue streaked out the open front door and terrified the already spooked horses.

Sega's and Seedy's two loose horses turned and bolted away, back down the trail. In reflex, the horses hitched to the half-fallen iron rail turned and followed the other two horses. Three of the four hitched animals pulled their reins loose from the rail. But Ozzie's smoky dun wasn't as lucky. The dun ran along at the rear of the fleeing horses, its reins drawn tight around the rail, dragging it along bouncing and clanging beside it.

Less than a mile down the trail, Ozzie, who had hurried as best he could on foot up toward the sound of gunfire, stopped when he heard the horses' hooves pounding down the trail toward him. As he saw the riderless horses come into sight, he stood in the middle of the trail waving his arms up and down, trying to slow them to a halt. But the spooked horses weren't about to slow down. They raced past him, his smoky dun bringing up the rear.

Seeing his horse, he pressed closer, hoping the dun would settle when it saw its owner waving it down. He was right. Upon seeing Ozzie, the dun started sliding to a halt on the rocky trail. But even as it did so, the iron rail, still bouncing and flipping at the horse's rear, made a vicious swipe through the air and struck Ozzie lengthwise down the left side of his head. Ozzie went down and out. The sound of the iron rail left a dull twang ringing inside his head.

As his horse slowed to a stop, it circled on the trail and came back at a walk, dragging the iron rail at its side. Settled now, the horse poked it nose at Ozzie's back, then stood over him and looked all around in the silence, as if wondering what to do next.

Chapter 23

The Ranger nudged his copper dun to a quicker pace when he saw how the rise of dust had moved closer across the sand flats. When he looked back a moment later and saw the dust moving up behind him, he pressed his horse even more. It might well be a posse of miners riding from the west, but he had no idea who would be heading this way from the southeast. Whoever it was from either direction, all he wanted was to get Ozzie and head out of here.

Even as he thought about it, he saw a single hatless rider meandering slowly—too slow to stir up dust—at the edge of the sand flats. A number of saddled horses moved along with the rider, none of them appearing to be in any hurry. Keeping watch on the rider, Sam reined his horse down, drew his telescope from his bedroll, stretched it out and raised it to his eye.

"And there he is, Copper," he murmured to the big sweat-streaked dun as if the horse would understand him. "It's Ozzie Cord . . . or what's left of him," he added, seeing the bloodstained bandanna that drooped from around Ozzie's swollen face and hung across his chin. He saw Ozzie's nose barely clinging to his face in a black lacework of dried blood. A wide swollen bruise ran full length down the left side of Ozzie's face.

"My goodness," Sam said. He shook his head a little as he lowered the telescope and shoved it shut between his palms. "Looks like he might welcome us taking him into custody," he said to the dun. But as soon as he shoved the telescope back into his bedroll, he drew his Winchester, checked it and laid it across his lap just in case.

He tapped the dun forward, keeping his eyes on Ozzie and the land surrounding him. After the shooting he'd heard from this direction, he warned himself to be prepared for anything. Yet, as Sam rode the horse closer at a light gallop, he noted Ozzie was making no move to even straighten in his saddle, let alone raise a firearm toward him.

Is he dead?

"Ozzie Cord, show your hands," Sam called out, stopping his horse, the Winchester up and in his hand.

At first Ozzie made no effort to respond. But before Sam called out again, he slowly raised his hands and held them out a few inches on either side of him.

"Nail me up," Ozzie mumbled in a slurred voice.

Nail him up?

Sam nudged the dun forward and stopped again only a few feet away. Seeing no weapon, and more important, seeing the shape the young man was in,

Sam reached behind his back and took out a pair of handcuffs.

"What happened to you, Ozzie?" the Ranger asked, laying the rifle back across his lap.

"When . . . ?" Ozzie said in a dreamlike tone.

Sam sidled in, clamped the cuff around one wrist and noted that Ozzie had enough comprehension to raise his other wrist into reach.

"Never mind," Sam said, both cuffs in place. "Who do these horses belong to?" He lifted Ozzie's big Colt from its holster and shoved it down behind his gun belt.

"Hell, everybody . . . I guess," Ozzie said. He shrugged and, answering the Ranger's first question, said, "My horse . . . did all this to me." He turned his face up a little to show the Ranger the long bruise and his disfigured face. "Nearly bit my nose off. Busted me upside the head . . . with an iron rail."

Sam winced a little.

"I've never seen a horse do such a thing," he said, not sure he believed a word Ozzie said in his dazed condition.

"I'll never . . . feel safe sleeping around him again," Ozzie said, sounding addled from the iron rail batting him in the head.

Sam looked off west at the closing rise of dust.

"Where's the payroll money?" he asked. "If the miner posse catches up to us, the money is all that'll keep them from—"

"It's gone," Ozzie said, cutting him off. "Don't even ask me where. . . ."

Sam stared at him.

"What do you mean it's *gone*?" Sam said. "Money doesn't disappear."

"No," Ozzie said with a thin, dreamlike smile. "But it . . . changes into pinecones and dirty long johns."

"Start making sense or I'll give you to the posse," Sam said, bluffing. "They've got as much right taking you into custody as I do, maybe more."

"I am making sense," Ozzie said. "Look back here." He nodded over his shoulder.

Sam stepped his horse back and picked up a half-empty canvas bag lying across Ozzie's saddle-bags. Spreading the bag open, he saw pine needles and cones stuffed against some wadded dirty clothes.

"This is what the shooting was about," Sam deduced. He stepped his horse back and faced Ozzie.

"Yeah. They're all dead up there," said Ozzie. "I rode up . . . found the woman and two Perros Locos shot all to pieces. Brought this back with me." He nodded again toward the bag behind him.

"Why'd you bring it back?" Sam asked.

Ozzie shrugged and said, "It changed once . . . who says it won't change again?" He gave a dark nasally chuckle that sounded as though it had to hurt. Sam looked at him, wondering if he was serious or just making a mindless joke in his addled condition.

Sam shook his head. He half turned in his saddle and looked back along the edge of the sand flats. The newer rise of dust had moved closer. He brought out his telescope and stretched it out in his hands.

"Step down and bury the bag," he said. "Hurry up, we don't have much time."

"Step down and *bury it*?" Ozzie said. "I'm cuffed. Look at the shape I'm in."

The Ranger wondered if this was how he'd be all the way back across the border. "You could be in worse shape real quick when the miners see it. They won't find anything funny about their money turning to pinecones."

"Then your job will be protecting me," Ozzie said, again with a dark chuckle. He raised the bandanna back across the bridge of his nose and adjusted it into place. He winced in pain while he did it.

Yep, this was how it was going to be.

Sam gave him a hard stare.

"Step down out of that saddle *now*," he said menacingly.

Seeing the look in the Ranger's eyes, Ozzie decided not to push it.

"All right, calm down," he said grudgingly. As he managed to swing his leg up over his horse and step down, Sam raised the telescope to his eye and gaze out into the cloud of dust. Now the riders were close enough for the scope to penetrate the heavy dust, the riders coming into sight. Seeing them, Sam stiffened a little.

"Get back on your horse," he said sidelong without taking the lens down from his eye.

"No, I just got down," Ozzie said in a childlike huff. "I'm going to bury the bag, like I was told to."

The Ranger jerked the lens down and stared at his irritating prisoner. "It's not miners, it's Lipan Apache. Get in the saddle or I'll leave you to them."

Ozzie scrambled into his saddle, yet even as he did so, he still had to make a comment.

"Lipans ain't near as bad as Mescaleros," he said. "They're just a bunch of gray-skin Texan horse thieves, got run out of their own lands—"

"That's interesting, Ozzie," Sam said, cutting him short. "I ought to leave you here to tell them all that—" He turned the copper dun toward the sand flats and grabbed Ozzie's reins from his hands. "But you're going with me."

"Wait, Ranger! My nose will fall plumb off on a running horse."

"Hold on to it," Sam said.

"I can't! My hands are cuffed." He wiggled his fingers.

Sam sidled in close and unlocked the cuffs from his wrists.

"Try making a run," he said to his grinning prisoner, "the last thing you'll feel is a bullet in your back."

Ozzie started to say something more, but before he could, the Ranger reached over and slapped his smoky dun on its rump. Ozzie's horse bolted forward at a run; the bandanna lying flat atop Ozzie's head flew away. Sam put his own coppery dun at a run beside him. Immediately the loose horses fell in, running behind the two, out onto the barren sand flats. Behind them the two clouds of dust closed in on each other from both directions.

*   *   *

Following close behind Ozzie, the Ranger looked back on the length of the flats, seeing the clearer outlines of the Apache, both man and horse emerging from the thick swirling dust. From the opposite direction he saw the tan-with-red-piping uniforms of the Mexican army, riding side by side with the dusty blue uniforms of U.S. Cavalry troops. Bandoleers of ammunition crisscrossed the soldiers' chests; brass bullet casings glinted in the dull dusty sunlight. He had to give it a second to realize that on the right flank of the troops rode Turner Bigfoot Pridemore and his mercenaries. They rode fast, loose and wildly, like demons unleashed from the gates of hell to do the worst on man's bidding.

This was the battle that had been the talk on both sides of the border for months, he told himself—a joint Mexican–U.S. alliance to eradicate the deserts and plains of the Mescalero and Lipan Apache. *Like it or not, here it comes,* he thought as his coppery dun pounded on right behind Ozzie's smoky dun, the rest of the loose horses running right with them. All he could hope for was to get Ozzie and himself out of their way.

Seeing the set of hoofprints ahead of them on his right, Sam quickly recognized them as belonging to Rayburn and the speckled barb from earlier. He figured Rayburn had seen the coming Apache and didn't wait until dark to clear out. *All right. . . .* With any luck and a canteen of water, Rayburn and the barb had made it well out onto the flats by now.

"Swing right, Ozzie!" he shouted. As Ozzie

glanced around, Sam waved him toward the dry wash Rayburn had taken shade in. The wash lay down out of sight from the flats behind them. If the stony wash had been good enough cover for Rayburn, it would be good enough for him. He almost wished Rayburn and his gun were still there. But the tracks leading away told him different.

Without hesitation Ozzie swung his horses toward the dry wash, and in moments, as rifle fire began cracking back and forth on the flats, the two slowed their horses enough to get over the sandy cut bank along the wash and slow to a stop.

"Up ahead," said the Ranger with a nod. "There's cactus shade and rock for cover." He nudged the dun forward, Ozzie beside him, the horses still following, but hanging back some now that the hard running appeared to be over.

Stepping down from their saddles, lawman and prisoner quickly led their dun horses to where a half circle of rock and an edge of ancient overhanging cactus provided good cover. Out on the flats rifle fire increased as the two forces drew closer. The thunder of hooves jarred the earth from both directions.

"You need to give me back my gun, Ranger," Ozzie said in a somber tone of voice. Sam noted he seemed to be coming to his senses a little, for whatever that was worth.

"I'll reconsider that when the time comes," Sam said. "Until then you sit down there and keep quiet—if you can." He gestured toward a short rock alongside the belly of the wash.

"Oh, I can," Ozzie said. "But you're crazy if you think I'm going to just sit here and be overrun by Apache without shooting back."

Sam wasn't going to waste time arguing with him. He turned away and climbed up the sandy cut bank with his telescope and Winchester in hand.

"Okay, we've got trouble," he said to Ozzie over his shoulder. He'd looked along the dry wash edge and saw the five loose horses milling about in full view, saddled and ready to ride. "This is too easy pickings for these warriors to pass up."

"What you've got to do is shoot the horses," Ozzie said, hearing him and slipping up the cut bank beside him.

"The shots would draw the Indians' attention," Sam said.

"So?" said Ozzie, as if nothing made sense beyond his own mindless half-cocked reasoning. "The warriors won't ride out here for five dead horses."

Sam didn't bother explaining the folly of the young man's flawed logic.

"Go back and sit down," he said. "Don't say another word."

Sam looked out through the telescope as Ozzie grumbled and slid down the cut bank. Looking back out at the dust, Sam saw a handful of warriors riding out of the swirl toward the dry wash in spite of the battle raging on the flats.

"They spotted the horses," he said. "Get back up here, Ozzie. Here they come."

Ozzie had just sat down on the rock. He shook his head and stood up.

"You need to make up your mind, Ranger," he said, disgruntled and peevish.

But his eyes almost lit up when he saw the Ranger draw the black-handled Colt from behind his gun belt and hold it out to him butt first.

"Don't make a move against me, Ozzie," he warned as the young man took his Colt and rubbed a hand over it.

Ozzie appeared not to have heard him. Instead he gave a slight grin. Sam took note and watched until the young mercenary leaned against the sandy bank beside him, the black-handled Colt up and cocked. This was not a man he could ever turn his back on. *No, not for a second,* he warned himself.

When he turned and looked back out through the shooting, he counted six warriors racing across the flat toward them.

Hold your pistol fire until they're in closer," he said sidelong to Ozzie.

"I know how to shoot, Ranger," Ozzie said with contempt.

"Good," Sam said calmly. "I'm going to try to turn them with my rifle."

As he took aim from under the shelter of the overhanging cactus, he caught sight of a handful of scalpers riding out of the other cloud of dust and racing diagonally toward the six attacking Apache.

"I'll take any help I can get," he murmured, leveling his rifle sights on the rider at the center of the six Apache.

Chapter 24

The Ranger's first shot fell short of the center warrior, just as he'd wanted it to. He'd hoped that a kickup of dust a few feet in front of his horse's hooves might send the riders back to join the battle along the edge of the flats. But no such luck. The fury of battle had them thirsting for blood. The lead rider veered slightly but still charged ahead in a full run; the five braves around him spread out abreast. This border fight had brewed too long and too hot for either side to stop it now.

"Watch that end of the wash," he said sidelong to Ozzie, seeing three of the five warriors cut away in that direction. Seeing Ozzie turn and direct his attention toward the right end of the wash, Sam leveled the Winchester at the lead rider again. This wasn't meant to turn the warrior; this one was for keeps.

A bullet whistled past between him and Ozzie as Sam squeezed off the next shot. The passing bullet didn't distract him. His shot caught the warrior in the top of his shoulder and flipped him backward from his horse. A mist of blood flashed in the air. The warrior hit the ground and slid in a spray of sand and broken bits of barrel cactus. Sam levered another round and settled in to take aim. Next to him, Ozzie's Colt barked twice as two of the three warriors rode into the dry wash, three of the loose horses running ahead of them.

"Got one!" Ozzie hooted and yelled. "I got one of these heathen 'Paches!"

"Keep shooting," Sam shouted as he took quick aim and fired again. But this shot flew over the warrior's head as he and his horse dropped down over the edge of the dray on the other end of their position. Before Sam had levered another round, the second warrior and his horse dropped out of sight also. All the braves were in the dry wash now, Sam reminded himself, turning on his side, away from Ozzie.

"*Yee-hiii!* Got another one!" Ozzie shouted and laughed as another warrior on his side fell off his saddle. "You going to help me out any, Ranger?" he taunted. "I'm doing all the work." He laughed insanely.

Actually laughed! This raving idiot, Sam said to himself. As he started to take aim along the wash, he caught a glimpse of four more warriors breaking away from the raging battle and heading this way to help their own.

"More coming, keep firing," he shouted at Ozzie.

"I'm out of bullets," Ozzie shouted as bullets zipped past them from either end of the wash.

"Grab some from my belt," Sam said, realizing what a bad mistake that could be, but also realizing he had little other choice at the moment.

"Got them," Ozzie said. He started pushing bullets into his Colt.

Sam fired. This time another warrior fell from his horse. As Sam relevered a round into his smoking rifle chamber, he caught sight of Turner Pridemore and his scalpers. The group rode hard, whooping, yelling and shooting toward the dry wash, as if the thrust of their whole battle had somehow shifted there.

On Ozzie's end of the wash, Sam noted that two warriors Ozzie thought he had shot were not shot at all. They had pulled an old Apache trick. They'd gone down from their horses and belly-crawled in closer. At less than fifty feet the two sprang up and charged on foot, shooting and yelping like coyotes. They ran with the loose horses between them and the Ranger. Sam and Ozzie both fired. One warrior went down, his chest blown wide-open—no faking there, Sam told himself. The other had taken cover in rocks and kept Sam and Ozzie busy while the additional warriors rode in and sprang into action.

The Indians were all inside the dry wash now. The fighting had moved in close. They had no intention of leaving, or slowing down. The only ending here was with one side dying. It was no longer about the five loose horses. Sam and Ozzie fired repeatedly, but the Indians were well entrenched among the rocks, creeping forward inch upon inch. Bullets ricocheted inches from the warriors' bare backs, their heads. Still they crawled in closer, waiting to charge when they knew their closeness and their larger numbers would overwhelm the single rifle and pistol fire aimed at them.

"Where's the scalp hunters?" Sam asked himself aloud, firing and relevering round after round.

A bullet whined through and lifted the Ranger's sombrero from atop his head. Another bullet ripped into his forearm at the wrist and left a deep slice the length of his forearm. Sam ignored the blood and pain, knowing it would only get worse before it ended. The only way he planned to go down was in dead-heat battle. Another warrior fell. Behind him he heard Ozzie firing, yelping, screaming, staying with the fight.

An Indian sprang up less than ten feet from him and bolted forward. Luckily the Ranger had just levered a round. He pulled the trigger as the yelling warrior reached out for the rifle barrel. The shot slammed through the warrior's throat, leaving a fist-sized hole and a large mist of blood. Sam sprang to his feet, knowing it would all be right here in front of him now.

As he rose, so did four Indians, too close for rifle work.

Sam drew the Colt, cocking it, getting off one shot, then another. Behind the Indians who came charging down the dry wash, Sam heard the scalp hunters' rifles exploding.

"Here come my pals!" Ozzie shouted.

Sam watched Indians fall less than twenty feet in front of him. He saw their bare chests explode into bloody rose petals from the rifle fire behind them.

One more Indian made it away from the scalpers' bullets. He charged through yelping and shouting and leaped into the air over a waist-high rock toward the Ranger. Sam sent a pistol shot through his chest and watched him fall sidelong streaming blood. Behind the downed Indian, Sam saw the scalpers running in with their knives out, slashing. They begin lifting the heads of both the dead and the dying and slicing their scalps away with one quick flick of the blade.

Sam turned away from the scalping. Seeing Ozzie backing away along the dry wash, he realized this was the break he'd been expecting him to make when the time was right.

"Stop right there, Ozzie," Sam shouted. "Drop the gun!"

The scalpers looked up from their grisly work, seeing the two squared off at each other.

"Go to hell, Ranger!" Ozzie said. "My pals are here now. You're not taking me anywhere! They'll kill you, if I say the word."

Sam gave no other warning. He raised his smoking Colt just as Ozzie raised his. Ozzie was fast, surprisingly so, Sam noted. He might well have gotten the first shot off. But for reasons Sam would likely never understand, instead of firing right away, the young mercenary gunman struck a pose, as if to make some sort of stage show of it. Sam thought he even saw Ozzie cut a glance toward Bigfoot Pridemore and his son, Fox, who had just ridden down into the wash.

Whatever Ozzie's reason, the Ranger wasted no

time. He dropped the hammer on the big Colt, felt it buck in his hand and watched as Ozzie flew backward and hit the rocky ground. Ozzie's black-handled Colt flew from his hand and hit the ground ten feet away. Sam walked forward, his Colt up, his elbow cocked, the gun barrel smoking near the side of his face.

"He's had enough, Ranger. Leave him be," Sam heard Fox call out behind him. But he didn't look around. He walked to where Ozzie lay writhing in the dirt, his hand pressed tight to his upper shoulder.

"Shut your mouth, Fox, before I box your jaws," said Turner Pridemore to his son. "This has nothing to do with you, or any of us. You're lucky this idiot didn't get you in trouble along with his stupid damn self. I knew he was no good first time I laid eyes on him."

Fox started to say something, but he stopped himself and sat staring as the Ranger rolled Ozzie up onto his side and helped him lean back against a rock. As Turner nudged his horse forward through the busy scalpers, Fox put his horse alongside him. Out on the sand flats the battle still raged.

"Just so you know, Ranger," Pridemore said, stopping a few feet back and looking down at Sam. "My boy here has had nothing to do with anything this fool's been into."

Sam just looked up at the father and son, knowing better, but not getting into it. Taking Ozzie Cord in for murder was his job, nothing else. Fox was Mexico's problem.

"Yeah, that's right," said Pridemore, "Fox has been with us all along. We'll all swear to that if it comes down to it." He stared at the Ranger with a poker face.

Sam turned and starred at Fox with a look that said he knew better, that this was all a lie.

"Is that right, Fox?" Sam said, letting the young man know that he knew better. "Then I'd be mistaken if I saw you this morning with a couple of the Perros Locos bandits?" He kept the stare strong and steady.

Seeing what was going on, Turner cut in on his son's behalf.

"You might have seen him talking to them, but he wasn't what you'd call 'with them,'" he said. "I sent him out scouting this morning, trying to see where these heathen Apache were." He looked from Sam to his son. "Didn't you tell me you run across a couple of bandits this morning?"

"That's right, I did," Fox said. Instead of looking at his father, he continued to stare at the Ranger. "Those two were bad hombres, I could tell just by talking to them. I was glad to get shed of them. Made up a story, told them my horse was going lame on me. Then I got away from them quick as I could."

It was time to let it go, Sam decided. He let out a breath and looked down at Ozzie, then back up at Fox.

"Good thing you left when you did," he said. "They rode up in the hills and got themselves killed, according to Ozzie here."

Fox looked down at Ozzie.

Ozzie said, "I didn't do nothing wrong." Then he looked away.

"I never figured you did," Fox said. Beside him Turner Pridemore stood staring curiously, not knowing exactly what they were talking about. Sam knew but he wasn't going to mention it. He knew that Fox had somehow set this all up to his benefit. But it was none of Sam's business. He looked back at Turner as the battle began to wane on the sand flats.

"I'm obliged you showed up when you did," he said, taking off his bandanna and wrapping it around his bleeding forearm.

Pridemore touched his hat brim.

"Don't mention it, Ranger," he said. "I'm always one to help the law when it comes to my best interest." He stared at Sam. "I take it we're square, then?"

"I got my man," Sam said. "That's all I was ever after."

Ian Pusser rode up carrying Sam's sombrero and handed it to him, the bullet hole showing in its crown. Sam looked at a bloody knife in his hand and the long line of scalps already adorning his saddle. He knew it was Pusser who'd killed the other scalper on the desert floor. Again, none of his business, down here in the deep Mexican desert, he told himself.

Pridemore saw him looking at the scalps and gave a wide grin.

"You know, Ranger," he said, "this land is tough

but fair, I always say. Where else can you tack a man's face to a board and sell it for big money as a novelty? We're wilder than darkest Africa."

"Sometimes it seems that way," Sam said.

Pridemore gestured around at his men busily taking scalps from the dead and leaving the bodies for the buzzards.

"Where else can you turn something like skinning heads into a business and watch it flourish?" He paused, then said, "You'd never guess that I started life as a lawyer." He nodded. "That's a fact. But I fell for a young woman in Texas and we come all this way to raise up two sons and start a trading post." He laughed. "A trading post, right smack on the badlands! Can you beat that?"

"No, I can't," Sam said. He took a folded cloth Ian Pusser handed him and passed it down to Ozzie. The wounded prisoner stuck the cloth inside his shirt and pressed it to his bullet wound.

"On your feet," Sam said to Ozzie.

"But I'm bleeding something awful, Ranger," Ozzie whined.

Sam pulled him up by his shoulder. He cuffed him, then raised his hands and shoved one back against his shoulder wound.

"How can I ride like this?" Ozzie said.

"Figure it out," Sam said. "We're crossing the flats tonight. We'll have you some help come morning." As unpredictable as these mercenaries were, he wanted to get his prisoner on his horse and get out of there.

"You're welcome to stay, Ranger," said Pridemore. "We'll find something to stick over a fire once we get all these scalps pulled and counted."

"Obliged," Sam said, giving Ozzie a shove up into his saddle. "I want to get this one across the border and turn him in."

"They going to hang him, Ranger?" Fox asked from his saddle.

Sam didn't answer.

"What do you care?" Turner Pridemore asked his son. "Be glad you ain't been a part of nothing he's done."

Sam saw Ozzie's and Fox's eyes meet, only for a second, before both of them looked away.

Turner and Fox Pridemore sat watching as the Ranger mounted and led his prisoner away, out across the sand flats, the same direction Jep Rayburn had taken.

"You're damn lucky we run into you when we did today," Turner said. "Think the idiot Ozzie will keep his mouth shut?"

"It doesn't matter. He don't know nothing," said Fox.

"Knowing how you are, this Ranger would've had to kill you and that idiot both if you'd stuck around."

"I'm not afraid of that Ranger," Fox said.

"So? Every man he's put underground has said that," Pridemore replied. He paused, then said, "I have to admit, you're the only one who come out of this standing up." He gave a proud, stiff smile. "I expect that comes from your raising?"

"Yeah." Fox smiled and said, "You should have

seen me, Pa. I had all the Perros Locos doing what I told them. Like I was some kind of big-shot desperado—"

"Well, you're back now," Turner said, cutting his son off.

"I'm not scalping anymore, Pa," Fox said.

"What will you do, then?" Turner asked, already having a pretty good idea.

"I'm going to ride up and get the money I buried. Then I'll figure things out from there."

Turner Pridemore saw one of his mercenaries gesture toward all the dead Apache strewn on out on the sand flats as the battle moved up into the hills.

"Suit yourself," he said to his son. "I've got work to do." He nudged his horse away. "If you're smart you'll stay down here in Old Mex, let that Ranger get your name off his tongue."

"I told you I'm not afraid of that Ranger," Fox said as his father galloped away. He looked out across the flats where the Ranger and his prisoner rode at an easy pace, barely stirring the sand.

"El Zorro . . . ," Fox said under his breath, recalling the name he'd been given, for a while anyway. He thought about it for a moment, then collected his horse beneath him.

On the flats, the Ranger had looked back over his shoulder for no reason and seen the young outlaw turn his horse and ride away at a gallop. Both man and horse looked small now from that far away. Small beneath the rising dust they'd kicked up behind them. Sam had a feeling he'd see Fox

Pridemore again. He'd remember his name and whatever else he could about the young outlaw, just in case.

Yes, just in case, he told himself, and then he put the matter out of his mind. He wrapped a bandanna around the bullet graze up his forearm, shirtsleeve and all, as he rode.

"Keep moving," he said to Ozzie riding in front of him. Then he rode forward, watching the trail ahead. The hoofprints left by Jep Rayburn and the speckled barb lay strewn out along the harsh sandy ground in front of him, as if marking him a path across the sprawling badlands—pointing his way home.

Turn the page for a look at Sam
Burrack's next adventure in

SHOWDOWN AT GUN HILL

Available from Signet in July 2015.

Big Silver, the Arizona Badlands

At first light, Arizona Territory Ranger Sam Burrack followed a series of pistol shots the last mile
into town. The shots came spaced apart, as if offered
by some wild-eyed orator who used a gun to drive
home the points of his raging soliloquy. Sensing no
great urgency in the shots, Sam circled wide of the
town limits and rode in from the south, keeping his
copper black-point dun at an easy gallop. At his side
he led a spare horse on a short rope.

Being familiar with the position of the town, he
knew if he'd followed the main trail into Big Silver
at this time of morning, he would have ridden face-
first into the rising sunlight—not a wise move under
the circumstances. Never a wise move, he reminded
himself, given his line of work.

His line of work . . .

A Winchester repeating rifle stood in its saddle
boot; his bone-handled Colt stood holstered on his
hip, hidden by his duster but close to his right hand.
Necessary tools for *his line of work . . .*

A block ahead of him, another pistol shot rang out in the still air—the *fourth*, he noted to himself. Along the street, townsfolk who had scrambled for cover a few minutes earlier when the shooting began now looked out at the Ranger from behind shipping crates, firewood and anything else sufficient to stop a bullet.

"He's in his office, Ranger!" a nervous townsman's voice called out from a recessed doorway.

"Thank God you're here!" a woman's voice called out. "Please don't hurt him."

"Hurt him, *ha*!" another voice called out. "Shoot that drunken son of a—" His words stopped short under the roar of a fifth gunshot.

"Everybody keep back out of sight," the Ranger called out.

He veered his dun into the mouth of an alleyway for safety's sake and stepped down from his saddle. The big dun grumbled and pawed its hoof at the dirt, yet Sam noted that the animal showed no signs of being spooked or otherwise thrown off by the sound of gunfire.

"Good boy," he said to the dun, rubbing its muzzle. The spare horse sidled close to the dun. As Sam spun the dun's reins and the spare's lead rope around a post, a townsman dressed in a clerk's apron hurried into the alley and collapsed back against the wall of a building.

"Man, are we glad to see you, Ranger!" he said. "Didn't expect anybody to show up so soon."

"Glad I can help," was all Sam replied. He didn't bother explaining that he'd been headed to Big Silver to begin with, or that he'd ridden all night from Dunston, another hillside mining town some thirty miles back along the Mexican border. As soon as the telegraph had arrived, Sam gathered his dun and the spare horse and headed out. He'd made sure both horses were well grained and watered. He'd eaten his dinner in the saddle, from a small canvas bag made up at Dunston's only restaurant. "Good eten," he could still hear the old Dutch cook say as he had handed him the bag.

He drew the Winchester from its boot and checked it. Hopefully he wouldn't need it. *But you never know . . .* , he told himself.

"Say, Ranger," said the man in the clerk's apron, eyeing the Winchester, "you're not going in there alone, are you?"

"Yep," Sam said. He started to take a step out onto the empty street.

"Because I can get half the men in this town to arm up and go with you," the man said.

Sam just looked at him; the man looked embarrassed.

"All right," he said, red-faced, "why didn't we do that to begin with? is what you're wondering. The fact is, we didn't know what to do, a situation like this." He gestured a nervous hand in the direction of the gunfire. "He claimed he's a wolf! Threatened to rip somebody's heart out if we didn't all do like he told us!"

"A wolf . . . ," the Ranger said flatly, looking off along the street. He took a breath.

"That's right, a *wolf*," the man said even though

Sam hadn't posed his words as a question. "Can you beat that?"

"It wasn't their hearts he said he'd rip out," another townsman said, cowering back into the alley. "It was their *throats*!" He gripped a hand beneath his bearded chin and stared at Sam wide-eyed with fear.

"It was their *hearts*, Oscar," the man in the clerk's apron said. "I ought to know what I heard."

"Throats . . . ," the old man insisted in a lowered voice as he cowered farther back.

Sam looked all around. The alley had started to fill with people pouring into it from behind the row of buildings along the main street. Another shot rang out; people ducked instinctively.

Number six, Sam told himself.

"All of you stay back," he said calmly.

As he stepped out and walked along the street, he knew that he only had a few seconds during *reload* to make whatever gains he could for himself. He pictured the loading gate of a smoking revolver opening, an empty shell falling from its smoking chamber to the floor. Another shell dropped, and another. . . .

As he walked forward he gauged his pace, keeping it deliberately slow, steady, trying to time everything just right. Now he saw the fresh rounds appear, being thumbed into the gun one at a time by a hand that was anxious, unsteady, in a boiling rage. Then, with the scene playing itself out in his mind, as if signaled by some unseen clock ingrained in his instincts, Sam stopped in the middle of the street—*it's time*—and faced a faded wooden sign that read in bold letters above a closed door Sheriff's Office & Town Jail.

Here goes. . . .

"Sheriff Sheppard Stone," he called out loud enough to be heard through the closed door, above an angry rant of curses and threats toward the world at large. "It's Ranger Sam Burrack. Lay your gun down, and come out here and talk to me." Looking around, he saw empty whiskey bottles littering the ground and boardwalk out in front of the building. Broken bottle necks lay strewn where bullets had blasted their fragile bodies into shards.

"Well, well, well," a whiskey-slurred voice called out through a half-open front window, "*Saint* Samuel Burrack. To what do I owe the honor of your visit?"

Saint Samuel Burrack . . . ? He hadn't heard that one before. Just whiskey talking, he decided.

"Territory Judge Albert Long sent me, Sheriff," he said. "He wants to see you in Yuma." He wasn't going to mention that the judge had heard outrageous complaints about Stone's drunkenness and had sent Burrack to persuade the sheriff to step down from office. A year earlier, *drunk*, Stone had accidentally shot two of his toes off.

"Oh . . . what about?" Stone asked in a wary tone. "Is he wanting my badge?" He paused, but only for a moment. "If he is, tell him to come take it himself. Don't send some *upstart do-gooder* to take on the job."

Upstart do-gooder . . . ? A couple more names he

hadn't heard himself called before—although he'd heard himself called worse.

He took a breath. All right, this wasn't going to be easy, he told himself, but at least there were no bullets flying through the air. Not yet anyway.

So far, so good . . .

"The judge said you and he were old friends," he replied, ignoring the drunken threat, the name-calling. "Said you once saved his life. Now he wants you to come visit him . . . spend some time on his ranch outside Yuma, I understand."

"Ha!" Stone said in more of a jeer than a laugh. "Spend some time on the judge's ranch . . ." His words trailed into inaudible cursing and slurred mumbling. Then he called out, "Let me ask you something, Ranger—does anybody ever fall for these yarns you pull out of your hat?"

Sam let it go. But he couldn't stand out here much longer. He had to get the gun out of the sheriff's hand. Whiskey was too unpredictable to reason with.

"I'm coming in, Sheriff Stone," he said. "Don't shoot."

"You ain't coming in! Take one step, you're dead!" Stone shouted, the whiskey suddenly boiling up again.

"I've got to. It's too hot out here," Sam called out calmly, taking a step forward. He ignored a gunshot when it erupted through the half-open window and kicked up dirt only inches from the toe of his boot.

"The next one won't be aimed at the dirt!" the drunken sheriff shouted.

"I'm coming in," Sam said in a steady tone. He knew a warning shot when he saw one. Whiskey or no whiskey, he had to gain all the space he could, get in closer. It was a dangerous gamble, but he took it. Another bullet erupted. More dirt kicked up at his feet. Realizing Stone had not made good on his threat, Sam took another step, then another.

"Hold it, damn it!" Stone shouted. "Come on in, then, but first lay that rifle on the ground! Don't test me on this."

All right . . . Sam let out a tense breath, calming himself.

"Sheriff, look," he said. "I'm laying it down right here." He stooped, laid the Winchester on the dirt, then straightened and walked forward, his hands chest high.

When he stepped through, crunching broken glass onto the boardwalk, the door swung open before he reached for the handle. In the shade of the office, Sheriff Stone stepped back five feet, a big Colt cocked in his hand. He weaved drunkenly. His eyes were red-rimmed and staring through a veil of rage. Sam glanced past him through a cloud of burnt gunpowder and saw two frightened eyes staring at him from the jail's only cell.

"You're a brazen bastard. I'll give you that, Burrack," Stone said, the gun level and steady in spite of the whiskey goading his thoughts, his rationality.